THE LADY'S LEGACY

DEB MARLOWE

Deb Marlowe

For Kim H
with many thanks for shared laughter, griping, tears and the soothing smell
of bleach

To Kater
With many wishes
For Happy Reading!

Deb Marlowe

Chapter One
LONDON, ENGLAND

Many of you witnessed it—the moment when I knew for certain that my greatest secret was out. Your eyes touched on me even as I felt my blood drain away. The whispers followed, the conjectures —but rest assured, none of what you might have said or thought could have hurt as much as my first view of that sculpture, of the sight of that toddling marble boy reaching for the woman in the painting and her outstretched arms . . .
from the journal of the infamous Miss Hestia Wright

W *hite.* Francis Headley sighed. Why must it be white? She took up her gloves and smoothed a hand over her skirts, pausing to touch the coral flowers and green leaves embroidered as trim. The fitted bodice and capped sleeves served to emphasize the modest curves that time and nature had finally pulled out of her. It was a lovely gown and she looked good in it.

But to a girl used to the stews and warrens of London, *white* didn't carry the same meaning as it did to the rest of the world. To everyone attending today's event, white represented gentility, innocence and means. But Francis was no debutante. To her, a girl in white had for a long time meant a *mark*. A victim. One to be plundered and pitied.

She wasn't that street urchin any longer. But neither would she ever be a delicate, young bloom of Society. Little wonder that grey was her normal, favored color.

Grey would not do today, however.

She set out, moving carefully down the stairs. No one waited in the entryway, here at Half Moon House. Was she the first one down? She stepped out toward the bench by the door—

Oof!

"Nestor!" She swatted at the youth who had bowled into her. "Can't you let me stay clean for five minutes together?"

"*Cor*, Flightly!" the boy answered, his eyes gone round. All of the street kids still called her by her old name. "What are you doing, all dressed to the nines?" Not waiting for an answer, he threw back his head and sniffed deeply. "Smell that? Rosemary bread! Callie's back!"

"I know she's back," she answered sourly. "We're going out this afternoon. That's why I'm dressed like this." Her old friend Brynne, now Duchess of Aldmere, was coming along, too, and bringing several of the most promising protégés from her orphanage program.

But Nestor wasn't listening. The call of fresh bread pulled him toward the kitchens. Francis rolled her eyes, and continued on her way, but she still hadn't advanced far when a group of girls poured from the classroom hallway.

"Oooh, Francis," breathed Molly. "Don't you look a treat?"

They surrounded her, offering up a chorus of compliments, making her feel . . . restless. It was a feeling that had plagued her over the last couple of years, since Hestia Wright had removed her from the ranks of runner/messenger/watchers and begun to train her in other duties. It wasn't that she missed the streets, not really. But she did long for the certain knowledge that she was being *useful*.

She would sacrifice far more than that, however, at Hestia Wright's request.

"I heard Callie say that you were all going to the Royal Academy of Arts Exhibition," said Molly. "How exciting!"

"Well, *I* heard that Marcus Moore is planning on attending today as well," someone said with special emphasis.

"It's open to the public," Francis replied. "Anyone may go."

"Why would the butcher's boy want to go and gawk at a bunch of boring old paintings," Jesse scoffed.

"It's art," she replied. "And a great deal of it. There is sure to be something for everyone. I really think some of you should plan on taking it in, as well."

"What? Go and stare at other people's relatives?" sniffed Jesse.

"Beautiful studies of interesting people," Francis corrected her. "And there's more—historical subjects, gorgeous landscapes—"

"Places I'll never go," the girl interrupted.

"Well, I think you're just mad because Marcus is going to see the pretty young ladies, not the paintings," said Molly with an arch of her brow in Francis's direction.

"Well, perhaps I'll just go and do the marketing while you are out." Jessie tossed her head. "Marcus may find he doesn't need to go down to Somerset House, after all."

"Yes, do that." Francis had had enough sniping. "Be sure to compliment his hearty haunches. It may just give you the edge you need." She moved off just as Isaac, Half Moon House's intrepid butler, opened the front door.

"Lady Truitt and her young companion are in the carriage already," he told her. "They ask if you are ready to go?"

"Of course." She bid the girls a good day and followed him out.

৩৫৩

The crowds lay thick all through Somerset House, and the stairs to the exhibition room were stifling. Society had come out *en masse* to view the Royal Academy's Exhibition, to see and be seen, to gossip over popular works and over which artists had found their work placed to advantage 'on the line.'

Francis helped Brynne and Callie keep a close eye on their group of girls. Hard to believe that her friends were now the Duchess of Aldmere and Lady Truitt Russell—but very easy to accept that they both were doing their best to help those less fortunate than themselves.

Brynne and her husband, the Duke of Aldmere, had founded an orphanage that took in young girls. They trained them for independent and happy lives, in business or service or even marriage, whichever way their inclinations led them.

Callie ran an inn, and also, very secretly, took in young women of all walks of life, often abused or compromised, who found themselves in the family way. In memory of her mother, she tucked them safely away, treated them well until they were delivered—and helped them and their children start life anew.

"Who is following today?" Brynne asked quietly in an aside meant only for Callie and Francis.

"Cade," answered Callie. She gave a little shiver.

Francis was entirely sympathetic. The wicked Marquess of Marstoke had men set to watch Half Moon House on most days. When Hestia's principal assistants went about Town, they often acquired unwanted followers. Cade, a tall, slender man, was one of the most disturbing. Not a discontented younger son like most of Marstoke's lackeys, no one knew where he came from. They all knew, however, that he was fast, mean and ruthless.

One of the young girls approached. As one, the three of them turned to greet her. "Your Grace," she said in an excited whisper. "Look at that group of young girls over there." She tilted her head in a perfectly discreet manner. "Their waistlines—they are lower! It is just as we heard from the modiste last week!"

Today's group was comprised of mostly Brynne's girls, and nearly all were interested in becoming a lady's maid, a dresser, or a seamstress. They'd been brought to Town to meet prospective employers—and to be taken out a bit to see the sort of results they would be expected to achieve.

Nodding, talking, Brynne herded them into the main room of the display. They all started out admiring the art. But the crowds grew, and they drew back, huddled together, more interested in discussing the attendees and what they were wearing. They perked up as the fashionable young Countess of Hartford entered, and Francis raised a brow as Brynne took her arm and again pulled her a little out of the way.

"The girls are all aflutter over the society ladies," the duchess said, low. "But I notice that you are watching the young men."

"Yes, well, apparently I have an assignation with the butcher's boy," she answered wryly.

"Good heavens, leave that young Moore boy alone, will you?" the duchess laughed. "He's not nearly so tough as his father's stew meat—and Half Moon House's kitchens will get the worst of it if you break his heart."

"Fine—then I'll leave him to Jesse. She appears to be interested."

"Far more his caliber," Brynne said approvingly. "But don't think to distract me. I know what you are doing. You are looking for *him*, aren't you?"

Him.

They exchanged glances. Brynne knew that for the last six months there had only been one *him* hovering in Francis's mind. A man she'd worried, fretted and obsessed over.

A man she'd never met.

Hestia Wright's son.

Almost nothing was known of him. Hestia had kept his existence a closely guarded secret for years. She'd done it to protect him from his father, her old enemy, the Marquess of Marstoke. But the madman had somehow discovered the truth. He'd found the young man and then sent a public message that had been clear only to Hestia.

It had happened at a ball. Marstoke, wanted for treasonous acts, had come out of hiding, risking capture in order to perform the flashy introduction of a new artist—and an unveiling of a sculpture that had pierced Hestia's heart to the quick.

But then both men had disappeared. The traitorous Marquess had vanished from his prison cell in Newgate to parts unknown—and the young man had faded back into obscurity.

Half the world had been looking for Marstoke ever since—or at least a good part of the Prince Regent's government—and a few foreign nations as well. Society was continually abuzz with news of a latest sighting. He'd been spotted in Paris, in Naples, or he'd bought an island in the Caribbean from which he would plot his revenge.

Of Rhys Caradec, in contrast, there had been no word and almost no talk. Her son was the artist, Hestia told them. She'd known that much about him and the sculpture that Marstoke had unveiled right before his capture had clearly cemented the fact.

"It was brilliant of you to sniff out his work in Yorkshire," Brynne began.

Francis nodded her thanks. It had been a coup, discovering the only further bit of information about the man—and a bit of a lucky break too. Hestia had sent her north to Yorkshire over the Christmas holidays—to assist one of the young women who'd come seeking help at Half Moon House—and to gain a bit of experience in dealing with the peerage. The mission had been a success on both fronts.

But her focus had taken on a whole new slant when the formidable old Duke of Danby had noticed how taken she'd been with the new, unusual pair of portraits of his twin granddaughters. He'd offered to show her the more informal, companion piece the artist had gifted him.

If she'd thought the formal portraits vivid and alive—well, then she wouldn't have been surprised if the giggling girls in the third piece might have stepped right out of their garden setting. But it was the pair of tiny figures in the background that had her gasping out loud: far-off, a blonde lady walking away, holding the hand of a tow-headed toddler.

It couldn't have been a coincidence. Another depiction of a faceless blonde and a small boy? Just like in the sculpture? A flurry of questions had revealed only that yes, the artist who had painted the girls had been Rhys Caradec—and no, no one knew precisely where he had gone once the commission had been completed. They'd obtained a good description of him, at least—tall, blonde with hair on the longish side, mostly good natured, strong willed and eccentric in his habits, but no further hint to help find him.

"But there's been no sign of him since. Clearly he doesn't want to be found," Brynne continued.

Of all of them, this concerned Brynne the most. Because everyone in Hestia's circles knew the evil that Marstoke was capable of, but Brynne had once been betrothed to the man. And having had the most exposure to the marquess, she feared the man's ability to turn Hestia's son against her.

"I know you are worried," Francis told her again. "But I just cannot believe that he would conspire against Hestia." How to explain? The man who had captured the essence of those laughing girls had treated them with . . . joy and reverence. "You've seen the sculpture—and you saw that painting. In both instances he created a blonde lady and small boy—and doesn't it feel *wistful* to you?"

"It was crafted to make us feel wistful," Brynne said darkly. "Who knows what the maker really feels?"

"I just can't believe the worst of him," Francis said with a shrug.

"I know," Brynne answered with a sigh. "And you are the most level-headed of us all. Your opinion is the only thing giving me hope."

She flushed a little, more pleased than she could admit. Reaching out, she gripped Brynne's hand in silent gratitude.

And that was why she was here today, was it not? She'd been given so much. It was what lay behind her fierce determination to solve this mystery—her fervent need to balance in some way her greatest debt.

There were so many kinds of debt in the world, and she'd seen them all. Money owed. Favors owed. The simplest of exchanges.

Family debts, moral issues. More complicated matters.

But what Francis had accumulated were life debts—two of them, in fact. She'd heard from a gypsy once, of an Eastern tradition—about a life saved forever becoming your responsibility.

It was worry about the reverse that kept her up during the nights. What if you were the one saved? That must surely become the biggest debt of all.

The first one she owed she would never be able to settle. Hatch was dead and gone. Francis liked to think that the work she did at Half Moon House, helping women of every class and situation, might tilt those scales.

But the debt she owed to Hestia Wright?

How to repay someone for giving you a life worth living? Shelter, safety and a purpose? A large, loose, oddball family of sorts and work worth doing? Care, concern and a path forward? She longed with her every fiber to be able to offer something in return.

And she knew Hestia well enough by now to know that there was a way. One thing she could give her that could come close to equalizing the balance between them.

Her son.

"Hestia doesn't think we'll find anything today, does she?" asked Brynne.

"I think she's afraid to hope," Francis sighed.

"Is that why she suddenly found such pressing business in the Lake District, of all places?"

"No, she wouldn't say what the business was, but I suspect it's something to do with Marstoke—and the government's search for him. Lord Stoneacre has been hanging around lately, and I think she was summoned before some members of the Privy Council." Her mouth quirked. "I don't believe she and Isaac know how much I can hear when they whisper together."

Brynne grinned. "Ah. I did wonder that she would leave when both Callie and I were in Town for a visit."

"Well, I know she hated to miss both of you. But I do think she was relieved to miss all of this." Francis waved a hand to indicate the crowd, the paintings . . . and the hope and expectation she could not suppress.

"Well, if anything is to be found of the missing young man, it would be here, would it not?" Brynne gestured around at the paintings mounted floor to ceiling around them.

"Exactly." Determination stiffened her spine. "We cannot leave any stone unturned. I'll talk to every artist, examine every painting, if I have to."

Brynne sighed. "Very well. Take Callie's girl along with you as you start, will you? She's a brewer's daughter and we've arranged an inter-view for her tomorrow here in the city. She's the only one along with us today who is not enamored with the hemlines and coiffures of the attending ladies."

Neither was the girl, Martha, interested in the art about them. Instead, she frowned thoughtfully around at the crowd as she followed Francis. "How many of these people already have suppliers for their household ale, would you guess?" she asked as they made their way through the crowd.

"All of them, I would imagine," Francis answered absently.

"And how would you convince them to shift to a new brewery, I wonder?" the girl said, almost to herself.

"Talk to their cooks, I would imagine. They would arrange the contracts. Or the butlers in some cases."

Martha nodded. "All right, then." She smiled at Francis. "Thank you."

"I wish you the best of luck in your interview and your new enterprise, but I need to examine the art here today. Would you like to help?"

The girl shrugged. "Might as well. What are you looking for?"

Francis thought about it. She remembered the reaction of those who had viewed the sculpture at Lady Pilgren's ball. The yearning between the figures had been nearly palpable. And the lady and the boy in the duke's painting had been unusual, but also pensive, somehow. "I expect I'll find what I'm looking for in a painting that grabs your attention, holds your focus. It might feel more immediate and alive. And it might hold something . . . different in the background. Figures that seem separate from the subject, but also . . . eternal. They might be of a blonde lady and a small boy."

Martha just shrugged. "I'll keep an eye out."

"Thank you. I'm going to start with the paintings 'on the line,'" she told the girl. "We'll move through the room and after that I'll take it wall by wall."

Putting old skills to use, she moved easily through the throng and started along the first wall. It didn't take long to lose herself in the art. There was so much of it—portraits to study, landscapes to be swept up in, and allegories to explore.

She was shying away from a particularly gruesome battle scene when Martha heaved a sigh. "I don't know why anyone would spend their money on a painting of someone they don't know." She sounded aggrieved. "If I had their sort of money, I'm sure I would spend it on a good wine cellar. Or invest in a promising business," she grumbled.

"Not all of the paintings are available for purchase," Francis told her. Some are here only to be shown." She surveyed the room with appreciation. "It's a lovely thing, don't you think, to show the public how much talent we have in Britain?"

"I suppose so." Martha brightened a little as they moved on to a sweeping landscape of greens and blues. "Now this I'd like. Mayhap I'd buy one o' the Downs, to remind me of home." She shook her head. "But look here—these are striking enough—but who would hang pictures of a bunch of rocks in their home?"

Francis paused. Striking was the right word for this set of related paintings. But something . . . A tingle went up her spine. There was something familiar about the bold brush strokes . . .

"Are you supposed to buy the set of three?" Martha asked. "They are pretty, in their own way. You could hang them in an office, I suppose."

Francis pushed past her, moving directly in front of the three landscapes. They were related, all of similarly odd shaped rock formations. She racked her brain. Weren't there supposed to be such rocks in the Yorkshire Dales?

"Well, no, then!" Martha suddenly declared. "That would do it for me." She was shaking her head and peering at the last painting. It featured a towering pillar that looked as if it were balanced precariously on a smaller rock. "Why put a picnic in the shadow of this one? I'd never get a lick of work done, always worrying that the thing would fall right over on the pair of them!"

Francis gripped the girl's arm, holding her breath. Yes, there, behind the curve of the rock base, a tartan blanket that blended in with the ground cover—and on it . . . a lady. Her face was hidden by a sweep of blonde hair—and she was feeding a tidbit to a small boy.

She gasped out loud. "Brynne!" she called.

"Oh, yes!" Martha leaned in, peering. "That's what you was looking for, ain't it?"

Francis could barely force her friend's name out. "Brynne!" She turned and gave Martha a huge hug. "That's it!" she crowed. "We've done it! We've found him!"

※

"Rhys Caradec? Yes. You've seen his depiction of the Brimham Rocks?" Mr. George North's eyes brightened. "Riveting, are they not?"

"Indeed. We are quite enamored of them." Francis strove for calm, but her heart was still pounding in anticipation and excitement. "We would very much like to meet the artist, sir. And when we asked, we were directed to you."

"Oh, well. Yes." The young man, suddenly discomfited, glanced around the small reception room they'd been shown to. "I suppose I am acting as his agent, for this showing."

"Excellent. Can you arrange a meeting for us?"

"Well, no."

"Why not, pray, sir?" Brynne brought out her most haughty demeanor.

"Well, he's not here." Mr. North flushed a little. "It's all very irregular, I admit, Your Grace. But I did obtain permission from the Academy members, I assure you." He looked a little sheepish. "Caradec has certain family connections, I understand, and at least one of the directors was eager to . . . ah, repay an old debt."

Francis spoke gently. The young gentleman had begun to twitch. "You are a student of the Academy, are you not, sir?"

"I am." He gave a little, nervous bow.

"And is Mr. Caradec also a student?" asked Brynne.

"Indeed, no, ma'am. But his work is stunning, is it not? I felt it just had to be shown. And I was very kindly allowed to submit it on his behalf." He rolled his eyes. "Certainly the gentleman himself refused to be bothered with the process—although he did say that the money would not go amiss, should they sell." He raised his brows. "And you did say you were interested in buying his work?"

"I am most definitely interested. But I'm afraid I must insist on meeting the man himself. If you are handling his business for him, one presumes you will know how to find him?"

The poor man flushed deeper. "Well, he did say that he would find me, when next he was in London. Highly irregular, as I said. But you must understand—he is . . . eccentric! Like no one else you've ever met."

Francis reached again for calm and kept her tone soothing. "Where did you meet Mr. Caradec, sir?"

"In Leeds. I was returning here from a visit with family in Durham. He had apparently recently finished some work in Yorkshire."

"Where was he traveling to?" asked Brynne.

"I'm not sure. I only know that he was . . . diverted."

"By a person?" Brynne spoke sharply. "A meeting, perhaps?"

"By his muse, evidently," the young artist answered with a shrug. "I first heard of him from the landlord at the Three Crowns in Leeds. When the man heard that I was a student of the Academy, he joked that his establishment had recently acquired an artist in residence. He kindly introduced me to Mr. Caradec." He shook his head. "I've seen my fair share of artistic temperaments in the grip of a mania—but this . . ."

"Was it the paintings of the Yorkshire rocks that gripped him?" Francis asked, curious.

"No! He was using them to drape rags over and to prop up his sketches! Can you fathom it?" Mr. North asked in disbelief and disapproval. "I had to rescue them! They are quite out of the ordinary. The grey in the rocks and the echo of color and depth in the sky—"

"Yes. We admire them tremendously as well," Brynne interrupted. "Do you know anything about the figures in the last painting?"

"The picnic?"

She nodded.

"I had to ask, of course. They are quite out of place! But he could only say that they lived in some of his work—and not in others. As I said—"

"Eccentric. Yes. So we understand," Brynne said dryly.

Francis had to know. "What was it he was working on, that had him so—"

"Excited? It was a sculpture. Apparently when he arrived at the Three Crowns he came upon something in the stables. One of the grooms had a small child, who had fallen asleep amidst a pile of puppies. The landlord said that Mr. Caradec began raving about innate trust and the abandonment of innocence. Apparently he caused quite a stir, banning everyone from the stable while they slept and he sketched like mad. Then he locked himself away in his room and barely came out while he did studies in clay and eventually plaster and marble. The innkeeper's wife complained about the layers of dust in there, but he won her over with a bag of coins and a devotion to her plum duff."

"We'll find him at the Three Crowns, then, if we travel north to Leeds?" Francis could not contain her excitement.

"Oh. Well, no."

"No?" She raised a brow.

Mr. North flushed again. "Well, I'm afraid I set him off. It rained buckets the first night I was there and the roads were impassable. I was forced to wait, and used the time to work on my own sketchbook. The next day, Caradec finished his piece and emerged from his room. We dined together and had a wonderful discussion—and he asked to see my book. He became intrigued with some of my sketches." The flush this time was one of pleasure and pride.

"Sketches of what?" Francis asked tightly.

"Of my father's hunting box in the Highlands—and especially my scenes of Edinburgh. He seemed quite taken with the notion of exploring the palace and the city."

"Edinburgh," Francis breathed.

"Francis," said Brynne, her tone a clear warning.

"Emily is right out there in the crowd," Francis countered, referring to the Countess of Hartford. "Her mother just opened her shop in Edinburgh. You know they would make arrangements for me to stay with her, should we ask."

"We will not ask! Francis dear, I know you love Hestia. We all do."

She was right. A great many people loved Hestia. A great many people owed her too—but none so much as Francis did.

"You know we must wait to talk to her about this before we do anything," Brynne continued.

"She won't be back for at least a couple of weeks. It will take days to get there as it is. If we wait, he could be long gone—and who knows to where?"

"We don't even know that he's there. Or how to find him."

Francis didn't respond, she was already plotting and planning . . .

"Francis! No!"

Blinking, she turned to Brynne and smiled, then reached out to pat her friend's hand. "I'm sorry, Brynne, but I'm going."

Chapter Two
EDINBURGH, SCOTLAND

I stood there in that ballroom and even as the terrible truth stabbed deep—Lord M—, he knew about my beautiful son—my mind drifted back. Back to those days when my parents had abandoned me, and Society labeled me a whore. Back to the day when I decided if they were going to discard and accuse me, then I would throw it back in their faces. I would become the Best Damned Whore Ever.

--from the journal of the infamous Miss Hestia Wright

F rancis charged down the narrow staircase. Saints, but it felt good to be in trousers again, although her scalp did itch under the wig cap she'd tucked her hair into. Worth it, though. The dirty mop of brunette locks sold her disguise far better than anything she could do to her own hair—save chop it off. And she was vain enough to want to keep her soft, reddish-gold curls.

Mrs. Spencer looked up as she entered the shop. Francis grinned at her. She heartily approved of her hostess's new enterprise. It was bright and welcoming and undeniably feminine. The place held ribbons, laces and sundries at all prices—and she'd seen Mrs. Spencer welcome a lowly fishwife with the same courtesy and grace that she showed the local noblewomen.

"Here now," the lady said as she approached. "Isn't it time you don your skirts again? Bad enough you should arrive here dressed like a lad."

"I probably should," Francis agreed. "It's far too easy to fall back into old habits. But really, you've no idea how much easier travel is for a young man," Francis told her.

"I can believe it, even though it is a scandal." The shopkeeper shook her head. "But my Emily says that you know what you are doing." She grinned. "And I suppose she knows a thing or two about disguises."

"A high compliment, coming from the countess," Francis answered with a smile. "And I thank you—and her—again for your hospitality."

"Och, no need. I'd move heaven and earth to help Hestia Wright, after all the good she's done—especially for my daughter."

"As would I," Francis agreed. And when word had come to Half Moon House that Hestia would be delayed in the Lake Country, her business taking longer than expected, Francis had known it was a sign that now was her chance. "Would you mind if I talked to your boy before I head out this morning?"

"Jasper? He's in the back, sorting out new inventory."

"Thank you."

"Will you be back for dinner?" Mrs. Spencer called as she headed for the back rooms.

"I hope so!"

She found Jasper in the first room beyond the main showroom, counting colored laces.

"Why're you still wearing boy's clothes?" he asked, clearly disapproving.

"Because I want you to introduce me to some of your friends."

"Ain't been here long enough to make friends." He moved a box with a grunt.

She merely leaned against the doorframe and waited.

He continued counting. After a few seconds he glanced up at her. And then again. "What?" he asked in exasperation.

"You know why I'm here. And you know who can help me find him."

"Who?" he asked, with a stab at innocence.

She laughed. "Once a street rat, always a street rat, Jasper. Now, are you going to make the introductions or not?"

He sighed. "And you are supposed to be a boy?"

She nodded.

"They won't go easy on you," he warned.

She straightened. "I wouldn't expect it."

It didn't take long to find Jasper's acquaintances, but it took half a day, rough words exchanged, proof that she could both take a punch and give as good as she got, and a promise not to knuckle any prizes in their territory before Francis found herself on good terms with a gang of local street urchins.

"The bloke I'm looking fer—he's an artist," she told them. "He shouldn't be too hard to find."

The leader of the group, Angus, rolled his eyes. "T'ain't London, but this *is* the capital city," he said with pride. "We've our fair share of artists."

"This one is newly arrived, and reported to be eccentric." She tilted her head back and scraped a measuring look over the lot of them. "A crew like this? I'll lay odds you know all the doings in this town."

"Wot's eccentric?" the smallest one asked.

"She means he's dicked in the nob." Angus pointed his finger at his temple and waggled it. "So, he's big and blonde, then?"

"So's I hear tell." She buried her excitement beneath a veneer of street *ennui*. "Where is he, then?"

"What'll ye give us for tellin'?"

"A shilling each," she said promptly. "That is, should you agree to help me run him down." She waited a beat. "And I mean that literally, lads."

"Two shillings fer me, as I'm captain," Angus countered.

"Done." Francis spit in her hand and extended it. Angus did the same and the bargain was sealed.

"He's up north o' the city proper these last days, I heard," Angus told her. "Painting the old St. Bernard's Well."

She grinned. "Good. Now, here's what I had in mind . . ."

※

He was losing the light.

Rhys sighed. It was all part and parcel of choosing a vantage point down in a narrow valley—but the view was worth it. The pastoral river, the old, many-columned temple of the well, and the lush greenery growing thick on the banks contrasted divinely with the hint of urban brick and glass just barely visible at the tops of the trees. The juxtaposition had captured his imagination.

But the depth of the location meant a limited amount of direct sun. He had to start late and finish early out here. Today he stayed until the last bit of useful light disappeared, then he began packing up his brushes and bladders, his mind on how he could thin the glazes back in his makeshift studio and perhaps capture at last the soft quality of the air that hung over the Water of Leith.

Taking up his case and his canvas, he started up the faint trail through the brush to the walking path at the top of the bank. His head was busy, full of plans for layering colors and for finishing his day with a grand slice of Mrs. Beattie's sticky pudding. He'd just reached the crest when—

Oof!

Something—someone—slammed into him, sending him staggering back. He threw his arms out for balance and managed to keep from tumbling back down the embankment, but his canvas went flying and his case flew open, scattering brushes, vials and bladders of paint everywhere.

"Clabber me!" His assailant, an adolescent boy, had been knocked backward onto his arse. "Sorry, guv!" He looked up at him with a set of bright, hazel eyes, then glanced nervously over his shoulder. Two other youngsters rounded a curve in the path at a run. The lad gave a squeak of alarm and dived into the foliage. "Don't give me away!"

Rhys didn't answer, but turned his back and bent to retrieve his sketch. He eyed the rapidly approaching boys. Both were taller, broader and thicker than the lad who had just bounced off of him. Ire flared in his gut. He knew what it was to be the odd one, the one always on the outside, the one who often had to fight to worm his way in.

"Oy!" the biggest bloke called as they drew near. "Seen a young shaver run through here?"

Rhys shot him a measuring look, read the determination and aggression in their demeanors, and made a decision. "Aye," he answered grumpily. "Do you think I made this mess myself?" He examined the still-wet canvas carefully.

"Where'd he go?" the other asked, his hands knotting into fists.

Rhys pointed with his chin. "Down the stairs by the well. And give him a dunk for me, when you catch him."

The boys laughed and hurried on.

Rhys propped up the canvas and began to gather his scattered supplies.

"I'll help." The whelp crawled from the bushes. "I'm that sorry, sir. I was watching over my shoulder instead o' in front o' me."

"Why are those toughs chasing you?"

"I'm new here," the boy answered, handing over a fistful of grime-covered brushes.

"Um-hmm. That's it? You didn't poach on their territory?"

"I said I was *new*, not daft."

Rhys sighed. "Never mind, let the bladders be or you'll spill my paint. Just go on and try to stay out of trouble."

"What? D'ye think I'm a lame duck?" the boy protested. "I pay my debts. I'll help you carry everything home."

"Um-hmm," he said again. "And you'll take advantage of my protection all the way back into the city?"

The boy's mouth quirked. "I did say as I'm not daft."

Rhys just grunted, closed up his case and handed it over. They started off and the boy marched along quietly, swinging the case. He ran another long gaze over the lad as they went. His features were sharp, his limbs thin beneath his baggy clothes. But there was something about him . . . was he familiar?

"That's a pretty enough spot you're painting." The boy craned his neck to look at the canvas Rhys carried. "It looks just like that, down there."

"It's just a sketch," he answered with a shrug. "The real work is done in my studio."

The boy's brows shot skyward. "You've got a studio here?"

"A temporary one."

"Ah, I didn't think you sounded like you were rooted here."

Rhys laughed. "No." He gave a dramatic shudder. "Not here, or anywhere, truly. No roots for me."

The boy stopped to stare.

Rhys just walked on.

After a moment, the boy ran after him. "That sounds . . . sad."

"What does?"

"No roots. What does it mean? No friends? No family?"

Rhys shrugged. "Do you find it pitiable? I assure you, I do not. Quite the opposite." The streets began to grow busier as they came closer to the city proper. He stopped to let a convoy of carriages pass and glanced downward. "And why should you? You said you were new here too."

"Yes. I'm just temporary here, too." He was quite a moment. "But I'm not rootless."

"Well, good for you, if it makes you happy."

The boy appeared to be thinking it over. He turned away and switched the box from one hand to the other. The lowering sun struck him, highlighting the delicate brow, the slightly pointed nose and the golden tips on a set of long eyelashes. Rhys frowned. What a waste, on a boy. And how serious he'd become. There was a puzzle here, somewhere. "What's your name?" he asked abruptly.

"Flightly."

Truth. He answered with a smidgeon of pride and not an ounce of self-confidence.

"It's interesting, down there by the water, isn't it?" Flightly gestured toward the canvas again. "The air is soft down in that ravine, and the light is too."

And the mystery deepened. Rhys set out again, his mind moving quicker than his feet. "You have a lot of opinions about my work."

The lad bristled. "And why should I not have them? Opinions are for everyone. They're free—and they don't weigh me down."

Fighting not to grin, Rhys raised a hand, capitulating. "No, no, don't take me wrong. You are, of course, entitled to your opinion. But you seem to have a bit of knowledge, and to have thought about it. Where did you say you were from?"

"I didn't say." The smudged chin went up. "But I'm from London, where there's plenty of good art in the streets and parks—and I seen my fair share otherwise, too."

"Have you?" A street urchin with fierce pride and opinions on art? "Do you perhaps fancy becoming an artist yourself?"

The imp laughed. "Saints, no, guv! If my handwriting is anything to go by, I doubt I could draw a stick house."

So he could write as well, could he? Turning a corner onto George Street, he gestured ahead. "I'm at the Hound and Hare." Half a block later, Rhys held out a hand for his case. "Many thanks for your help."

"As I thank you for yours." The boy gave a quick, little bow and Rhys's curiosity inched up another notch.

"What is it that brings you to Edinburgh, Flightly? You didn't say."

"Oh? Didn't I?" His eyes sparkling, the boy skipped backwards down the street. "Well, I should have made that clear from the start. I'm looking for someone, you see."

"Oh." Wait a moment . . . there was something in the lightness of that step, in the quality of his movement. Rhys's heart began to pound. "Well, good luck to you. I hope you find him."

Flightly turned and flashed a grin over his shoulder.

Abruptly, Rhys lost his grip on the heavy case. He never moved, merely let it go as it slid down his leg while he carried on, staring at the cheeky urchin.

Another flash of white teeth and a wicked grin. "Who's to say I haven't already?"

The figure darted away and disappeared around a corner. Rhys just stood there, his mouth gone as slack as the tension in his fingers.

Damnation.

Flightly was a *girl*.

Chapter Three

But I was a gently bred girl. Lord M— might have abused me mercilessly, but that only taught me how to hate—and how to survive. I needed to know much more if I was going to become an accomplished courtesan.
--from the journal of the infamous Miss Hestia Wright

The hour was late when Rhys collapsed into bed. Late enough that the inn had gone quiet around him and the quantity of candles he'd lit earlier had all burned low.

With a sigh, he pulled his hair loose and rubbed paint-stained fingers along his scalp.

The thin glazes were doing the job. So close he'd come, to capturing the unique quality of that lush valley. He'd been working feverishly for hours, trying to summon magic into his fingers—and avoiding the storm of conflicted conjectures in his head.

They caught up to him now, though, despite his best efforts.

So Flightly had come to Edinburgh looking for him? She hadn't said it in words, but the implication lived in the glint of her eye and in the mischievous slant to her grin. Well, he didn't give two damns why she'd searched him out. There were several possible answers to that question —and he wasn't interested in any of them.

He was interested in *her*, however. With his artist's eye he looked back, and realized that the clues had been there all along. The clear, high tone of her voice. The narrow set of her shoulders. Her fair skin —it had the peachy undertones of a blonde or redhead. Surely that dirty mop of dark hair was a wig. She'd been smart enough to darken her eyebrows, though, and to wrap her dirty neck cloth high around her throat.

How old was she? Older than she appeared as a boy, he'd wager. The quickness of her mind, the confidence she exuded—and the almost unconscious allure in that last exchange—it all made him believe she might be small in stature, but not in number of years. He'd guess she had close to a score of years, if pressed.

And how on earth had she come to be so comfortable in her role as a boy? She had the walk conquered, the bravado, the street cant. Hellfire—she'd even fooled him for a significant period of time, and he counted himself as far more observant than the general population.

All of those questions kept him tossing about and unable to sleep. But one followed him as he finally dropped off into the depths of slumber.

What did she really look like? As herself? What bounty had she hidden away beneath that wig and those baggy clothes?

His prodigious imagination set to work and his sleeping mind conjured one hazy image after another. She transitioned from slender to curved, from ash blonde to vibrant redhead. But every incarnation called to him, beckoning with laughing eyes and sultry smiles. She moved effortlessly through the mist in his dreams, drawing ever nearer —until he abruptly awoke—grumpy, hungry and hard as a pike.

The sun was just up. He crossed to the washbasin and dumped the cold contents of his pitcher over his head. Shaking like a dog, he tied his hair back into a queue and went to stand in front of his painting. Moments later he was back to it, brush in hand. Caught up in a furious push to finish, he paused only for a bite of toast and to toss back cup after cup of strong, black coffee.

When the sun finally reached a spot high enough in the sky, he gathered up a blank canvas and his case and went back to the Water of Leith.

The small valley was empty this morning, the well abandoned for the moment. Rhys set to work again, concentrating only on capturing the sky, the light on the lush growth and the sparkle and glint of industrialization peeking through and above the foliage on the opposite bank.

Only gradually did he become aware that someone had intruded on his isolation. The weight of attention tingled along his spine and raised the hairs on his forearms. Was she watching him? Casting discreetly about, he searched for a sign of the street urchin.

It took several minutes before he spotted her. No urchin now—but a young lady seated up at the well. She was nearly hidden by the shadows of the columns, and yet he knew it was she who had set his instincts alight—all while doing a convincing job of looking elsewhere entirely.

His heart rate climbed, pulling him along and into a heightened awareness.

Her. It had to be.

He strained, trying to see without letting her know. He had to know what she looked like—in her natural state. At this distance he could only make out bits of fair skin, light green skirts and a straw bonnet with matching ribbons.

It wasn't enough. Taking a step back, he stretched and tilted his head, examining his work. After a moment, when she didn't move, he gathered up his brushes and a small pail and went to the water to rinse them—at a spot a good ten feet closer.

She appeared not to notice. In fact, she appeared to be absorbed in the view that had so captured him—leaving him with little more than a glimpse of her profile.

He went back, burning curiosity slowly being replaced with a sense of bitterness. Did she think him so unobservant? Her disguise so foolproof? She flaunted her presence, seemingly secure in his imagined ignorance. And the question remained—which of his parents had sent her? It had to be one of them—who else would care?

It scarcely mattered in any case. He was interested in hearing from neither.

Moving stealthily, he packed up his case while she continued to appear lost in the beauty around them. Taking up his things, he crept quietly up to the walking path above.

At the top, he hesitated. Torn.

Slowly, he turned to look at the well.

She'd risen to her feet and walked to the other side of the round area. Was that a length of reddish hair escaping the confines of her bonnet?

Briefly, he imagined marching up to her to find out. But she took the initiative again. Leaning both hands on the railing, she shifted her weight forward, but turned her head to glance directly back at him. He was far enough away so that he could only really see the curve of the smile she tossed him.

He wanted to drop his things and stride over there. Get a really good look at her. Question her to discover why she'd sought him out—and at whose behest.

But what good would it do, in the end? He had his own life to live—and no plans to engage with either of his warring parents.

So he merely raised a brow at her, then spun on his heel. Resolutely, he turned toward the other direction and set out on a longer, alternate path back to the Hound and Hare. It was time put to good use, though. He spent it convincing himself of the folly of temptation. His course was set. He was having a grand time living just as he'd always wished. Why veer astray now? It would be foolish to even think of risking his carefree, hedonistic lifestyle.

He remained utterly convinced of his own wisdom, right up until he passed through the gate into the courtyard.

There she sat, looking prim and proper, even though she perched on an upturned stump near the inn's front entrance. Surely she must have run, to have reached the place so far ahead of him—but how then, did she look so completely unruffled? He couldn't decide if he was more impressed or annoyed.

She looked up as he approached—and everything changed.

That wide grin hit him full on. Her eyes, turned quite green in proximity to her walking dress, lit up. Mischief and glee and triumph—and *challenge*—oozed from her.

He stumbled to a halt. He could better see the outlines of her bones without the overlay of grime. She was everything sharp—high cheekbones, tilted nose, pointed chin. It might have given her a look of shrewishness, were it not for her large, expressive eyes and generous mouth. Her expressions saved her as well—and right now she looked piquant and almost . . . fey.

His fingers twitched.

He wanted, quite desperately, to paint her.

"Afternoon, guv!" she called in her street urchin's tone. Then she stood and strolled toward him—and a shiver went down his spine. Her boy's clothes had indeed hid a host of feminine curves, but they were pleasingly showcased now. It all felt eerily like the dreams he'd had the night before. Breathlessly, he waited, while she stopped, still several feet away. "I'm so sorry that I missed you at the well this morning, Mr. Caradec." She tilted her head. "Did you think to avoid me?" Her voice had changed, flowing smooth and cultured without even a hint of street taint. "How disappointing. But I am determined, sir."

"As am I," he answered.

"Does that mean you are not interested in speaking with me?" she asked. Amusement lived in her lively expression, not insult.

Who was she? Urchin? Lady? Messenger? Distraction? All he knew was that she was challenging him yet again. He stared back at the red-gold curls dancing around her bright face, at her cocky stance—and he knew that it didn't matter why she was here.

He gave her a long, considering look. "Someone sent you. And while I could not be less interested in whatever it is that they mean for you to say—I find I am quite interested in *you*, Miss . . ." He raised a brow and waited.

She didn't give in to the hint. "Well, that does leave us at an impasse, does it not? Whatever shall we do about it?"

It could have been said with innuendo and flirtation. Perhaps it *should* have been delivered so—it would have been the expected thing. But she said it with humor and quiet confidence and it piqued his interest more.

There it was—that prickle of inspiration. The tingle that began when his imagination caught fire and wouldn't let him go. He had to know her. He felt awake and alive and animated in a way that usually only came to him at the height of a project. There was no way he was going to back down from the provocation she was throwing in his direction.

Hitching his case up, he stepped forward until he'd drawn even with her—and then he leaned in close, so that the warmth of his breath would caress her cheek. "So. Flightly, you said your name was?"

She lifted a noncommittal shoulder.

"Very well." He fought back a smile. "Do I think to escape, you ask? I confess, I haven't yet decided. Would you chase me?" He paused to savor the surprise that flashed in her eyes.

"Or would it be more pleasurable if I chased you?" He walked on past her and tossed the last bit over his shoulder, just as she had done to him last night. "Let's find out, shall we? Tomorrow. If you can find me, we'll speak, then."

Chapter Four

How to learn such things? I turned to books first—my first loves, my best teachers. I learned of the great courtesans of Venice, who wrote poetry, composed music and advised powerful men on affaires of state. I read of the sophisticated beauties who moved through the courts of France, influencing politics, Fashion and many aspects of Society. . .
--from the journal of the infamous Miss Hestia Wright

"Oh, he's no' here." The next morning had dawned bright and clear, with a sea wind blowing steadily. Mrs. Beattie, the inn's landlady, spoke around the clothespin in her mouth. Crisp, clean linen fluttered in the breeze, filling half of the walled courtyard behind the Hare and Hound. She nodded toward the top of the building. "Yon large beastie was up there painting into the wee hours—the candles that man does go through!"

She snapped another piece of linen from the basket at her feet. "He came down at mid-morning, ate a breakfast fit for two men his size, then headed out into the city."

Francis, dressed in her breeches once more, buried her pounding heart beneath a mien of annoyance. "D'ye know where he meant to go? I'm supposed to put this message straight into his hand and nowhere else."

"Sorry, lad. Ye might check back here later." She nodded toward the stables. "Or wait if ye like—jest don' go distracting the lads from their work, aye?"

Francis thanked the woman and made her way around to the front of the inn. Excitement fizzed through her veins, as it had ever since she'd realized the truth—Rhys Caradec had seen right through her disguise.

She'd suspected it that first afternoon, when he'd gone slack-jawed and let his case slip from his fingers. She'd known for sure when he'd abandoned his painting yesterday, while the sun was still high and the light still favorable.

She was still savoring the surprise of it. She'd learned her role from the best—and she was good. The last person to recognize her trick straight out had been Brynne, long ago. The fact that he'd unearthed her on their first encounter—it meant that he was quick and observant —two of her favorite qualities.

But it was his reaction that had truly set her alight. He'd shown no sign of disapproval or disgust—and she'd encountered both in the past. The men, in particular, who had been let in on her secret had always found it distasteful. Not Rhys Caradec. Instead he'd looked . . . fasci- nated. And that was nearly as alluring as the kindness in his blue eyes —or the appealing height and breadth of him.

She felt fairly certain he'd *flirted* with her, too—and she had no idea how to feel about that.

"He's out and about in the city." She gave Angus a twisting grin as he approached. "Likely tryin' to avoid me."

"We'll find 'im," Angus answered with confidence.

But it wasn't easy. One of Angus's crew had spotted the man near St. Giles, but there was no sign of him there when Francis arrived. Another street boy heard talk of an artist sketching at the castle, but no one had managed to spot him.

At last, Francis got lucky and they found her quarry on Cockburn

Street. She paid the boys their fee and they melted away, while she tucked herself into a recessed doorway to reconnoiter.

Caradec had found a stool somewhere and was perched on it, right at the entrance to a narrow close. He was facing away from the alley, though, and staring intently at the rounded windows of a coffee shop.

Was he watching someone inside? She waited a while, and then began to ease slowly toward him, using the occasional pedestrian and successive entryways to conceal her movements.

She needn't have bothered. He had his sketchbook out and was utterly absorbed in whatever or whoever he was drawing. Gradually she drew close enough to see that he was focused on a gargoyle perched atop the decorative lintel above the windows. Not the usual, distorted human figure, this gargoyle depicted a cat with demonic blank eyes, huge fangs and enormous, clawed feet. Its likeness took shape on the page beneath his rapidly moving fingers, and she leaned against a nearby wall to wait.

It gave her the chance to observe him undisturbed—and she took full advantage of the opportunity. He truly was stunningly good look-ing. She'd never seen such long hair on a man. It fascinated her. He wore no hat and his long locks were the brightest thing in this dim spot tucked between tall buildings—blonde like Hestia's, but streaked with highlights honeyed by the sun. He wore it tied back in an untidy queue, but it would surely reach his shoulders when loose. Softly, her hands rubbed against her breeches, even as she imagined her fingers exploring that thick mane.

Almost. She was nearly close enough to catch his scent. She sidled a little closer. There. Linseed oil and a faint whiff of . . . trees. Like the faintest aroma of pine. She studied his long form, bent almost protec-tively around his sketchbook. In profile, his strong jaw stood out and when he looked up to study his subject, she could see his eyes had gone smoky in the shadows.

She'd just leaned forward to study the graceful movement of his hands when he suddenly stopped. Straightening, he gently blew on the page, then closed the book and tucked it away. He stood and gave a mighty stretch—and Francis swallowed.

He was so *big*, his shoulders so broad—and yet he was lean at the same time. Long and strong and lanky, like some Viking warrior of old. The combination was . . . tantalizing.

So many times she'd seen it—the tug of attraction. Everywhere from Covent Garden, to the ballrooms of the *ton*. She could certainly recognize it. Had put it to use more than once. She'd never fallen victim to such things herself, though. But now—Rhys Caradec had started something blooming inside of her and with each glimpse of him it stretched and awakened further.

He bent to catch up his bag—and caught sight of her.

And now she found herself the object of that intense focus. Their eyes met. Her breath caught. A prickle of sensitivity spit and sparked and traveled all through her like a flame following a long and winding fuse.

A slow, ironic smile started in the corner of his mouth, then widened to light up his whole face. "I wondered when you would find me."

She lifted her chin. "I wondered when you would notice me."

"Been here long, have you?"

"Long enough." Abruptly, she grinned. "Although I will admit it took a while to track you down. You did a good job of avoiding me."

"I wasn't avoiding you, precisely."

"No?"

The smile twitched again. "No. But I didn't try to make it easier on you, either."

She laughed. His eyes were still running over her, their weight almost alive, as his gaze darted about, assessing all the finer points of her disguise.

He looked away, picked up the stool, then glanced back at her. "Are you hungry, then?"

She shrugged.

He placed the stool just inside the coffee house door, before continuing on down the street. "Well, come on," he called. "I'm starving."

She hesitated. None of this was going as she'd imagined. There was something alive in the air between them. It wasn't simple. It was . . . distinct. New. Unexpected. She found she wanted to know more.

A strange ache started up in her chest, watching him walk away—and she shook her head and chided herself for succumbing to dramatics. Scrambling, she hurried to his side as he walked on. "Where are we going?"

"Just up here."

She followed, silent—and feeling decidedly dainty beside his large form. Surprisingly, she didn't resent it—as she sometimes did at home, when a hulking man from the streets stomped about, throwing his bulk into the faces of smaller mortals. But Caradec moved quickly and lightly on his feet. He carried his strength with ease and she found herself appreciating the difference.

They'd nearly reached Market Street when he stopped at the wide steps leading upward and into Warriston's Close. At the base stood an old woman tending a steaming cart.

"Have you had a bridie, since you've been in the city?" he asked.

"A what?" She watched him exchange a coin for two handfuls of something in flaky-looking crust. "Meat pies?" she asked. "We have those in London."

"Not like this." He handed her a pie, fragrant and warm, and bit into his.

Francis blinked—then quickly grew caught up in the sight of his enjoyment. She hadn't even been truly hungry, but watching him, she was suddenly starving.

He had his eyes closed. His teeth looked strong and white as he took the first bite. His tongue darted out to catch the escaping juices. He moaned—and something fluttered in her stomach.

It wasn't hunger pains.

"Come, sit down and try it." He coaxed her over to the steps, still warm from the sun. They sat together. But not too close.

"Go on." He gave her a nod and she lifted the pie and took a bite.

Her eyes widened. As with his, the juices ran. Without hesitation, she stuck out her tongue and licked them from her wrist and hand, unwilling to let a drop escape. "This is . . . wonderful," she said fervently, before taking another bite.

He stared, watching her avidly, forgetting his own meal. She pointed with her chin.

"Oh, yes." He bit in again. "Mab makes the best bridie I've ever tasted." He smiled his appreciation at the older woman.

"The secret's in the spices." The older woman leaned in confidingly toward Francis. "Me darter moved to Italy with her husband. She sends me the freshest herbs—and fine stuff like you cain't get 'round here. Makes all the difference."

"It surely does," Francis agreed. She laughed suddenly. "You know, I knew a young woman with a baby, back at Ha—" She caught herself. "Back at home. When you gave the little tyke something particularly good, he would mumble the entire time he was eating it. Mmm, nmmm. Mmm, nmmmm." She grinned up at Mab and cast a saucy glance at Caradec. "I absolutely understand the urge, now."

He laughed and the old woman thanked her, then moved on with her cart. She and Caradec finished their meal, sighed and sat back, replete and happy. The stone radiated warmth, the street lay as quiet as the contented silence between them.

Now. This was the time that she should tell him. She'd met his challenge, now she could tell him why she'd come. Let him know about Hestia, how wonderful she was. How much she missed him. How much it would mean, if he could go back with Francis to meet her.

But that comment about not having roots—it still worried her and made her hesitate. He'd sounded so adamant, almost defensive, about it. She suspected that it was going to be a job to convince him—and likely an argument.

And she—who had scrapped her way through numerous street brawls and traded insults with everyone from pimps and thieves to constables and even dukes—suddenly had no wish to fight.

"That was an unusual gargoyle you were sketching," she said instead, surprising even herself. "I've never seen one quite like it."

"This city is full of them, I'm finding. I saw a Green Man on the Royal Mile this morning. Someone saw me sketching it and directed me to St. Giles—but many of theirs are high and difficult to see. This street, though, hosts several interesting specimens."

"Is that what you'll paint next? Gargoyles?"

"Perhaps." He yawned. "I nearly finished the river painting early this morning. I need a certain color to finish the sky, but I'm out. Now, while I wait, I'm ready to rest and explore again. I found the gargoyles interesting today—so I sketched them. They'll bubble in the back of my brainbox, along with whatever else I find to store away. Eventually, an idea will pop up."

Francis had never felt less like yawning. She thought about what he'd said as she watched the traffic on Market Street, visible from their perch.

"What are you thinking about?" he asked—and she turned to find him examining her again.

She blinked. "I was wondering what *they* would think." She gestured. "The people of the city. Surely they are used to great artists coming here—but likely to paint the palaces, the churches, and the views. What would they say, if they knew you were thinking of painting their gargoyles?"

He shrugged. "I should think they'd be happy enough. They love their capital, and the gargoyles and grotesques are just another wonderfully unique aspect of it." Eyeing her askance, he continued. "And in any case, the people here rather remind me of their gargoyles."

She snorted. "Weathered?" she asked quietly, indicating old Mab's retreating form.

"Enduring," he corrected. "And unique. Fanciful, but practical about it, at the same time."

Slowly, she nodded. "Yes. I think I know what you mean." She gazed at him, sure that this must be the strangest conversation she'd ever had—and equally sure she wanted it to go on. "Is that always how you choose what to paint? Wander about until something strikes you?"

"Yes. That's exactly how I do it." He laughed. "Do you disapprove? I'm sorry to tell you that I am likely exactly what your elders always warned you about." He waggled his brows. "The insidious, itinerant artist."

He said it like she should picture him with horns. But in truth, he was a far cry from what she'd grown up worrying about. She had no desire to start that conversation, however. She let him continue, instead.

"I wander." He threw an arm skyward. "I go where my urges take me and I stop when I find something interesting, beautiful or meaningful."

It sounded . . . She wasn't even sure how such an existence sounded, so opposite it was from her own. Wonderful? Terrifying? *Free?*

He was studying her again. "Sometimes," he said softly. "Sometimes the thing that is interesting, beautiful and meaningful—is a person."

Perhaps he was trying to unnerve her. Her. She almost laughed out loud.

Except, damn him, it was working.

She stood. She wasn't a street rat any longer. Hestia was teaching her many things—including how to understand a situation and help mold it to suit her purposes. She hadn't come all this way to let Caradec scare her off. She was here on a mission. She would tell him about Hestia, convince him to establish a relationship with her.

"You said yesterday that if I found you today, we could speak. I could tell you why I've come."

He sighed. A big, massive breath full of resignation. "I did. And you could. But we don't have to, do we?"

"We do. At some point."

"It's bound to be unpleasant," he warned. "And this—this has been exceedingly pleasant. I'm very aware that you must have come from one of two persons—neither of whom I'm interested in hearing from. I'll be irritated and you'll be frustrated." He shook his head. "Instead of ending our . . . acquaintance . . . on a sour note—wouldn't you rather put it off, and perhaps . . . do this again?"

Search him out again? Meet the challenge he'd thrown out at her? Sit in the sun and talk with him? Share a meal and learn a bit about him, again?

She stood up. Perhaps that's what she needed to make this work. It might help to know more of him. She could gauge the best way to approach what was sure to be a sticky subject.

She wasn't intimidated. Or intrigued.

Oh, saints. She was a little of both. But she'd handled far more difficult situations.

"How old *are* you?" he demanded, looking up at her.

She sighed. "Older than my years."

He nodded, as if he approved of this answer. "Going somewhere?" he asked.

"Home."

Silence stretched out for a few moments. It felt heavy with . . . what? Disappointment? Expectation?

She straightened. "Not to worry, though, I'll see you tomorrow."

He laughed. "Perhaps."

"Oh, don't doubt it," she said loftily, and then she turned on her heel and walked away.

Don't look back. Don't look back. Don't look back.

"Flightly!" he called.

She looked back.

He was on his feet.

"Are we going to do this?" His voice carried down the curve in the street. "Enter into this . . ." His hand waved in the air.

She pressed her lips together. He was asking about more than just their game of hide-and-seek. But how much more? She had no idea—was suddenly afraid that she couldn't even yet conceive of all that he meant—but she burned to know.

She nodded.

"I won't hold back," he warned. "I'm going to give you a run for your money."

She tossed her head. "You can try."

Then she blended into the traffic and disappeared.

Chapter Five

In the end, I decided I needed a mentor. Not just any woman, but one of elegance and grace, intelligence and beauty. But how to find such a paragon?
--from the journal of the infamous Miss Hestia Wright

R hys found himself making a special effort with his neck cloth the next morning—and cursed when he realized what he was doing. Tying it off, he abruptly quit his room, throwing his bag over his shoulder as he strode downstairs.

"Weather's changing, Mr. Caradec." The landlady approached as he headed for the door. She followed him and peered at the sky. "Rain coming midday. Mark my words. If you will just hold a moment . . ." She turned and went to a cupboard behind the desk that held the register, returning with a folded length of brightly colored wool. "Take a spare plaid, it'll keep you dry enough."

"Thank you, Mrs. Beattie. I'll be sure to return it." Pausing, he looked from the tartan to the sky. "If you don't mind, might you have one more to spare?"

"Aye. I do indeed. Wait here." She shuffled off and returned with a similar fold of fabric. "Found a friend, have you, Mr. Caradec?" she asked knowingly.

"I hope so, Mrs. Beattie." He grinned at her. "As you appear to have your finger on the pulse of the town, perhaps you'll let me know?"

Her laugh rang out, a peal of delight. "Oh, go on with ye, lad—and enjoy yer day."

Chuckling, he left the inn behind. He wandered a bit, letting the flow of traffic take him where it would, watching the people and the scenery with a casual eye. The city was old and venerable—and pulsing with life. From ancient kirks to new public spaces, it bustled with energy but contained plenty of quiet spots for reflection, as well. He quite liked it. He continued on, absorbing the city's atmosphere, and keeping his eye peeled for a sign of Flightly.

It was a point of pride, not to let her find him too easily today. And after the multiple challenges she'd thrown at him, he was due one of his own. But he had to admit, he was looking forward to seeing her again—and seeing how this all played out.

He was a man who enjoyed women, it was true. And they liked him in return; he was not loath to admit. Fair dealings, openness and honesty—it was his way. Women were no different.

Except, he was forced to acknowledge, this one was different. He didn't even know her real name. He did know that she was an appealing mix of innocence and worldliness—and he wanted to know more.

Impatience tugged at him, but it was more than his usual anticipation of some easily scored, good-natured bed play. This girl had depth. She would require finesse.

It wouldn't be easy. She was like a finely formed puzzle box. One wanted to trace gentle fingers all over her, probing until all of her secrets lay open. But for her, he would proceed slowly. Show patience. If he let her set the pace, he felt certain that the reward would be . . . substantial.

But first, she must find him. And he had work to do—and inspiration to seek. Looking around, he realized he was near Holyrood Palace. The entrance to the park lay just ahead—and a few bars of discordant music sounded from that direction. Curious, he followed the noise.

The park was surprisingly full. Perhaps everyone had Mrs. Beattie's weather eye—and hoped to absorb the last rays of the sun before the rain came again, for the rough, open field had taken on the air of an impromptu fair. A couple of tinker's wagons were set up, doing a steady business. Students sat in groups, holding precious books and earnest discussions. A baker wandered, selling sweet buns. Men played chess around a couple of portable tables. Children ran with hoops and balls. Women watched them and sewed in contented circles.

He cast an eye to the skies—there were definitely clouds moving in —but for now Rhys followed an ear-numbing chorus of unrelated notes to a group of musicians beneath a spreading chestnut tree. He took a seat with his back to sun-warmed rock and settled in to watch.

"Let's start again, mates, with the old *Hamilton House*, eh? Ready?" A big man waved his hand and nodded his head in time and they were off, four of them with a pipe, a fiddle, a bodhran and a set of spoons, all tripping along well together on the rollicking song—until suddenly they were not. The pipe lost the melody, which set the fiddler off. The spoons gradually died away until only the quick, heart-thumping rhythm of the drum forged on.

"Hold on," the piper called and a muted discussion ensued.

Rhys finished off a quick sketch of them, then looked around for something else to draw. The view of the Abbey and the Palace was not bad here. He worked for a while on capturing the grandeur and was just making a note in the margin about the quick-changing color of the sky behind it, when a cry of distress brought his attention back to the misfit band.

A young child had joined them. The piper's son, by the sturdy look of him—and by the miniature pipe clutched in his small hands. He was attempting to mimic the simple run of notes his father played for him. The other musicians had wandered over and gathered around a smiling woman with a basket—presumably the child's mother.

Almost without volition, Rhys began to sketch the pair. Fingers flying, he raced to catch the determined furrow in the child's brow, the clear affection in the father's eyes and the flush of pride and relief that glowed from the boy when he won the man's praise. What must that feel like? That unconditional support? The open fondness?

"That's the first time I've seen you frown while you worked."

He looked up with a start. Flightly sat cross-legged on the ground only a few feet away. Her gaze was curious—and a little triumphant.

And his reaction was immediate—and physical.

"You found me quickly, today." He closed the sketchbook.

She shrugged. "I thought about what you said yesterday, and I thought you might feel like sketching people today. Everyone's talking about the rain coming." She gestured overhead and he realized that the predicted weather had grown decidedly imminent. "I figured a lot of people might be out to enjoy the weather before it turned—so the parks. I tried the Royal Botanical first, but . . . here we are."

"Very quick witted of you." And too observant by half. Had he been frowning? He glanced quickly over to where the boy and his father had finished their lesson and had gone to help the others pack up their things.

She watched them too, alight with curiosity. "I'm sorry I missed their rehearsal. I've been hoping to hear the Highland pipes."

"They are very . . . singular."

She grinned. "Then I shall be sure to enjoy them. When isn't singular better than common?"

She was dressed as a boy again. His first reaction was disappointment. He had been looking forward to seeing those curves showcased again, instead of hidden so thoroughly. But all around them people were gathering up their belongings and starting to leave—and her attention shifted quickly from one group to the next, to the sky and on to him, and her thoughts flowed like water across her face. Dressed like this, there was no distraction from her fascinating, quicksilver expressions.

And right now her expression told him that her attention had been diverted. "Excuse me for a moment?" she said to him, her gaze focused somewhere off behind the musicians. "I'll be right back."

He watched her go, watched her face go blank and wary as a group of gentleman passed her by, their heads together and their conversation low and muttering. He watched her smile and nod to a couple of small girls gathering flowers at a small hillock. She spoke to them a moment, then bent and wandered about a bit, gathering up a handful of flowers herself. Were they violets? He narrowed his eyes, trying to see and saw her wave at the girls as she headed back towards him, her expression now one of satisfaction.

He could do a whole series on her, he mused. One aspect after another, each featuring that creamy skin, that trail of freckles across her nose and those incredibly expressive, changeable eyes . . .

"Oh, I forgot!" She stopped in front of him, paused in the act of pulling a knapsack from her shoulder so that she could deposit her flowers inside. She dug into it, coming out with two, linen-wrapped bundles and held one out to him. "I owe you a meal."

He gazed down at the offering—and something softened in his chest. "You didn't have to do that."

"I wanted to. Since you gave me a taste of the Highlands, I thought I would return the favor." She held it out. "Fresh baked oat bannocks, slathered with honey, and scotch eggs. My friend grew up here and assures me this was regular fare at tea time."

His stomach growled and they both laughed. But an alarm thumped inside of him, as well. He'd always been a popular fellow. His size discouraged most mischief. His cheerful, even nature made him a fair amount of friends. His willingness to reward good service and loyalty generally ensured that he was welcome everywhere. But his solitary and wandering ways meant few opportunities for others to reciprocate—and now he found himself unexpectedly moved and . . . restless.

"I thought we might—" Whatever she meant to say was cut off when a great raindrop splatted right on her nose. Her eyes widened. A similar drop hit his forehead—and then the heavens opened up.

Around them people laughed and cursed and whooped and headed for the gate in a steady stream. Flightly slung her bag back over her shoulder and made to follow, but he held out a hand.

"Wait."

Pulling out one of Mrs. Beattie's plaids, he draped it over her head and let it hang down over the rest of her. Grabbing his own, he pointed toward a thick grove of elms and weeping ash not far beyond the spot where she had picked the flowers. "We'll stay mostly dry in there, I think. Shall we?"

She hesitated but a moment, giving him a long look, then turned and dashed for the shelter of the copse.

He'd been right. The leaves were thick above them, and only a few drops made it through the protective canopy. The light shone dim. A carpet of old leaves and needles lay thick beneath their feet. The branches of the ash trees drooped low, enclosing them in a protective bubble, with only the patter of the rain overhead to remind them of the world outside.

"Well, this is cozy." Flightly removed her plaid and folded it, using it to soften a seat on a wide, low branch. She tossed him the packet she'd offered before, then took her perch and dug into her food.

Rhys shook his head, immeasurably pleased with her *sang-froid*. Not many women of his acquaintance could adapt so easily—but neither did they run about town in breeches. He took a seat against the base of a tree and unwrapped his own lunch. "This is not the oddest meal I've ever enjoyed, by far," he told her placidly. "But it's the oddest one I ever shared with a female."

"At least you won't forget me," she said, unconcerned, and took a bite of egg.

He snorted. "Forgetting you won't be an issue." He cocked his head. "But I would like to know more about you. Your name, for example?" He raised a brow.

She sighed. "Why is no one ever happy with just Flightly?" She tipped her head back, as if asking for patience and he fought back a laugh. "It's Francis," she said at last. "Francis Headley."

"Frances." He tested it out. "Convenient. Suitable for either a male or a female."

Her chin rose. "I spell it with an *i*. F-R-A-N-C-I-S. Always. No matter the clothes I'm wearing."

"Why take the masculine version?"

"It's a long story." She lifted a shoulder. "Maybe I'll tell you, another day."

He nodded, allowing the retreat. "Well, it's pretty enough." Her knapsack was getting in the way and she reached up to hang it on a higher branch. Her sleeves fell back and he stared at the firmness of her arm and the toned musculature beneath her silky skin. What must she look like, without clothes? As fascinating and unique as she was in them, he'd wager. "But Flightly suits you better."

"I know," she answered glumly.

"I can guess how you came by the nickname. I gather you are fast?"

"Like the wind," she said with pride, her grin the widest he'd seen from her yet. His fingers literally twitched—and so did his cock. He wanted to snatch that wig from her head, let her hair free, watch it stream out behind her as she ran—and he gave chase.

"I was faster than any of the—" She stopped and the smile faded. "Faster than anyone. She shifted on her branch and he knew she'd had enough of sharing. "So what was your oddest meal?" she asked, clearly diverting focus onto him.

"Let me think a moment."

"So many to choose from?" she said, slightly incredulous.

"You don't believe me?" He sat back against the tree. "The tales I could tell! A Danish sailor once shared his rye bread, raw beef and fresh pickle sandwich with me." He smirked at her crinkled nose. "But that does not compare to the night I shared a bottle of wine and a boiled calf's head with a French executioner."

Her jaw dropped at that one, he was pleased to note. "How? Why?" she demanded.

"His sister was married to the mayor of a little French village. I was staying with the couple while I painted her portrait. The brother came to visit from Paris and asked me to join him for dinner. Truthfully? I went because I was afraid not to, after he was done telling me how much he enjoyed his job."

She laughed, and he felt triumphant. Her smiles were a joy, a transformation. They spoke of ancient mischief and shared laughter. He was struck, suddenly, with a very vivid image of her in his bed, wrapped in tendrils of red-gold hair and dissolved in helpless laughter.

Damnation. She made him yearn with all the zest and zeal of an untried boy.

"You've traveled widely, then?" she asked with a note of approval.

"I have. I grew up in France. But I've been through Prussia and

Austria. As far north as Copenhagen. And now England and Scotland."
He did not mention how it was that he came to England. If she was
Marstoke's creature, then she knew his father had arranged it. If she
was Hestia Wright's—then it would be better if she didn't know the
particulars. "Italy will be next. Soon." He shrugged. "I can feel
her pull."

"It would seem the natural destination for an artist," she agreed.

"It's possible that I'll be diverted again, but I'll make it there. And
what of you? Have you traveled?"

"A bit. All within the confines of England."

"And yet you've seen much in your meager years." He could tell.
Knowledge lived behind those changeable eyes.

"I've seen the ocean." She deliberately didn't answer his true
statement.

"Where?" he asked.

Her gaze had gone unfocused. "In Dorsetshire. Near Weymouth."

"And?" he asked softly. "What did you think?"

She didn't answer for a moment. "The beach was silt and pebbles.
So odd under my feet. The water was cold. It was so . . . vast. The sky
so large and blue. I found it to be beautiful, of course."

He waited.

She blinked and turned to him. "I felt small," she confessed. "But
also connected to something very large. To everything."

He nodded, satisfied. He'd known she had an artistic soul. "I
believe that there are some places on this earth that are meant to make
you feel—truly *feel*."

"Are those the spots you paint?"

"Some of them." His mind cast back. "Some are too perfectly beautiful to be translated by the hand of man."

She drew a deep breath and blew it out. "Tell me."

"The mountains," he said in a low voice. "Gorgeous crags and
alpine lakes, so smooth, like glass. They act as a perfect mirror. You
stand there, suspended between two sets of wooded slopes and snow
peaks. Two brilliant blue skies." He closed his eyes. "I think surely they
are there for God's use. And we are just fortunate to be able to experience them."

They sat, for a few moments, in comfortable, contemplative silence. A rarity in itself, in his experience. The light was still dim, but the rhythm of drops overhead had slowed considerably. Rhys watched her lay her head back against the tree and examine the roof of sheltering limbs. A relief, really, to know that she had the ability to turn all of that quick wit and inquisitiveness off, for at least long enough to rest a moment.

Eventually, though, she shifted on her branch to watch him. She'd gone serious. That wide mouth pressed thin and her eyes had widened. "I may not have seen as much of the world as you have, but I've seen enough to know that I like the way you look at it. And the way you translate it, through your art."

He froze, uneasily certain that she'd just shattered the peace between them. "You've seen . . . what?" he scoffed a little, trying to diffuse the sudden tension. "A preliminary landscape and a handful of charcoal sketches. How could you know such a thing?"

She turned her head. "I've seen some of your other work."

His mind raced even as he sat very still. "The Royal Academy?" he asked after a moment.

She nodded.

No chance of retrieving the quiet now. His heart was pounding too loudly in his ears. "Ah. I suppose Mr. North told you where to find me, then?"

"Yes. I saw your renditions of the Brimham Rocks." She hopped down, took a step toward him, then retreated again to lean against the branch. "They were magnificent. I was caught up in the small details—right down to the striations in the rock. They felt . . . real. And I suppose you know Mr. North could not stop rhapsodizing about the color of the sky."

He didn't answer.

"I truly enjoy the way that your art transports the viewer. I could feel the awe that place must inspire—almost as if I were there myself."

Would she continue to surprise him every time she spoke? He wanted to delve into her reactions, ferret out the details, ask a hundred questions. Instead he stood. "The rain's not so heavy now. I have work to do."

She folded her plaid and handed it over. Pulling down her knapsack, she waited, as if it were a foregone conclusion that she would accompany him.

He strode off, feeling dreadfully conflicted and more than a little resentful about it. She followed him at a run and he bit back a sharp remark, then surprised himself with a surge of irritation when she paused.

He walked on, but looked back as he reached an intersection, to see her talking to a girl. The mite was huddled under a lamppost as if it would protect her from the still-steady drizzle of rain. A flower seller, she had her ragged cloak spread wide at her feet to protect the bucket holding her wares. Rhys watched Flightly pass over the bunch of violets from her knapsack.

Snorting, he crossed the street, but it didn't take long for the intrepid girl to catch him up. He held his silence as she dogged his heels all the way until Holyrood Road turned to Cowgate. As the traffic thinned a bit, he shot a terse question over his shoulder. "You've seen more than the Brimham paintings, haven't you?"

Her hesitation spoke volumes.

"Yes," she said at last. "I thought your portraits of the Duke of Danby's granddaughters were . . . amazing."

He stopped, right there on the street and ignored the mutters of protest as their fellow pedestrians were forced to break and flow around them. "You've seen *Danby's* paintings?"

Yet again, it was not what he had been expecting. He'd thought she was going to admit she'd seen the sculpture that Marstoke had . . . appropriated.

"Yes." Her spine went ramrod straight. "And the companion piece, as well."

He was aghast—and struggled to understand why. He'd already known she'd come looking for him.

But he surely had not imagined her following in his footsteps across the country, examining the artwork he'd left behind him. The thought of it made him feel . . . a little wild.

"Damnation." He spun on his heel and stalked on. Stubbornly, she followed. When it suddenly began to rain in earnest again, he ducked into an alley, reached out and pulled her in with him. Half dragging her, he continued into the gloom until he reached a doorway. He shoved her in, under the scanty protection of the recessed doorframe.

It was a world of shadows and haze back here. The street they'd left was hidden in the mist. Everything, the stone building, the mud at their feet, and the rain in the air—all was slick and dim and grey.

But her face shone bright up at him. Her cheeks glistened and her eyelashes were damp and spiky. He pushed her further into the doorway until her back came up against the wooden door.

Her eyes went wide. Her mouth hung, pink and tempting and slightly agape. "Pixie," he said roughly. "How did I ever mistake you for a boy—even for a second?"

His hands were still on her, clutching her arms. She reached up and grasped him, just behind his wrists. "You saw what I wanted you to see."

He snorted. The rain was cold on his back but all of the rest of him was surging with glorious heat. "Don't think it will happen again."

She laughed. "It will," she said with slight derision. "But you won't even know."

Another challenge.

This time, he answered. Holding her tight, he bent his head and kissed her.

Chapter Six

Fortunately, my friend Pearl, owner of The Oyster, had connections in varied circles. She knew just the woman, had met her back in her own heyday. The woman had fled Paris with a group of artists and intellectuals and was living in Vienna. We wrote to her and made plans while we awaited a reply. We thought we had plenty of time.
--from the journal of the infamous Miss Hestia Wright

S hock hit Francis first. Shock at the sensation of his warm, masculine body pressed abruptly all along her front—and then wonder at the feel of his mouth moving over hers.

Her second reaction was a sudden, thorough comprehension. *This explained so much.*

She'd thought kissing a small thing. The touching of mouths, the sharing of breath, the mingling of tongues. But it was more—so much more.

This was huge. A massive wave that separated into a multitude of feelings, all spreading in ripples from their point of contact. They touched her everywhere, muddled her thoughts. His kiss was a wind-storm, blowing away everything she thought she knew, ushering in a whole new world of revelations.

He kissed her with aggression, deep and insistent, before catching her lower lip, and then the upper, tracing all the contours of her mouth. He was learning her, tasting her, making the rest of the world disappear and all of the bones in her legs dissolve.

Abruptly, he pulled away, hauling her upright as she leaned against him. "Damn it." He looked into her eyes. "Have you never been kissed, Flightly?"

Heat rose in her face, but she refused to be intimidated. She lifted her chin. "I have now."

She'd flummoxed him. It felt good. She decided to do it again.

All of it.

Moving her hands up, she explored the solid strength of his arms, the breadth of his shoulders. Then she clutched behind his neck and pulled him down to kiss her again. Greatly daring, she kissed him in the same, unrelenting way he had her. And she did a good job of it, judging from the sound that emerged from down deep in his throat. It made her shiver as it went all the way through her and settled, molten and heavy, in her belly.

His hands slid to her waist and clutched her closer. The tip of his tongue coaxed its way inside. She held on tighter, feeling the strange wonder, the delicious heat of their mutual excitement. And it was mutual. She wanted this as much as he did—and kissed him harder still, reveling in the excitement of so many conflicting feelings.

This was madness. It was amazing. How could she feel the power and danger of what they were about—and yet feel so . . . treasured and safe . . . in his arms? How could she not yearn for more?

With a sound of regret, he pulled away. "Minx," he said fondly.

She just rolled her eyes and tugged at him again.

"Slow down a moment."

She didn't want to. The knowledge of all that she'd missed had been dropped in her lap and she was ready to catch up.

"This is going to require . . . discussion." He looked up in exasperation at the rain, still pelting his back. "Here." He dragged one of the plaids out again and wrapped her up in it.

"What about you?" she asked, grateful for the hefty weight of the wool.

Reaching back, he squeezed a trickle of water from his hair. "It's too late for that—but let's find somewhere warm and dry."

She followed him from the shadowed alley, back out into the street. They hadn't gone far when they encountered a pub on a corner. A group of men exited, allowing tantalizing smells and laughter to waft out. Caradec eyed the place with longing, started to pass it, then stopped and looked back at her, running a measuring eye up and down the length of her. "Well. We might as well make use of that get-up." He beckoned for her to follow as he headed in. "But we'll leave if it gets too rowdy."

Francis tugged off the plaid as they entered the taproom. Should she reassure him that this was hardly her first tavern? This one was noticeably cleaner than some—and it was full. On the far wall a couple of men drained their pints and stood. Caradec moved at once to claim their spot. He pulled both chairs and the table a little closer to the fire before sitting down with a groan of satisfaction.

She took the other seat and kept her head down when the serving girl approached.

"Do you have coffee?" he asked.

"Aye. But it's this morning's brew," she warned. "Might do better with the ale."

"No, we want something hot—and I like it nice and strong."

"I'll jest bet ye do," she said with a purr.

"One for me and one for the boy," he told her. "No, wait. Just bring the pot."

"Won't be but a moment."

She returned directly with a tray and Francis ignored her fawning over the artist in favor of cradling a warm cup in chilled hands. The girl flirted a few moments longer. Once she was called away, Caradec took up his cup, as well. With a sigh, he took his first sip.

"Ahhh. Dark and hot as a sinner's soul," he breathed. Eyeing her over the brim, he raised a brow. "But let's have none of that between us, eh?"

"Sin?" she asked, returning the raised brow.

"Darkness," he answered firmly. "Let's keep all between us open and honest and out in the light."

"Fine, then." She gave him a direct stare. "You can start by telling me why you kissed me."

He choked on his coffee. "What kind of question is that? Why do you think I kissed you?"

She lifted a shoulder.

He leaned in and spoke low. "Because you were—are—damned near irresistible, minx."

She gave a disbelieving snort and looked down at her ragged clothes.

He made a low, urgent sound. "Do you think it's not intoxicating, knowing what lies beneath there? Knowing that I'm the *only* one who knows?"

Her doubts must have shown, because he put down his cup and sat back in his chair with another long sigh. "Perhaps it would be well if I start this by sharing some things about myself." He glanced over, waiting on her permission.

She gave a slow nod.

"As I said before, I am a wanderer. That's the best explanation, the best description. I just wander where the fates take me, soaking life in and letting it roll around a bit inside of me before I send it back out through my fingers."

She smiled. "You remind me of a chef I saw once. He was choosing wines from a merchant. With each new vintage, he would take a drink, swish it around in his mouth, then spit it out."

"Ah, but I'll wager he smelled it first, did he not? Closed his eyes and breathed it in? Did he hold it up to the light to look at it closely?"

"How did you know?" she marveled.

"It is what connoisseurs do with a fine wine—and it is the perfect metaphor for life. You must drink it in with all of your senses, savor it, extracting all of the lovely flavors."

"And spit it out?" She made a face.

"Onto the canvas, in my case," he said seriously. "There is pleasure to be had in life. All of the tastes and smells and joys and wonders. I love my unfettered life—it leaves me free to experience it all—and to wander where I will, following inspiration where I find it. In a gorgeous vista, in a strange custom, in delicious food and friendly people."

"You make it sound lovely, but I am sure there are complications."

"None worth dwelling on. There is nothing so sweet, nothing I love more than the unexpected—the experience of something I've never seen, tried or tasted before."

Passion lived in his words, in the tension of his large frame, in the bright earnestness in his blue eyes. She heard it—and coveted it. But did she want it for herself—or focused on herself?

Either. Or both.

He leaned closer and she inched back a little, cognizant as always of the picture they presented to the room.

"You," he breathed. "You are entirely new. Beyond expectation. I find that—"

"Here we are!" The serving wench was back and she had a determined air about her as she eyed Caradec. "I made you a fresh pot."

"Thank you," he said absently.

The girl had lowered her bodice, Francis noted, and she bent low and lingered as she poured him a new cup. "If there's anything else ye'd be hankering for, jest let me know."

He looked up. "Actually, we were wondering if there's anything sweet to be had from the kitchen?"

Straightening, she put a hand on her hip. "I'm the sweetest thing to come out o' that kitchen, sir."

He chuckled. "Well, and I have no doubt that's true. But I was thinking more along the lines of something to feed the boy. He needs fattening up."

The girl never looked Francis's way. "We have mutton stew, and oat bread to go with it."

Caradec shook his head. "We'll stick with the coffee, for now."

Her lips pursed in disappointment. "I won't be far, should ye change yer mind."

He nodded. "You'll be the first to know."

Francis smirked as the girl sashayed away. "Saints, but I'll bet you get that everywhere you go."

"Not everywhere," he protested.

She shot him a look of disbelief.

He rolled his eyes. "It's only my size. A woman once told me that they all look at me and think: *The bigger they are, the harder they fall.*"

She smirked again. "Bigger and harder feature in their thoughts somewhere, I'm sure."

He feigned shock. "Large talk for a girl who's only just had her first kiss."

"I've eyes in my head and blood in my veins. Just because I haven't acted on it doesn't mean I don't feel anything." She cocked her head. "Looking at you, I'd say it's as likely to be your hair as much as your size."

Now he really did look surprised. "My hair? Mostly the ladies tell me how unfashionable it is—and urge me to cut it."

"Oh, no. Don't do that." In fact, she wished he'd take it from the queue and spread it to dry in the fire's heat.

"You like my hair." Bemused and a little pleased, he shifted in his chair. "I have to say, I'd like another look at yours." He gave her a look that started another fire in her belly. "In fact, I'm quite vehemently interested in getting to know more about all of you—but there are a few things that must be discussed first."

He had no idea.

"Everything I told you earlier was to a purpose," he continued. "We are attracted to each other. I daresay we even like each other. I would be interested in pursuing those feelings. But you should know that I offer nothing permanent. I find this city to be fascinating—and you more so—but eventually the muse will call me elsewhere—and I will answer."

Her spine straightened in indignation at being warned off even before they'd begun—but a moment's thought had her appreciating the honesty of it. "What exactly are you offering, then? Temporarily?"

"Whatever it is that you wish. I'd like the chance to get to know you. How far we take that friendship—the decision will lie with you. You set the limits and I vow, I will heed them."

Oh, how he tempted her. This giant of a man with his big hands and his too-long hair, with his ready laugh and his hot kisses—he could be her first *affaire.*

The blood singing in her veins urged her to agree. The silky heat in her belly did too. She wanted to say yes. The very air between them vibrated with their . . . mutual appreciation. She knew he would treat her well.

But he was Hestia's son. It was Hestia who longed for a connection with him. How would she feel about a former street rat taking up with her son?

An unworthy thought—she knew it before it had finished. Hestia would never begrudge either of them a bit of happiness.

But therein lay the danger. She liked Rhys Caradec. She was unexpectedly and wildly attracted to him—and she was very much afraid that *temporary* would not make her happy. She'd had enough of *fleeting* in her life. Hestia had given her a taste of safety and solidity and she'd liked it very well indeed. She'd chosen to stay and acquire more, all those years ago—and to try and spread it around a bit too.

When she gave in to a man, she wanted to jump all the way in. She wanted big and bold and all encompassing—what Callie and Brynne had found. She wanted a love so deep it would engulf her—and change everything.

"There's one more thing," Rhys said, suddenly sober. He took up his coffee again.

"Yes?"

"You came to Edinburgh looking for someone. It was me."

Her breath caught. "Yes."

"Then that's the one limit I must put forth straightaway. I am not stupid or uninformed. It was not always the case, but I know now who my natural parents are. I'm aware of the hostility between them—and I know one of them must have sent you. I don't give a tinker's damn which it was."

She started to speak, but he raised a hand.

"I don't even *want* to know which one sent you. Whether it was to learn something, offer something, or merely to plead a case—I don't wish to hear it. I don't mean to offend you, but I will not take part in their games, or war, or whatever they wish to call it."

She straightened. "I don't think you understand—"

"No. I'm sorry. Clearly you have chosen a side in their conflict, but I will not be drawn into it." His tone grew harsher. "And I will not be used as bait or ammunition or be thrust into the middle of it, in any way." He sat the cup down. "That is my only restriction. The one limit I *must* set."

His shoulders were rigid, his jaw set. "Think before you answer—because I predict this will not be easy for you—to cut the person who sent you out of all conversation—and I will not be moved."

She narrowed her eyes. He was giving her an easy escape. She should take it.

His expression drooped a bit. "I very much look forward to getting to know you, but I will end it if you cannot leave the subject alone." He sighed. "And if the failure of your mission makes our . . . friendship . . . impossible, then I am very sorry."

Not half as sorry as she was. She could hear the pain that lived behind his declarations. Something had happened to him. Something that had soured him toward both of his parents. Hestia hadn't had any contact with him since he was but a babe, so it must be something that Marstoke had done—and she knew from experience that it might have been very bad indeed.

And what of Hestia? She'd sworn to do anything she could to give her friend and mentor the thing she wanted most. Him.

What should she do? She knew what she yearned to do. Saints, even he might blush if he could see all the things she'd pictured earlier.

She snuck a glance at him. He was watching her with sympathy and more than a little yearning of his own.

"Have I ruined it?" he asked quietly. "With your quest turned aside, will you have to return to London straightaway?"

She considered. Truly, she didn't have to go. It would be days, still, before Hestia returned. And even then . . . She glanced down at her knapsack, hanging on the chair, and thought of the violets that she'd carried inside. The kind of work she helped Hestia with could be done anywhere—although not as easily without the weight of her mentor's name behind her. But it could be done, here.

Maybe that was the key. She glanced at Caradec again. Maybe it was the sort of message that she could demonstrate, rather than tell.

She was the only one at risk, here. And he, generous, foolish man, had given her control. All she had to do was to keep things light between them, keep her heart tucked away while she learned what she could of him and showed him Hestia's generous and giving ways. She could do it. For Hestia.

And perhaps for herself, too.

"No," she whispered. "There's no hurry."

"And you?" he asked. "Do you have any objections to continuing . . . this?" He circled a finger in the air between them. "Any obstacles?"

Objections? No. Francis had always held a thoroughly pragmatic view of relations between males and females. She'd seen every sort imaginable, in her days on the streets. She was no debutante, with expectations of behavior and proprietary. Before she'd actually experienced passion, she'd expected she would find it someday, be perfectly willing to act on it, and move on. But now, having had her first taste, she felt like there would be more involved than easing bodily demands.

"Obstacles?" she asked.

"Of any variety," he answered with a shrug. "A husband, perhaps? Betrothed? Irate father or other invested males?"

"Only an interested butcher's boy," she said with a laugh. She ran a heated gaze over him. "And he never tempted me as you do."

"Damnation." He shifted again in his chair. "I take it that means you are free of moral objections."

"Nary a one," she said cheerfully. "But there is one thing. My . . ." she hesitated.

"Inexperience?" he said gently.

"I'm not sure I'm ready for a . . . physical *affaire*."

His gaze grew heated but he sat back. "We will do nothing you are not ready for. I swear it."

She believed him. He was a kind man—and a cursedly irresistible temptation. Intentions were one thing, but Francis had been in a thousand sticky situations. She well knew the folly of not preparing for every contingency.

"My virginity," she said bluntly. "It is mine to give. And if I decide to wrap it in a bow and gift it to you, I will let you know."

She hadn't known it was possible for a man to moan and laugh at the same time.

"It's no foregone conclusion," she warned. "You said I could set the pace and the limits."

"And so you shall, even if it kills me," he said in a strained voice. He laughed suddenly. "Yes, everything about this enterprise is going to be a new experience."

She met his gaze directly. "If I agree to your condition, then you must agree to mine."

He sobered and waited.

"As you said earlier, I've seen things. I understand how most of this works, even if I've no experience myself. And as you've promised only a temporary run, then I must be sure that I will not be caught with . . . consequences."

"I've never had the pox," he vowed. "And as for pregnancy, well, there are precautions."

"French letters," she said clearly. "A supply of them. Worn every time—or we part ways now."

"I do so promise," he held up a hand. "Very wise of you."

"Very well, then. We are agreed." This trip was taking a very different turn than she'd expected when she set out. But she felt hopeful—and excited and nearly breathless with anticipation and a few dozen other emotions. "How do we begin?"

"Slowly." The strain was back in his voice. "We begin slowly."

Chapter Seven

But then it happened again. One of Lord M—s lackeys came looking for me. I cowered in the attics while Pearl again told the story of the girl who had arrived broken and bloody. He demanded further proof. Pearl let him speak to the chambermaid, who described with great relish the bloodstained floor and sheets she'd had to clean. Still, he wasn't satisfied and left to travel the nearby countryside, asking after a noble girl, alone and with child.

--from the journal of the infamous Miss Hestia Wright

*S*lowly was going to kill him.

Clearly, Francis Headley did not understand her own appeal. He looked forward to rectifying that situation—and to making sure she knew her worth, too.

But the *slowly* bit—that was going to require all of his control.

"Well," she said brightly. "I'll leave the first steps to you, then?"

She might have been discussing a hand of cards or a shopping expedition, but this felt altogether more serious to him.

Standing, he threw coins on the table. "Come, let's leave before someone notices how I'm looking at you."

She scrambled to her feet. "Perhaps you should just stop."

"Stop looking at you?"

Her mouth quirked. "Stop looking at me *that way*."

He raked her with another scorcher. "Impossible," he rasped.

Wrapping up, they headed out. Fortunately, the rain had slackened, leaving only a drizzling mist in the air. As before, she fell in behind him, in keeping with her guise. "I should just hire you as my errand boy," Rhys mused as they paused at a busy corner. "It will give us time together—and no one will blink an eye if I keep you in my studio for hours."

"I will," she objected. "I thought you understood I'm not ready for that."

"When you are," he said, low and intense, "it will look entirely natural." His stirring manhood approved of the plan.

"I suppose so." She sighed. "I would like to wear my own clothes occasionally, when we are about."

His cock twitched in agreement.

"Perhaps we can put it about that you are painting my portrait?"

"Perhaps." Interest flared in his gut. He would paint her, he knew. The desire was fierce, but unformed. He needed a focus, an idea—and he was content to spend time with her while he waited for it to strike.

"Where are we going?" she asked as they set out again.

He noticed she was keeping a little further back than she had this morning. So, she might throw brave words around, but she was nervous. *Slowly* really would be key here.

"High Street. Mr. North was so kind as to give me the name of the best color man in the Highlands. I'm to pick up an order of paint today."

It wasn't far. He bit back a grin when she ran ahead of him up the short stairs and held open the door. The mischief in her face captivated him—as did so much about her. She was utterly different from anyone else, and resolutely at ease with it.

Fascinating.

"Mr. Caradec! Come in, come in."

"Mr. Dunbar. Good day to you."

"Your order is nearly complete." The color man set aside his mortar and moved behind the counter.

"Nearly?" The shop was small. Rhys left Francis examining jars of powdered pigment and crossed to speak with the shopkeeper. He kept one eye on her as they spoke, though, so he was angled to see when the door opened and another gentleman entered.

He relaxed when the man passed Francis without a second glance, but straightened in surprise as he stepped closer. "Andor!" he exclaimed as the man tucked his hat beneath his arm. "Is that you?"

He stepped forward and grasped his hand as a great smile broke out across his friend's face.

"Rhys Caradec! I cannot believe it!" Andor's Norwegian accent brought back a wave of memories. "What are you doing here?"

"Oh, it's the same story." Rhys shrugged. "Inspiration pulled me into town. But I had no idea you were here as well."

"But yes! I live here now. My wife and her family have business interests here and we have agreed to watch over them for a time."

"Wife?" Rhys reared back in shock. "Wife?"

"Wife, yes! But you are shocked, are you not?" His friend grinned at the joke.

"Shocked? Yes. Surely it was not so long ago that we traveled together—and you were the most infamous seducer of . . ?" He paused and looked over where Francis watched them with interest. "Well, you were very NOT married," he laughed, thinking back. "Was it a year ago that you left, headed to France to paint portraits for a wool merchant?"

"Yes, a little over a year. And yes, I did paint the portraits—then married the eldest daughter once her portrait was done. Oh, but you must meet my Lorette! She has a head for business to rival any man's. Her father wanted offices and a warehouse here, close to the source of so much of his stock. Lorette will get it up and running, so we will be here for a brace of years, at the least."

He sounded content and proud—and Rhys could not fathom it. "But, what of your painting? Surely you haven't given it up?"

"Of course I have not! Not even the birth of our first child has slowed Lorette. I could do no less! I have a studio and I've done several pieces I'm proud of—and even found a way to derive a steady income from my work."

That bit of speech sent several jolts down his spine, but he focused on the first and most important. "Your first child?" he repeated, stunned.

"It is true!" Andor laughed. "I am a papa. Is it not wonderful?" He glanced over at Mr. Dunbar. "Oh, but do not let me get started on all the amazing qualities of my son, or I will never stop—and I have clearly interrupted. My apologies."

"No, we are finished." Rhys stopped him before he could back away. "Mr. Dunbar has filled my order as much as he was able."

"I do apologize," the color man said. "The ash of ultramarine which gives that particular grey its blue undertones can be difficult to find. But a shipment will arrive shortly and then I will fill your order first, Mr. Caradec."

"Oh, but you need the Natural Grey—yes, it is perfect for so many of the skies here, is it not?"

"It is. I have a painting nearly complete, but I'll need it to finish."

"Well, you must not wait, and there is no need. I have some of that color in my studio. You are welcome to it."

Rhys frowned. "I would not want to impose upon your own—"

"No, no, I insist! And should love to show you what I have been up to, in any case."

He hesitated.

"Here you are." Mr. Dunbar pushed a small box of supplies across the counter. "The rest of your order."

Out of nowhere, Francis stepped up to take it.

"Is this your boy?" asked Andor.

Rhys had to work not to glance her way. "Yes. I've just hired him. I was about to take him back to my own studio and get him started on his duties."

Bless her heart, she did not make a sound.

"Bring him along to my place, first." Andor smiled at Francis. "I daresay you'll like the surprise I have for your master." He clapped Rhys on the back. "I'll send you both back in our carriage."

They both stared at him, awaiting his decision. Francis's face held carefully blank. He felt a strange reluctance to see the place where Andor lived such a changed life, but he couldn't say that—if only because Francis would scoff at him. And she would be right. If she had only been his hired errand boy, he would have gone—and he had no wish to raise suspicion, either.

Sighing, he nodded his head.

⚜

R hys was glad for the carriage, as Andor's home was situated well away from the Old Town, near the docks. They stopped before a massive, square building, whitewashed and with a long stairway leading along the front of the place to a door on the first floor.

"Below are the offices and warehouse space," Andor explained. "We'll go up." He opened the door at the small landing and they entered a small entry hall with two wooden doors.

"There we live," his friend waved a hand toward the right. "I suspect my young Erland is sleeping, so we will stay in the studio, for today." He turned toward the left and held the door for them to enter.

Francis let out a sigh as she moved in and Rhys, following, couldn't blame her. The space was large and open.

"You had the windows added?" he asked. But he knew the answer, for the place was flooded with light—and with color. It assaulted the senses, but once he stepped in a little further, he had eyes only for the large canvas in the center of the room.

"Gorgeous," he told Andor, moving to contemplate it from one side, then the other. It was a lovingly detailed rendering of Edinburgh Castle, the vantage from below. On Prince's Street, most likely. Unlike the cloudy, grey sky of his own current work, Andor was in the midst of portraying a vivid blue sweep behind the imposing edifice. "Was it commissioned?"

"Yes. I've done a few portraits since I arrived, but this one was ordered by my father-in-law. He wants something impressive in the offices back home—something he can point to when he discusses his Scottish warehouses."

"Well, it is impressive, indeed. Well done, my friend."

"Thank you. Now, let me show what else I have been doing . . . ah, I see your boy has discovered it."

Rhys swung around to see Francis bent over a smaller work. A triptych piece, the three panels were only a couple of feet high and propped on a long counter, leaning against the wall. She appeared to admire the fanciful scene. It depicted a forest grove, with the moon peeking from behind leafy trees and small, fey creatures peeping from the undergrowth.

"It looks like a set piece—something you'd see in the theatre," she marveled.

"Exactly right," Andor said with delight. "This is for a Midsummer Night's Dream."

"I would have guessed that one," she said with a nod. "It looks as if Puck might be just behind a tree."

"So small?" Rhys looked down the counter and saw several more, similar works, but each with a different scene painted. "What are they for? Theatre companies?"

"Yes," Andor grinned. "But toy theatres."

"Toy?" Francis asked before he could. "Theatres?"

"Have you never seen one, lad? Many a nursery or schoolroom boasts one. I met a man in France who manufactures them. Rather than restricting his buyers to a general background or just one play, he had the idea to make sets you could change out—and I got the charge to design them."

"And is this the fair Verona?" she asked, moving on to the next one.

"'Tis indeed. I'm surprised you haven't seen a toy theatre, then. They've been popular for quite some time."

"Not in my circles," she said wryly.

"Yet you know of Puck and recognized Verona?" Rhys pointed out.

She shot him a glance. "Yes, well, I know a fair number of actresses. And I was hired as a puffer once, when one of them, a friend of mine, won the role of Hippolyta. She shook her head. "It was a rare beauty of a thing, that play."

"A puffer?" Rhys repeated.

"I thought it was a failure of my English," laughed Andor. "What is this, please?"

"Damned if I know," Rhys answered. They both eyed her, waiting.

"Neither of you?" Francis rolled her eyes. "Well, let me tell you, when Molly won that role, the other actress under consideration was right hot over it. The rumors flew that she and her friends meant to show up on opening night and hiss Molly off the stage. So the manager hired me and some others to do the opposite—to cheer her to drown out the spite." She lifted a shoulder. "See? Puffers." Her head shook in reminiscence. "That was a good night. Got to spend it in out of the cold, got to see the spectacle of the crowd and the play—and was paid tuppence, besides."

Rhys lost all interest in the set pieces, transported by all the things Francis had revealed in that little story—and all of the questions it raised. What had she been through, his disheveled little urchin? How had she come through it with her confidence and quirky humor intact —not to mention her virginity? And why was he so drawn to her, and determined to discover the answers?

"It sounds a good night indeed," Andor said kindly. "So . . ." He moved off to one end of the room and pulled out a drawer in a cabinet. "Here is your paint, Rhys."

"Thank you," he answered, moving to take it. "I'll be sure to replace it once my order is filled."

"Yes, and you must come to dinner and meet Lorette and my son."

"Thank you. I appreciate the kind invitation." He clasped his friend's arm once more, than turned to Francis. "Let's go, lad, and allow Andor to get back to work."

Chapter Eight

How had my secret got out? Who would have told Lord M— that
I had managed not to lose my child? I kept my hand curled
protectively over my belly for days. I couldn't know who it was.
And neither could I wait to leave. My plans had to change.

--from the journal of the infamous Miss Hestia Wright

They had to walk to the livery where the carriage had gone to
await them. Francis didn't mind. Caradec had taken the box of
supplies from her and stomped off, a formidable scowl upon his face,
and dutifully, she'd fallen in step behind him, wondering what was
bothering him.

She had no idea what it was, but she was enjoying the sight of him,
strolling along with his long steps, the escaped ends of his hair blowing
in the sea breeze and his dark expression clearing the pavement ahead.

She was having a grand time, in fact, imagining him as a warrior,
striding along these same streets in the last century, wrapped in a

colorful plaid with a broadsword strapped to his back. He had the shoulders for it, the long, lean back, the strong brow and set jaw. She was very busy conjuring up how heavily his arms would be muscled and staring daggers at the very correct, modern clothing that prevented her from comparing, when he abruptly turned into the livery yard.

He bundled her and the supplies into the coach and they set out. He spent a few more minutes staring broodingly out of the window and she'd just settled in for a quiet ride when he turned to her.

"So, you enjoy the theater, do you?" His tone sounded gruff.

She was slow to answer. "Well, I don't really know, to be truthful. The night I told you about, I missed a lot of the meat of the story, worrying for Molly and thwarting her hecklers. The only other night I set foot in a theatre, I was mostly . . . behind the scenes."

And she wasn't ready to discuss that night with him or anyone else. The infamous night that the Duke of Aldmere foiled Marstoke's plan to incite an international incident. The night that Hatch died—and Francis's new life emerged out of the ashes of the old.

She considered him. The skies outside were patchy with clouds. There must be one sunbeam in the entirety of Edinburgh, and it had found him, slanting through the window to set his hair to gleaming with hints of gold. "Are you?" she asked. "A fan of the theater?"

"I hardly know. I've hardly much experience myself, of the formal variety. Now, the traveling troupes, those I know a bit about. My first commission was for a mural on the side of a prop wagon."

He unfocused a little, clearly reminiscing—and the memory obviously brought him some pleasure.

The sight of it made Francis thankful, not for the first time, that she hadn't been born a lady. There were no rules governing her behavior or feelings, none to stop her from enjoying the light that slowly chased his morose expression away. Nothing telling her to look away from the attractive crinkling in the corner of his eyes.

This big, handsome, charming man had proposed a seduction—of *her*. Even if she didn't mean to let things go that far, still the wonder of it made her slightly dizzy.

"Was that how you first started wandering? With a player's troupe?" she asked, to distract herself.

"No, but it is where I got the idea. They were . . . irresistible. So carefree and full of fun and mischief. It was a window onto another world."

Had there been no fun or mischief in his early life? She filed the question away for later. "So you followed in their footsteps and have wandered—but alone instead of with a group?"

"Not always alone. I've shared paths with others from time to time. Andor was a fine companion. We traveled through three cities together."

Understanding dawned. "Ah, is that why you've gone scowly? You don't like the idea of your friend settling down?"

He straightened. "I don't like it. No."

"He seems happy enough."

"Happy *enough*? He's a talented artist! He did a series of landscapes of the frozen fjords of his home—and they hang in one of the royal households!"

"He still possesses the same talent," she said reasonably.

But Caradec's attention had shifted. He leaned forward and stared out the window for a second before signaling the driver to stop. "Stay here. I'll be back in a moment."

He was out of the carriage before she could object. Gripping the handle, she watched him open a door and enter a building under a sign that read *Jacobs and Sons, Wine Merchants.*

It took considerably more than a moment and more than once she considered going in after him, but he finally emerged carrying a box that he placed on the bench next to him. "No questions." He held up a hand. "You asked me how we were going to begin? Well, I'll show you once we get back to the Hound and Hare."

He would brook no opposition and they rode the rest of the way quietly. When they reached the inn, she took up the smaller box of art supplies while he took the other.

"Mrs. Beattie!" he called as he entered, moving ahead of her with his long stride.

"Yes, Mr. Caradec?" The landlady came down the stairs carrying a load of linen. "I see ye did not melt in the rain."

He laughed. "No, thanks to your plaids. And I do thank you for the loan of them."

"Keep them for now, ye'll have use of them again," she said sagely before she turned to eye Francis. "And is this the lad who wore your extra? I'm that disappointed for you, sir. I thought you had a lady friend to keep company with."

"I hope to see my lady friend tomorrow," he confided. Francis wondered if the matron noticed the twinkle in his eye. "But I did find myself an errand boy today. I mean to put him to good use fetching supplies, carrying my easels and such."

"Aye? Well, feed the boy, and you have the chance. Heavens, but are you naught but skin and bones, lad?"

"No, ma'am," she answered truthfully. "There's more to me than that."

Caradec laughed out loud. "I'll have one of your private parlors for the evening, if it's available. I'm going to discuss his new duties with the boy and go over the properties and manufacture of quality paints."

"Aye?" He'd lost Mrs. Beattie's interest. She hefted her linens back up and nodded toward the back of the inn. "The blue parlor is empty. Go on with ye, then."

"Thank you. And could you send along a couple of wine glasses?"

"Ah, I thought I saw the old Jacobs mark on that box." The landlady tucked behind the small desk that held the register, reached up and pulled a bell pull before taking her linens up again. "We've a new girl working tonight, Mr. Caradec."

A brunette came breathlessly from the green baize door just beyond the desk. She approached and curtsied. "Yes, Mrs. Beattie?"

"This is Malvi," the landlady said, her voice tight. "She made a special request, Mr. Caradec, to meet the artist we had staying with us." She lifted a brow in his direction. "She'll bring your glasses and anything else you'll need, but please don't make me regret making her known to you."

Francis saw Caradec straighten, most certainly affronted, but the servant girl spoke before he could.

"I'm sure the gentleman would never, Mrs. Beattie." Malvi breathed in, emphasizing the way she'd tied her apron to mold to her ample curves.

She never—never looked at her employer, that is. Francis didn't think she'd taken her eyes off of Caradec since she'd stepped out of the servant's corridor.

"Never *what?*" she asked, as rude and condescending in two words as only an adolescent boy could manage.

The girl's gaze still didn't lift from Caradec. "Never do anything untoward. Would you, sir?"

"Why would he?" Francis snorted. There. That got Malvi to turn away—if only to shoot a dark look full of malice in her direction.

"I hope you know I shall continue to treat all of your staff with the utmost courtesy, Mrs. Beattie," Caradec said stiffly. "Exactly as I have done."

"Aye, sir. Ye've been naught but the perfect gentleman and I mean no offense, but I did wish ye to know of the . . . state of things." Now the landlady tossed a warning look at her new girl. "Ye're welcome to the parlor and Malvi will be with you shortly."

Francis followed him into the back of the house and entered when he held a door for her. The parlor was small, but the fire was laid and ready and two plush chairs sat before it. A round table and chairs occupied the other side of the room and light from several covered lamps made the place feel cozy.

Caradec eyed the chairs before the fire, but then moved to the table. He set the box down, went over to set a light to the fire, then crossed back.

"Now, we begin—and we do it just as we discussed—by absorbing all the rich wonders of life."

"Wine?" Francis asked, moving closer to watch him open the box.

"Not just any wine." He took out a bottle, slightly dusty. "Sit," he motioned.

The look he gave her along with the order had a temperature of its own—and it slid over her skin like silk. She sat, worrying that they hadn't even started yet and she already needed to worry about keeping her resolve.

"When I was a boy, there was a winery near my village," he began.

"It had been there as long as the village, everyone said, and had quite a good reputation. The children, myself included, were sometimes hired to help in the fields or at the presses. The patriarch of the family who owned the place was a legend. Nearly eighty years old and still a man with an eye for the ladies." A smile broke out on his face as he remembered. "Oh, he was a character and we loved to hear his stories. His palate was renowned. He could taste a wine and tell what region it had come from and sometimes what year it had been bottled."

He shook his head. "At assemblies and festivals, men would test him, setting up a challenge, asking him to name several different vintages. Old Gabin nearly always knew. One time he sat all the children down and taught us how to appreciate a good wine—much in the way that your chef did."

The door opened and a subdued looking Malvi came in, carrying a tray with two glasses.

"Ah, just in time," Caradec said. "We'll take those—and if you could bring two more glasses and a pitcher of water? And ask the kitchens for a bit of cheese, if you please?"

The servant girl set down the tray. Staring at him, she hesitated a moment, then whirled around and left the room.

Francis would have rolled her eyes, but Caradec appeared oblivious. She watched him open the box and take out a bottle, handling it carefully. "Is that from the winery?" she asked, bursting with curiosity. "The one near your village?"

"It is. I think you will enjoy it." He leaned in and the narrow space between them filled with heat and a jolt of something that traveled right down to her belly. "And now," he breathed, "we begin."

She could not resist the urge to needle him. "Begin what?"

"Your education."

She might have laughed, if she hadn't been caught by that slow, anticipatory smile.

With smooth movements and deliberation he poured a glass of wine and set it before her. He poured himself one too. When she would have reached for hers, he stopped her.

"Look at it first. What do you see?"

"A glass half empty?" Her mouth twitched.

"Very amusing, but we'll save philosophy for another day." His heavy lidded eyes fixed on her face. "I'm an artist, Flightly. I want to know what you see, learn how you view the world."

Swallowing, she nodded.

"Tell me," he ordered.

Carefully, she examined the wine.

"Don't frown so," he told her. "There is no wrong answer."

She looked, really looked. "It's like a jewel. A garnet. And there is a brownish line around it, where it touches the glass."

A flash of curiosity showed in his face, but he didn't ask anything. "Hold the glass—by the stem, not the bowl—and leave it on the table while you swirl it around a bit."

She obeyed.

"Now, breathe it in."

She lifted the glass and took a cautious sniff. "Oh!" she said in surprise. "It's not sour at all, but sweet. It smells like berries."

He followed her example. "It does. Anything else? Close your eyes and see what comes to mind."

"There is something." She frowned. "Something . . . wet?"

"Earth?" he suggested.

"No." Her eyes popped open. "Leaves. I can smell wet leaves, like after a rain." Amazed, she looked at the glass.

"Interesting, isn't it?"

"I never knew there was so much to it." She smirked over at him. "But then, I've probably never had wine this fine before, either."

"Not even at Danby Castle?"

Oh, my. The bitterness with which he made his remark told her how bothered he really was about that particular point. "Well, I never saw a bottle that looked so old, even there," she told him.

He took a deep breath, letting his pique go and gathering himself. "Now, we taste. Take a sip. Move it around in your mouth, letting it touch everywhere. Hold it a moment before you swallow."

"We're not spitting it out?" she asked with a grin.

"No." His tone lowered. "We are enjoying the full experience, if you will recall."

Something happened to her insides when he spoke in a rasp like that. To cover her reaction, she lifted her glass. After a small hesitation, she took a sip.

"Did you taste the fruit?"

"Yes. And something else. Something tangy at the end."

"Did you enjoy it?"

"I did." She drank the rest of the small glass and held it out. "May I have more?"

"In a moment. Where is that girl?" He looked at the door just as a thump sounded on the other side. With a glance and a raised brow, he went and opened it. Malvi stood on the other side, both hands occupied with a large tray carrying his requested items.

"Oh, thank you, sir. I couldn't manage the latch, too," she said, a little breathlessly.

"Of course. Leave it all on the table, if you would."

The girl crossed the room and did as he said, then turned, putting her back to Francis and facing Caradec. "If you please, sir, I'll apologize for what was said earlier, with Mrs. Beattie."

"There's no need." He waved a hand in dismissal.

But Francis saw her straighten her spine and spin the tray in her hands. "It's just that . . ."

Caradec sighed. "Yes?"

"I . . ." She took a step closer to him. "I would like to model for you."

Francis craned her neck around so she could see his reaction. He'd recoiled a bit in surprise. Not in revulsion, she was sure. Malvi might be a bold piece, but she was pretty, in a sulky, voluptuous way.

"That's very . . . enterprising of you—"

"Models are paid well," she interrupted. "That's what I've heard."

"They are fairly compensated. And I thank you for your interest, but I am not presently in need of a model."

She slid forward another step. "I'm not shy. I'll take my clothes off for you." She lowered her voice to a seductive whisper. "All of them."

Francis had had enough. She pushed back her chair with a clatter and stood. "The nob done give you his answer," she said in heavy street cant. "Toddle off to the taproom, lovie. Mayhap ye'll find a customer there to strip for."

The girl whirled on her. "Mind your business, gutter rat!"

"He's hired me ter mind his business," she said, thrusting her chin at Caradec. "And he's not interested in yours."

"That's enough from both of you," Caradec said with a sigh. He walked over and held open the door. "Go on, now," he told the servant girl, not unkindly. "We won't be needing anything else this evening."

Turning, she gave him an injured look, then swept out, clutching the tray like a shield.

Caradec closed the door behind her. "Now, what did you do that for?" he asked with genuine curiosity. "I assure you, I could have turned her interest aside."

"I knew I was right. You are besieged everywhere you go," she said, shaking her head. "But be careful of that one." Her instincts were sharply honed by experience. Even Hestia commented on her ability to read people. "She's on the hunt for something."

"A protector, most likely," Caradec agreed. "But there's no need to worry." He tilted his head at her. "My hands are quite full enough, already."

"Not yet, they aren't," she said, lifting her chin. "Now, may I have a bit more of that wine?" Perhaps it wasn't the best idea, but she wanted nothing more than to go back to that intimate atmosphere—to hear more of his past, to learn more to share with Hestia, she told her prickling nerves.

It had been a long time since she'd told herself such a big lie.

"Yes, come. Pour us some water and have a bite of cheese while I open the other bottle. I'm interested to see how you compare the two."

She did as he asked and he poured two more glasses of wine from the other bottle in the box. Sitting it before her, he nodded. "Come on then, show me what you've learned."

She pulled the glass toward her. "Oh, lovely." She lifted it to the light. "This one is a ruby. It looks like a great ruby pendant, without the sharp edges." Dipping her nose into the glass, she gasped a little. "It smells like smoke!" She had to taste it then, to see if the smoke lived there too—but was surprised again. "No smoke. No berries, either. Plums. And it feels soft and velvety, almost heavy, like it fills my mouth."

He made a faint sound and she glanced at him with heavy eyes. "I'm afraid you've ruined me for lesser wines."

"You've ruined me for tasting wines," he shot back, his eyes alight with more than the reflection of the lamplight. "Have you ever seen a ruby? A real one?"

"Yes. Have you?"

"Not up close," he admitted. "Only adorning a lady's neck. A lady far beyond my reach."

"Well, rubies should have always been beyond my reach, but circumstances don't always go the way they should." She glanced over at the low fire. "Real rubies have a sort of weight to them. It's nothing to do with scales and everything to do with the fire inside of them. Like they have desires of their own. Like they are full of life."

"Sounds familiar," he whispered. "It sounds like you."

She set her glass on the table. "Are you going to kiss me again?"

The air between them heated several degrees. "Regrettably, I am not—but only because that door has no lock, and Mrs. Beattie has the habit of barging in to ask after my comfort. Were things different . . . were we in private . . . well, I'd wager I'd already be kissing you—and I cannot guarantee that my hands wouldn't be wandering about your person, as well."

She swallowed, and tried to hide her disappointment.

"You are disappointed?" he asked.

So much for that. "Yes," she said, tossing her head. "But you can make it up to me by telling me why you are so disapproving of your friend's new situation."

He straightened. "I'm not *disapproving*. I just think it's . . ." He sat back and scrubbed the heels of his hands across his forehead. "It's just that . . . all of that talent focused on children's toys?"

"Perhaps the significance of that has changed, since he's become a father himself," she offered. "In any case, he still has time for other work. That landscape of the castle was magnificent."

"Yes, it was." He exploded out of his chair, taking a wine glass with him. "Less than a year ago we were having the finest of times. Nothing but paint, wine, and . . ."

"Women," she said when he paused. She got to her feet as well and watched him pace.

"Well, yes. He was even more popular with the ladies than I was. For several months we traveled together. It was always a new town, a new vista, new people, new inspiration."

"Perhaps he's ready for more," she said softly.

"Well then, he should not have settled for so much *less*," he bit out.

She stilled as he tossed back a long drink of wine. Did he truly feel that a wife and child, a welcoming extended family, and a steady, creative enterprise all measured short against the freedom of his wandering ways?

"Don't look at me like that," he growled.

"Like what?" She retreated when he stalked toward her, not stopping until he fetched up against the wall between the door and a small table.

He drew closer, radiating heat. Her hands, flat against the wall, curled into fists. She pressed them into her hips to keep from reaching out.

"Like I've disappointed you," he whispered, setting the glass down on the small table.

"Why not?" He smelled of the wine that they'd shared. And rain. And the small, ever-present tang of linseed oil. She breathed it in and let the smell of him roll through her, savored it, just as he'd instructed her.

"Because I don't like it." He loomed closer and then leaned in until his lips brushed her ear. "I like it better when you look at me like . . . this."

He touched her nape. Just the lightest touch, the softest brush of his fingers, but she felt her color rise, driven high by the feel of liquid want spreading from that one point of contact, curling into all of her most private places.

"The door," she whispered.

"The door can go hang," he said gruffly.

The moment was heated, charged with surging passion—and still she could not ignore the inadvertent humor in his words. Her eyes widened. She saw the moment it hit him—and they both laughed softly.

But it faded quickly and he watched her intently while his hand slid around to the back of her neck.

She'd never imagined that she could feel like this, hung in suspense while waiting for a man to kiss her. Even when she knew it was not wise. When she'd vowed to keep things between them light and uncomplicated. Yet here she was, entirely willing and waiting impatiently for it to happen.

And then it did. One moment they were sharing breaths, and the next he was kissing her with a hungry passion.

She leaned into it, so glad that they had shared that laughter. It freed her somehow, made it easier to give over, to open her mouth and invite him in. It made the raw desire that welled up inside of her lighter, more frothy.

He felt it, too. He made a sound and pulled away, buried his mouth in the curve of her neck.

"Ahh," she said on a long sigh.

The door opened.

"Mr. Caradec?" Mrs. Beattie said.

She was right there, on the other side of the door. They had been saved from discovery only by the thin panel of wood.

"Mr. Caradec?" The landlady, sounding puzzled, took a step inside.

He took a step away from Francis, reaching for his glass at the same time. "Right here, Mrs. Beattie."

The older woman peered around the door. "What are you doing back there?" she asked.

"Comparing colors," he answered. He held the wine glass aloft. "See how much darker and richer it looks, without the light going through it?" He looked at Francis with a raised brow and she nodded, trying to look earnest. "Heart's blood—that's what this particular shade is called. Learn it well, for it is used often in portraits."

"Sounds macabre to me," the landlady said with a shiver. "I was just wondering if you were both ready for a bit of sticky pudding?"

"Thank you, but no, Mrs. Beattie." Caradec tossed back the rest of his wine. "I promised to escort the lad home, as the hour is late. But I shall be up early for breakfast."

"As you wish." She nodded at Francis. "Good evening to you both, then."

They stared at each other when she'd gone.

"Tomorrow," he said fervently. "We are going to find ourselves some privacy."

Chapter Nine

The glittering courtesan came up with a plan. She had an artist friend who would take me in, a Frenchman living in Brittany. I packed my bags immediately.

--from the journal of the infamous Miss Hestia Wright

The people of Edinburgh were an industrious lot. The hour was early, the sun still hung low in the sky, but the streets were busy and the mood seemed generally light. Rhys's humor matched it. He'd asked Francis to be ready early and his insides had all gone airy with anticipation. He'd also asked her to wear her skirts, which might have a bit to do with his eagerness.

He pulled in close to the place where he'd left her last night and shook his head yet again. A shop for ribbons and notions? Not where he would have imagined her dwelling.

He set the brake and motioned with a hand. The skinny boy who'd come with the rented gig—to act as his tiger—moved forward to take the reins. Rhys stood—but the door opened and Francis emerged before he could descend to the pavement.

His breath caught.

She twinkled back at him, her face alight. She wore a walking gown of soft rose pink that should have clashed with that strawberry blonde hair, but made her look fresh and alive instead. It brought out a blushing sheen to her skin that had him making a noise of appreciation —and mentally mixing paint in his head. The white pelisse she wore over it was everything correct—and yet it was cut to highlight the pleasing curve of her bosom. She looked . . . delectable and tantalizing.

And he was developing an appetite that had nothing to do with his gut and everything to do with the ache in his groin.

"Good morning to you, Miss Headley," someone called as he hopped down. "Heading out so early?"

Rhys turned to see an older man, rail thin and impeccably dressed, standing outside the music shop next door. He held a broom in his hand and smiled at Francis. "I wanted to tell you that I ordered that Russian waltz music," he called.

"A good morning to you, Mr. Fritz. You should have luck with that waltz." She smiled as she straightened her gloves. "It's all the fashion in London right now."

"That's all I'll have to say, to insure its popularity," he called. "Thank you for the hint."

She nodded and turned to Rhys. A charming, small hat perched askew atop her curls, its darker pink ribbons matching the trim on her pelisse.

"You look ravishing," he said, taking her hand to assist her into the gig.

"So do you," she returned.

He'd made an effort, abandoning his comfortable, paint-stained garb for a rust-colored, embroidered waistcoat and a deep green coat. Mrs. Beattie's kitchen lad had polished his boots until they shone in the morning light.

"A ribbon shop?" he asked, nodding toward the place as he climbed in on his side.

"Owned by a friend," she told him. "A new establishment, but already making a name for itself." She glanced back to smile at the tiger. Looking at the basket at the boy's feet, she glanced further around. "Where's your case?"

"Only my sketchbook today," he said. "I'd prefer to concentrate on you."

He enjoyed the slow flush of color that crept upward into her cheeks. The sight of it tugged at his heart—and his conscience. It had been a long time since he'd spent time with one so innocent. The prospect was both delicious and daunting.

"Actually, I realize I've been remiss." Her flush triggered a thought. "I'd planned a picnic for us."

"That sounds lovely."

"Yes, Mrs. Beattie's weather sense assures me that there will be no rain today—so I meant to show you something . . . special. But it's outside the city. A forty-minute drive into the countryside. I should ask first—are you comfortable with the idea?"

She glanced back at the boy.

He gave a shrug. "Actually, I promised him a day off." And a shilling besides, but she didn't need to know that.

A wry grin tugged at the corner of her mouth. "Without your master's knowledge?" she asked the boy.

The lad turned as red as his hair and ducked his head.

She laughed.

Rhys was tempted to touch her. To reach out and absorb some of her quick, good humor. He did not. He ought not. But he did meet her gaze and ask, his tone low and questioning, "Will you trust me?"

She gave a little shiver, but didn't answer right away. He could see her considering the question. Considering him. He was glad, because he didn't know the particulars, but in some ways she was *not* innocent. She'd seen some of the sordid, evil things the world had to offer. She knew what she was risking.

"Yes."

His chest swelled. "Thank you," he said tenderly.

She held up a hand. "I'll agree, if you'll agree to stop by the palace on our way out of town."

It was out of the way, but he would have done far more. "Agreed."

He wove the gig through the streets, trying to keep his focus on the traffic and not the curve of her cheek or the closeness of his knee to hers, or the sweet memory of her kiss. It wasn't easy—but it was necessary. The crush of traffic grew as they neared the end of the High Street.

Suddenly she reached out to touch his arm.

He only just stopped himself from flinching. It was just a touch, through gloves and layers of clothing, yet the small warmth of that little hand threatened to flood his senses.

"If you'll just pull over there, I'll only be a moment." She indicated an open spot ahead.

He took it, then hopped down to help her descend.

"I'll be right back," she promised.

He watched her glide away, amazed all over again that this delicate seeming young lady was the same scamp who had scrambled through the rain with him yesterday in breeches and boots.

She reached the corner ahead, waited, then crossed the street with the flow of people heading for the simple, functional gates that led to the Castle.

Finding it difficult to keep her in view, Rhys climbed back up into the gig. There. She reached the far street with a crowd of others.

Rhys glanced back at the boy behind him. "Will you head out now?" he asked. "We can arrange to meet here at sundown, if you like, so you can accompany me back to the livery."

The tiger's gaze appeared to be fixed in the same direction that Francis had gone. His mouth pursed and Rhys turned to see that Francis had stopped near the gates. A flower girl stood there, offering her wares to the visitors passing by. The same girl she'd given the violets to yesterday?

No way to tell from here. They spoke for a moment. Francis reached into her pelisse and pulled out . . . a ribbon? Yes. A long, lacy length of ribbon. She wrapped it around the stems of the bouquet the girl held in her hand.

A smile lit up the younger girl's face as the ends fluttered in the breeze, then spread wider when an older gentleman stopped and bought the bouquet. Francis withdrew several more ribbons and pressed them on the girl. After a few more words exchanged, she turned to come back.

Their gazes met across the distance. His chest felt tight but she smiled and then concentrated on the traffic in the street.

"You got enough food for three in that basket, yer lordship?" the tiger suddenly asked.

Francis had started alarm bells ringing in his head. Rhys ignored them long enough to raise a brow at the child. "I'm no lord, lad. And a Scotswoman packed that basket. It likely has enough to feed a regiment." He turned in his seat a little. "Were you thinking to change your mind, then?"

The boy shrugged. "I wouldn't mind a day in the country—and I promise to make myself scarce at all the right times."

"It's a bargain."

Francis approached. Rhys climbed down, his head awhirl with indecision.

"Miss Headley? I say, Miss Headley!" Again, her name came from another direction, from another man. "It is you, isn't it?"

Her attention diverted to a young man hurrying toward them, doffing his hat as he came.

"Good day to you!" he called.

"Mr. Larson. How nice to see you." She dropped a perfectly elegant curtsy.

The gentleman's bow was just as smart. "I saw you and had to tell you—that collar you helped me choose was exactly the thing!"

She smiled. "I am so glad."

Rhys's hackles were rising.

"My wife adored it," the gentleman gushed.

And all of that completely inappropriate tension in Rhys's chest abruptly eased.

"I promised to bring her to Mrs. Spencer's shop before too long," Mr. Larson continued. "She spends quite a bit time alone while I am working, and the more senior partner's wives . . . well, they are already established. She'll enjoy an outing." He shook his head and smiled. "But in the meantime, may I escort you somewhere?"

"Thank you, but no. Mr. Caradec is waiting on me. He's been very patient." Francis smiled at Rhys as he stepped closer. "Mr. Caradec, may I present Mr. Larson?"

Rhys bowed and the pleasantries were exchanged.

"Mr. Caradec is quite an accomplished artist, Mr. Larson. One of his landscape series is right now causing a stir and earning high praise at the Royal Academy showing in London."

"Oh? Congratulations, sir. Are you here to paint fair Edinburgh?"

"I am," Rhys said through a suddenly clenched jaw.

"He's done a fabulous depiction of St. Bernard's Well, but now my friend the Duchess of Aldmere hopes to persuade him to paint *me*," Francis said with shy delight.

"Well! How lucky for you both." Mr. Larson's brows rose. "Perhaps when you are finished with Miss Headley, we might discuss a portrait of my wife, sir?" He reached into a pocket and patted fruitlessly. "How unfortunate. I seem to have used my last card. But please, call on me at any time." He beamed at Francis. "Miss Headley can arrange it."

"I would be happy to," she said easily.

"Thank you." Rhys nodded and swallowed his indignation and irritation. It wasn't the poor man's fault.

"Well. Very nice to have met you." The young man replaced his hat and nodded. "Good day to you both."

She turned to Rhys with an air of satisfaction, and he managed to hold his anger in check while he handed her up. Using the traffic as an excuse, he eased the gig out, remaining stiff and silent.

Francis waited a few minutes while the silence stretched out. She watched Caradec, but he drove on, his face blank. Eventually, she heaved a long sigh. "Oh, dear. Let's have it, then."

He merely grunted at her in reply, pulling the horse up as a clattering cooper's wagon recklessly passed by.

Once they were started again, she nudged him. "Out with it. It must be dire. Scarcely a man alive could be sullen on a beautiful morning like this, with the prospect of a picnic and the company of a woman who *might* agree to become entangled with him—but here you are, managing it."

He shot her an unreadable glance. "How long have you been in Edinburgh, Francis?"

She thought about it. "Nearly a week."

"So short a time. And yet you've made so many acquaintances."

She nodded. "I've made some."

"So I see. And so many have come to know Miss Headley, rather than the street urchin I've known."

She tilted her head at him. "Well, there are more hours in a day than the ones I've spent running around after you."

"And you've put them to good use, I'm sure you imagine," he said coldly. "Not content with a nod good morning or pleasantries exchanged, are you? You've progressed straight to Russian waltz music, ribbons, dress collars. Do you look at everyone you meet as a charity case, in need of your interference?"

She stilled. "No. I do look carefully at everyone I meet, though. There are a great many sorts of people in the world. Some are worth knowing. Fewer have the potential to become friends. But I like to be helpful to those who might appreciate it."

He snorted.

"Come now, out with it. What have I really done to offend you?"

He shot her another dark look. "I am more than capable of obtaining my own commissions," he ground out.

"Of course you are," she answered simply. "I know that."

"Your coarse attempts to procure one for me would lead me to think otherwise. And do you think me so desperate for work that you must blot your copybook with such a lie?"

"What lie?" she asked, bewildered.

"The one about your dear friend, the duchess." Almost, he sneered. Not quite.

It was the *not quite* that saved him. Otherwise she'd be tempted to plant him a facer.

"Brynne Russell, the Duchess of Aldmere, is one of my closest friends," she told him. Icicles might have hung from her words.

"*Mmmph.*"

A completely male, utterly irritating response. Did he not believe her?

He rounded on her before she could ask. "Do you have any family, Francis?" He asked it intently, as if the answer was important.

"Anyone waiting at home while you are pursuing your *good works* here?"

"No." She waited a beat. "Unlike you."

"*No.*"

One savage syllable that spoke volumes.

She let the silence stretch out a moment. "I'm sorry if I offended you. I only meant to help."

Her apology only seemed to anger him further. "Is that what you thought you were doing with that flower girl?"

Now Francis's ire was beginning to flare to life. "You can't be offended because I gave a flower girl a bit of ribbon?"

"Oh, I can, let me assure you."

"How?" She blinked. "Why?"

The dense cityscape had begun to give way as they'd approached the western edge. Buildings stretched out a little, giving each other some room. She wished she could take a step or two away, get a new perspective on this cranky version of Caradec.

He heaved a sigh. "It's clear that you are Hestia Wright's creature," he began.

He shook his head at her when she would have spoken.

"You don't have to say a word. You obviously share her damnable impulse to fleetingly interfere in everyone's business."

She drew herself straight. "There are multiple untruths in that statement."

"I beg to differ. I know you think you helped that girl today, but such interference can do more harm than good."

She blinked. "You think I've harmed her?"

"No, but you think you've helped her—and I think you should look closer." He shook his head. "So many people think they are helping. A gentleman throws a coin in a crippled veteran's cup. A temporary ease- ment, at best. The man needs employment and independence. Or at least care and a feeling of worth. Society ladies gather pennies for orphans, when those children truly need a home, support, and the love of a family. Pennies and ribbons don't accomplish anything. It's just hubris."

"Hubris?" she asked incredulously.

"It means pride——"

"I know what it means! I just didn't know that you think so little of me."

"That's not it, precisely."

"I've harmed her with few bits of scrap ribbon and the idea to brighten up her bouquets? Pray tell me how?" She was growing frustrated and wanted desperately to understand—both his reasoning and the darkness she suspected lay behind it.

"A stripling lad helped that girl yesterday. A young lady, today. Perhaps you'll even come up with something for tomorrow. But what of next week? Next month? You'll be gone back to London. And she'll be waiting in vain for the next person to help her when she should have been learning all along to rely on herself."

A tangle of negative emotions lodged in her chest, stealing her breath. Everything she knew, everything she was, pulsed with rejection of his words. "There is no shame in offering help. And none in accepting it, either," she forced out. Where would she be if that were so? Dead, likely. Or on her back in a hayseed brothel.

"No, but there can be harm in coming to expect it. That child likely has many trials ahead. Hunger. Cold. Hell, a blight on blooms could set her sorely back. It sounds harsh, but in the long run, she will do so much better learning to count on herself to solve such issues."

Francis groped for calm. Their views were so entirely opposite, they might never come to agreement. And if he would only look closely, he'd see that child faced far worse threats than the ones he'd named. "Let me tell you what I've accomplished, with just a couple of conversations with that child. I've learned quite a bit about her. I've discovered that she's clean and well spoken and honest. She didn't tell me, but I know that she is indeed often hungry and often cold. And I've seen that she has someone who watches over her, at least part of the time that she's out in the streets, but not all of the time."

"Your ribbons will help none of those conditions. I'm sorry, but I know that to truly make a difference in someone's life, it requires a serious commitment of time, effort and emotion."

"I agree—and sometimes that even isn't enough."

He mulled that over a moment. "I can see that that might be true.

I suppose that some people cannot be helped. But more often than that, I believe that the lack comes from the other direction. Flitting in and out of someone's life can cause more harm than good."

"I've never flitted in my life," she insisted.

"I'm just trying to explain that a half-hearted commitment can lead to a great deal of pain."

"I gave her an *idea*, a bit of creative thinking. Perhaps now her nimble brain is thinking about other ways to make her wares stand out."

"I hope you are right. I hope she learns that her own hard work and acquisition of skills—or ideas—will serve her best in the end."

"I don't dispute that—"

"Good. Because only the effort she puts forth for herself will stick, in any case. Everything else will just slide away."

Denial bubbled inside her, white and hot. But she breathed deeply and glanced over at him. The early sun struck his profile, turning him into a study of earnestness done in planes and angles and shadow. He looked a tower of masculine confidence—but she knew vulnerability lived beneath.

The realization calmed her boiling need to argue with him. He meant what he said and he meant well in sharing it.

He risked a glance at her, waiting for her response.

She couldn't give him one quite yet. Truth be told, she'd spent the night reevaluating her decision to stay, her notion to show him Hestia's work—and her very real desire to enter into her first *affaire*. She'd been thinking that she might indulge in this one, sunny, perfect day and then head back to London to report to Hestia and allow her to deal with her reluctant son.

Now, though, the light of purpose shone on her, much like the sun had found Caradec yesterday. He was far more guarded than she'd suspected.

She'd encountered a good number of people who had closed themselves off from the world. Many were flippant and jaded. Most were sullen, reserved or disagreeable. Caradec, the clever, tricky man, had fooled her longer because he was friendly and full of wit and charm. But where it counted he was the same. Not open. Cut off. Closed to people, relationships and even the idea of one, if his reaction to his friend's news could be judged. It was as if he drew a line before everyone he met. *This far you may come. This far and no further*.

And she'd seen enough to know how it would turn out. Caradec might break a few more hearts along the way, but in the end he would be in the same place—alone and small and unhappy.

And what of his art? Surely his work would suffer if he went on this way. He talked of the places that made one feel, but what of the people? What of the abiding understanding that comes with real friendship? What of that bone-deep contentment and surety that she'd seen blossom in her friends along with their love for their husbands? What of birth and death and the paralyzing fear and boundless hope and unconditional love that came with a child? How could he cut himself off from all of the best and worst of humanity—and still be a great artist?

Her path was clear. He held on to too much resentment and pain for Hestia to reach him yet. Francis had to make the attempt. And she had to do it so very carefully. If she struck just the right balance and used a light touch—she could perhaps set his feet on the path.

She must protect herself, though. A street rat with a fast mouth and a history of spending her time as a boy was not the sort to tempt him fully over, while he was everything that called to her. This time, to save her own heart, she might need to draw her own line.

This far and no further.

"What is it?" he asked, glancing her way. "What are you thinking?"

She smiled at him. "I'm remembering you saying that you wanted to know how I see the world." Reaching over, she patted his hard, muscled thigh. "And I'm thinking that I'm going to show you."

Chapter Ten

Saying goodbye to Pearl . . . I barely managed and cried buckets of tears. But she bade me go. See the child safe, she told me, and then learn your lessons well. Find your own power, she whispered in my ear.

--from the journal of the infamous Miss Hestia Wright

The sun had climbed only halfway to its zenith when they finally arrived at their destination. The grasses were still damp with dew.

Rhys heard Francis's breath catch in gratifying fashion as the old, overgrown track rounded a copse and the spot came into view. Her hand clutched his arm as he lifted her down, her gaze locked on the charming picture before them.

Truly, it might have been one of Andor's scenic sketches. A forest of old trees, thick with shadow, opened up onto a meadow of low grasses and wildflowers. In the midst of it squatted the rambling ruins of an old castle—with one stone tower still mostly intact.

He'd seen a rough sketch of the place back in Leeds, in North's book. He'd known at once that he must see it for himself. North had given him the information and in fact, Rhys had stopped here first on his journey, spending an afternoon here even before he continued on into town.

He wanted to share it with Francis. He'd known she'd love it. She and this place shared so many of the same qualities—strong bones and wild beauty and an almost joyous refusal to give in to the elements that worked against them.

Her reaction was even better than he'd hoped. Her grin stretched wide with delight, she reached up to unpin her hat. The gloves were next, then the pelisse—she left them all on the seat of the gig and with a laugh she scampered off, ignoring the dew dampening her skirts as she darted from one delight to the next.

He watched her go, happy to have pleased her and grateful for the small respite after their . . . disagreement.

Perhaps he should not have said anything to her, but he'd felt compelled to do it. He'd seen the damaging effects of Hestia Wright's transitory attention. He'd seen the truth of it in action—her notice could be the greatest blessing, her indifference akin to a death knell.

Hell, he knew firsthand how it felt to bask in that glowing warmth, and how the empty, aching loss of it felt, too. He liked and respected Francis. Enough to break his own habits in order to keep her from making the same mistakes—and to prevent someone else from suffering a painful, confused aftermath.

He brushed the issue aside for now, though, and looked up at the boy still waiting on the back of the gig. "Well, since we're to spend the day together, I should know your name, at least."

"I'm Geordie, yer lordship." The boy tugged a forelock. "Geordie MacNeal."

Rhys doffed his hat—and then tossed it after Francis's onto the front seat. "Call me Rhys, Geordie. I'm not a lord. Can you hobble the horse in a likely spot? And then feel free to explore as you will. I'm going to do some sketching while the lady looks about. We'll call you when it's time for luncheon, though."

"Yes, sir. Thank you, sir."

Rhys strode through the calf-high grass, headed for the far end of the ruins, opposite the tower. A short section of stairway had survived there, leading up to a spacious stone-floored room. It stood mostly open now, with only one exterior wall still standing. But it had a thick, recessed and arched window in it that lent inspiration to quite a few images in his head.

The sun slanted down on it now, coming over the trees to warm the stone beneath his feet. He crossed to the edge to enjoy the view of the rest of the castle—and the girl scrambling through it.

He settled down to draw as she explored. She was drawn to the stone tower first, just as he'd been. He knew what she would find in there. Narrow, spiraling stairs and small rooms, dust and cobwebs. Pretty views of the countryside and perhaps a dream or two of the past. He did a quick sketch of a tall window, a panorama below and the flutter of red-gold hair in the breeze as a girl gazed out.

She came down slowly after a while and set out to follow the outlines of the old foundations and walls. She ducked down to inspect crumbling, old fireplaces, and stopped to pick up forgotten roof tiles of slate.

His fingers lay idle as he watched her, but his brain was busy. He had not yet set upon an idea of how to paint her, although the urge grew with their every encounter. She was busy too, moving lightly, flitting from one discovery to the next. When her wanderings brought her close, he called out to her.

"Come up? I'd like to show you something while the sun is right."

She came running up the steps, but slowed, pausing in wonder when she reached the top. "How lovely!"

Just as he had, she crossed to the lone wall with its deep-set window and ran her fingers along the rubble of what must have been a wide window seat. "Oh, can't you just imagine them sitting here?"

"I can. Tapestries on the walls. Women gathered together, sewing and laughing. Colored pillows and a girl sitting here, reading by the light of the afternoon sun."

"Or giggling while she spies on the men training below?" she answered with a laugh. "Will you hold me?" She held out a hand and when he took it, she lifted her skirts and stepped into the depression where the stones had crumbled away. Twin windows arched high and she braced a hand on one and leaned over to look out.

"Ooh, I might have been right! It could have been a training yard down there—and it looks like the remains of a forge on the corner!" She spoke further, caught up with the view, but Rhys was caught, literally and figuratively, by her hand.

So small and warm, and it told him so very much. Her grip was unselfconscious and trusting. He could see clipped nails and several reddened knuckles. He could feel calluses on her fingers and a rough patch on her palm. Such a tiny, useful, functional hand. He felt a raw, sensual need to feel it moving across his skin.

Unconsciously, he gripped her tighter.

She glanced back.

He cleared his throat, pointed with his chin. "Look up, Flightly."

She did. "Oooh, how wonderful," she whispered.

The sun shone in at a perfect angle to light up the carved Green Man. Rhys had discovered him at a similar hour in the morning—and wondered if he might have missed him at another time of day.

Tucked up high in the thick curve of the arched bay, he looked as if he'd been placed there to watch over the occupant of the window seat.

"He was the first one I saw here. I liked him, somehow. It's what made me search out the gargoyles and other green men like him in town."

"I've never seen one look so sad," Francis said.

Rhys nodded. The face had been fashioned long, the nose wide, the eyes turned down with bags heavy beneath them. Oak and ivy framed the face and curved twigs made up a drooping mustache and long beard.

"Usually they look fierce, but this one appears . . ."

"Weary?" Rhys asked. "Maybe he grew tired of all the women and their chatter," he teased.

"No, I think he rather misses it. Perhaps he's lonely and sad because of what's become of his home." She took a last look outside and then turned to climb down. "This place is still beautiful, but it is sad, when you think of what it once was."

Instead of letting her hand go, he took up the other one. "Well, that won't do. I didn't bring you out here to make you sad."

Unblinking, she stared up at him. "Did you bring me here to seduce me?"

"What?" he choked. "Of course not!"

She raised a brow.

"Well, perhaps . . . just a little."

"A *little* seduction?" She ran a bold gaze up and down the front of him.

Lustful approval smoldering, he laughed. "Slow and steady wins the race."

"Oh, that old tale." She rolled her eyes. "I should have known you'd take the side of the tortoise. *I* was always partial to the hare."

"I could have guessed that all on my own." Rhys began to walk backward, pulling her by both hands to follow. "You are always in motion. Even when you are sitting, your eyes are darting, your head tilting . . ." He stopped, realizing the reason why even as he said the words. "Always ready to *fly*."

She said nothing, but her lips pressed together for just a moment before her expression began to grow defiant. Challenging.

He shook his head. "No need to fly today, Francis. All is well. I want to share something with you."

She gave a little snicker.

"Hell and damnation, girl. I've said I wasn't going to seduce you."

She gave a pout. "You said a *little*."

"Fine. A little. Since you are insistent about it." He blew out an exasperated breath. "But not now."

"Fine."

"Now, come and sit."

"Where?"

"Here." He moved to the edge of the stone floor and sat, letting his boots dangle over the edge.

She made a face. "I'll stay back here, if it's all the same to you."

He frowned. "You just stood on a broken seat and looked down over a greater height than this. You cannot be afraid."

"I'm not afraid of heights. I'm afraid of *drops*." She gestured back from where they'd come. "There was a wall in the way over there—and you had a hold of me."

"I won't let you drop. I promise."

Sighing, she came forward and gingerly sat down next to him. He scooted away a bit. "Do something for me, Francis?"

"What is it?" She looked wary.

"Concentrate. Let your worry fade. Forget about everything for a bit—even that seduction you're insisting on. Forget about yesterday and tomorrow. Just . . . breathe in today. Now."

She looked a little sad. "I don't know how to do that."

"It's not hard. Try closing your eyes."

She grimaced.

"Grip the edge if you need to. Just for a moment. Come on, then. Close them."

Still reluctant, she curled her fingers around the edge of the stone, her spine echoing the curve. "And now?"

He shrugged. "Feel the warmth of the stone. The tickle of the breeze." He waited a moment. "Breathe deeply." She obeyed, but still did not relax. "What are you thinking?"

"I'm thinking about keeping my feet arched."

He blinked. "Why?"

"Because if I do not, my slippers are going to fall off of my feet."

"Oh." He laughed. "Let them."

Her eyes popped open.

"It's not that far. They'll land in the grass—and I'll fetch them for you when we go down."

Grinning, she looked down. "There they go!" Laughing, she wiggled her toes.

Her feet were dainty and clad in silk stockings. When she lifted them straight out in front of her, he pretended to be shocked. "Careful! You'll start a scandal! Your ankles are showing."

She tossed him a look of pure mischief. "Just a little scandal."

He rolled his eyes. "Keep poking the fire, lassie. You're bound to get burned."

"Oh, are you on *fire*?" she asked in a stage whisper.

"Not yet. Now, come then. Eyes closed," he ordered.

With a huff, she obeyed. He said nothing this time, just let her adjust. Ever-so-slowly, she stilled. Her breathing slowed. Her eyes opened. They sat there together for several quiet minutes.

Eventually, she turned to him. "Why?"

He merely lifted a shoulder. "Listen. There's an angry squirrel in the trees behind us. Can you hear him scolding?"

She listened, then nodded.

"And look ahead and to your right. That lacey patch of mead-owsweet—can you see it swaying?"

She stared. "Yes. Why—"

"A hare at the base, perhaps? Or a vole at the roots?" He swept a hand across the view. "There's a panorama of light and shade in here. And do you hear the birdsong?"

She nodded.

"And your heartbeat too. The breath moving in and out of you. It's a gorgeous, simple slice of life—and you are part of it. Breathe it in. Let it fill your soul." He tilted his head back. "Think of it as ballast. It will keep you afloat during some dark time in the future."

She drew a deep breath. "I like it," she declared softly. "Like I told you before, I like the way you see. With all of your senses."

For a while, they lingered. Rhys was watching the grasses dance in the breeze while his mind drifted, mentally choosing the separate colors it would take to create all the red and blonde tones in her hair, when he became aware of a shift in the atmosphere.

Her gaze rested upon him. He felt it like the weight of an actual touch. And his focus shifted. He wasn't hearing his own exhalations, but the slow and deep rhythm of hers. All the desire banked in him began to glow again, warming his belly—and throwing heat higher—and lower. Surely she must feel it—hotter even than the sun-warmed stone.

Slowly, he turned his head. She watched him with a gaze that was both knowing and curious. She'd left off gripping the edge and had leaned back, propped on her hands. The posture thrust her bosom to the sky.

So fortunate, the sky.

But fortune favored the bold—and luck often followed the seizure of circumstance. So he edged closer to her.

She watched—and then looked up to his face with a clear invitation to come closer.

With a surge of triumph, he answered the call.

Clearly she believed in helping luck along too. She tilted her head, achieving the perfect angle for his kiss.

Leaning down, he gave it to her.

She didn't shift position, only kissed him back with a long, shuddering sigh.

So he kissed her softly, reverently. He kept his hands to himself, even though her thrusting bosom was a nearly irresistible temptation. He gave her soft kisses and light, teasing flicks of his tongue. He kissed her cheek and along the curve of her jaw, then pressed a tender, worshipful tribute to the delicate spot beneath her ear.

She sighed again and stretched a little, giving him better access. He complied with the silent request and kissed down to her nape until she squirmed.

He pressed closer still, moved to return to her mouth and was just about to deepen the direction and intent of the kiss—

When her stomach gave a long, demanding rumble.

He stopped. His eyes popped open just as hers did—and they both broke out in rueful laughs.

"Well." He pulled away. "I know an order when I hear one."

"I am sorry," she said sheepishly. "I took too long fussing with my hair this morning. I missed breakfast."

He glanced up at her soft curls, disheveled from her earlier exertions. "Time well spent," he assured her. "And don't worry. That was so small a seduction, it couldn't even be termed *little*."

"I probably should not confess how glad I am to hear it. I wouldn't want to think I'd wasted my chance."

He laughed. "You'll get your chance. But let's feed you, first."

Chapter Eleven

I kept to myself as I traveled, thinking about what Pearl had said. Men held the power in my world. And the men who should have used theirs to protect me—had betrayed me, instead.

--from the journal of the infamous Miss Hestia Wright

This was going to be so much more difficult than she'd hoped. Such a lovely, big man, he was. How small she'd felt as he'd hovered over her. She shivered now, thinking of it. He was so large, with so much physical strength—all held in check for her sake—it made her feel both delicate and oddly powerful at the same time.

And he was so damned tempting when he wasn't actively rejecting any form of true intimacy. Although clearly he felt capable of indulging in physical intimacies with her without putting himself at risk.

How lowering.

Well, she had an agenda of her own to pursue, and perhaps she could fit in a bit of conversion to go along with a *little* seduction. Right after luncheon.

And a delightful one it was. The basket was packed with simple fare—roast chicken, creamy yellow cheese and bread—and there was plenty of it. A good thing, too. Francis might have been hungry, but she didn't come close to consuming the amounts that Caradec and Geordie, the livery boy, did.

They gave every evidence of enjoyment, too—until Caradec woefully held up a slice of oat bread. "In all of my travels, I've found nobody does bread so delightfully well as the French do."

"Ah. First wine, now the bread. Is there anything else you miss about France?" *Anyone* else, she knew better than to ask.

"The desserts!" he answered promptly.

"Spoken like a true Frenchman," she said wryly.

"*Mais oui*," he responded with a flourish. "*Toutes les pâtisseries. Ils me manquent tous les.*"

She peeked into the basket at the cloth-wrapped, round bundle still left in there. "It would seem your landlady knows your taste. I can smell the sweetness from here."

"She does indeed. In fact, it is by design."

"Did you flatter her into making you a pudding?" she asked with a grin.

"No, actually, it's how I choose my lodgings."

She pursed her lips. "According to the *desserts?*"

"You may laugh, but I *am* a Frenchman. Wine, women and song, a rich cigar, fresh bread, lush desserts--these are the things that make life sweet. So, I come into a new town and I ask around at a taproom or two—Where are the lodging houses with the best wine cellars or the most flavorful food?"

"It's as good a method as any, I suppose."

"I have an arrangement with Mrs. Beattie, in fact. Her husband's back is not what it was, so I agreed to chop firewood for her—"

"And in return she keeps you in sticky pudding?"

"More or less," he said with a shrug.

"Well, I look forward to enjoying the fruits of your labor. Shall I dish it out?"

It was delicious, rich with dates and dripping with a caramelized sauce. Francis closed her eyes at the first bite. "I hope you are cutting her cords and cords of firewood."

"Oh, I am," he assured her. "Both in appreciation of her talent and to counteract the effects of eating this—"

"Ambrosia," Francis declared. "Food of the gods."

"It's that good," Geordie agreed. He picked up his plate and licked it clean, as if to prove his point. Francis was tempted to follow his example.

"That's enough of that." Caradec took the plate from him. "There's a stream just over there. I'll go rinse these so we don't attract ants. Geordie, if you'll pack the rest, we'll allow our guest to rest up for the afternoon's exertions." He shot her a loaded look and she tried to ignore the sudden galloping of her heart. Watching him stride off—all wide shoulders and long lines down to narrow hips—didn't make it any easier.

The favorable view disappeared as Geordie leaned across the blanket for the cheese. He gave her a curious, sidelong glance, then stared back over his shoulder, looking back and forth until Caradec disappeared amongst the trees.

He turned then and looked her directly in the eye. "The gentleman seems a good sort, Miss. But I'll ask ye not to listen to him. Least-aways, as far as young Janet goes."

She contemplated this for a moment. "Young Janet?" But then understanding dawned. "The flower girl, you mean?"

"Yes. She needs all the help she can get."

Francis craned a look over his shoulder to be sure Caradec was not on the way back. "I saw the bruises when her sleeve fell away. And the woman with the infant, who lingers near, wherever she's set up. Is it her mother?"

"Yes, but she's not the cause of the bruises. It's wee Janet's uncle, him that they all bide with." He leaned down, urgency in his expression. "If ye know someone what could help them . . ?"

"All three? Are there any more?"

He shook his head. "Just those three. But it does seem to grow worse, as time passes."

"It won't be easy. But I'll look into it." She raised a brow. "What are you to them, Geordie?"

He flushed. "Only a friend. They lived in the same building, back when Janet's dad still lived."

She let it go. "Fine, then. I will see what may be done—but don't mention it to them until I know more?"

"Yes, Miss. I mean, no, Miss." He tugged at his forelock. "Thank ye ever so—fer yer help."

"Save your thanks for when I can do something for them." She nodded over his shoulder. "The gentleman returns—and you were right to ask me when he was not here. Let's not mention it before him yet, either."

He nodded and finished loading the basket, then hoisted it high to walk it back to the gig. Passing Caradec on the way, he paused to take the clean plates from him.

"It's actually quite pretty down there by the water," Caradec said, approaching her. "Would you care to stroll with me?" He reached out a hand.

She let him pull her to her feet. "I would, thank you."

They set off, not touching, but close enough. The forest around them was alive with bird song and the sound of small creatures. She heard the frogs singing before they reached the water and sighed in pleasure when Caradec pulled back a branch to expose a short bank above a small stream.

"How lovely."

The water was clear and swift flowing. Moss, grasses and low growing shrubs covered the bank in sections. The sun shone warm and the stream burbled pleasantly—and they were alone.

"A far cry from London, eh?" Caradec bent down and gathered up a handful of pinecones. Like males everywhere, he could not resist tossing them in to watch them be swept away.

"Indeed. Would that the Thames was so clear." She smiled and wandered a little upstream to where an oak encroached all the way to the dropped edge of the bank. Rooting about, she found some old acorns and brought them back. She tossed one in. "Shall we race?"

"No." He let go of his remaining pinecones and wiped his hands on his thighs. "There are other things I'd rather do."

She watched him expectantly. "Such as?"

"I'd like to talk a little, if you wouldn't mind." Her surprise must have shown, for his mouth quirked. "I'm no monk. I've confessed as much already. I fall in with a pretty woman easily and often—as long as the wanting is there, and mutual, and I'm sure I'll slip easily out again. I don't usually look for much in the way of conversation."

He shook his head. "But as I've already said, with you, everything is different. Oh, the wanting is there. I am intrigued by you, Francis. And now I begin to wonder if it might not be better if I understood more about you—*before* we indulge ourselves any further."

She hunched her shoulders a little, torn. She guessed she already knew far more about him than his women usually did. He would doubtless try to learn more than he would reveal.

"You mentioned a story behind your name, once," he continued.

"Yes, but you already guessed that it came from being fast. Though you might not have imagined how fast I can go backward—"

"No." He shook his head and she fell silent. "Francis. Always with an i—in the masculine version. You said you might tell me about it—and I confess, the mystery has been niggling at me."

"Has it? I must apologize, then. It's not all that mysterious. Just sad, in truth."

"Will you tell me?"

She watched him as she considered it. Not many people knew the story. They were similar in that regard, at least, preferring to keep much of themselves private. The imbalance of it would be unusual for her, knowing less of him than he of her.

With anyone else she would find it an irritant. But it would serve as a reminder to them both—the gap between them was wide. Too wide to contemplate anything but a quick fling.

Too, sharing her secrets just might lead to him to be more open with his own . . .

"I suppose I'll tell you, if you'll share something in return," she said slowly.

He grew instantly wary. "What would you wish to know?"

But Francis was not fool enough to rush her fences. "I'd like to hear about—the first dessert you remember." She grinned. "What started this life-long obsession?"

His eyes widened. "Oh, I recall it perfectly. It happened at a street fair in the village next to ours. The baker set up a tent and the boys hovered around it, hoping for a handout. My friend Gilles was very brave. He waited until a large party came to distract the man with an order and used the cover to steal away a couple of pastries."

He sighed. "It was *choux à la crème*. Light and airy dough filled with cream and covered with a sugary glaze. I'd never tasted something that filled my mouth in such a way—and also my *soul*. I thought I'd died and gone to heaven."

She sighed. "That's a much nicer memory than the one you are asking for."

He sobered. "I'm sorry. Am I asking too much?"

"No." But the answer came slowly.

"Don't tell me if it will make you uncomfortable. We don't really know each other well, after all."

"No, but as you said, isn't this the point of today?" She waved a hand.

Now he looked a little uncomfortable.

She took a deep breath and turned away. Walking to the edge of the high bank, she settled down onto a mossy spot. For several minutes she let the babble of the brook soothe her, but eventually she started to speak.

"I had a different name once, when I was very small." She gave her words to the water. They came out a little easier that way. "I only have a couple of memories from that time. Just flashes of my mother, kneading bread in a small, dark kitchen. The sparkle of water as we walked along a dock. Her whispering my name in my ear as I fell asleep."

He moved closer behind her, the better to hear her, she assumed.

"I don't know what happened. Perhaps my father died. Or left. My next memories are of the brothel."

He made a small sound of protest but she didn't turn or otherwise acknowledge it.

"It was in a different place, but I'm not sure where. The country. We had a room to ourselves, near the top of the house. I was still small when we moved there. Everyone there called me Rosey—and pinched my cheeks because they were pink." She sighed. "When my mother was . . . busy, I was sent down to the kitchens. Eventually I stayed there, training to help the cook, acting as her maid-of-all-work."

She lifted a shoulder. "Shockingly, it wasn't a bad life. The madam and most of the girls were indifferent to me. A few were kind. The cook drove me hard, but was never harsh. My mother's tears were the sour note—and the lingering cough that turned worse—and eventually stole her away."

"How old were you?" he whispered

"Six or seven? Too young to be put to the men, thank goodness."

He sighed.

"I did have a burden to bear. I think his name must have been Stuart—but everyone called him Stew. He was a stable boy, boot boy, whatever they needed, just as I was maid of all work in the kitchens. A couple of years older and twice as big as me—and he hated the sight of me."

"Why?" he asked, indignant.

"Who knows? Maybe he just didn't like girls. Or red heads. Or pink cheeks. I never did anything to him—not until his 'pranks' started to become more regular, and more painful."

"What did you do, then?"

"I began to give him as good as I got. He used to trip me every time I went by him, so I accidentally knocked him in the head with a ladle or broom or shovel, afterwards. If he put my only pair of shoes in the water barrel, then I left his too close to the fire so the soles scorched."

"I don't imagine it went over well."

"No. Things began to escalate. It came to a head one day when he caught me in the stable, bringing apple peelings to the horses. He'd prepared for it. He had set an iron hook in the wall, up high. He grabbed me from behind, tied my over-sized apron into a harness and hung me up by the hook—so that he could beat me at his leisure and without worrying that I could hit back."

This time there was no sound, but the soft weight of a large hand came down on her shoulder.

She appreciated it. "It was bad," she admitted. "It might have been worse if a guest hadn't come in, looking for someone to take her horse."

The hand fell away. "Her horse?" It momentarily diverted him. "The guest was a woman?"

"After a fashion." Francis glanced over her shoulder. "Have you ever heard of Hatch? She was a bawd. A pimp. Quite famous for never wearing skirts, but always dressing like a man." She glanced down. "Much like you are, in boots and breeches, coat and waistcoat."

He shook his head. "No, but how would I have heard of a London bawd?"

She turned around completely and searched his face. She had no idea what his relationship was with Marstoke—the wicked marquess who had sired him. She knew only that they had had contact at least long enough for Marstoke to have obtained Caradec's sculpture—the one that had caused Hestia such pain and let her know that he'd discovered the child she'd tried to hide from him.

Had it been only a brief acquaintance? Or had he spent time with the father he'd never known? Perhaps that was the source of his antagonism toward Hestia? Had he, in fact, worked with the marquess to hurt his mother? She couldn't quite believe it. She didn't want to. One thing she knew, though, Hatch had at one time been in service to the wicked man.

"You never know," she said quietly. "She was quite famous in some circles."

"What did she do when she found you like that?"

"She took me down from the hook and set me on shaking legs. Then she pried the hook out of the wall, handed it to me and stood back, waiting and watching."

"What did you do?"

"I could barely hold the thing. I could scarcely stand. But I gripped it tight and stepped toward Stew. He didn't even move. I must have looked too weak to worry about. He was right. I collapsed right there in front of him. But on the way down, I made sure that hook went through his foot and anchored him to the stable floor."

Caradec's eyebrows jumped high.

"Hatch picked me up. She left Stew there, screaming, and she took me into the house and got me cleaned up. I knew the madam wouldn't be happy to see her. She only showed up in the country brothels to poach the best girls and take them back to London. But when she left the next day, she only took me."

His voice tight, Caradec asked, "And what did she do with you?"

"Took me to the next town, cut off most of my hair and bought me a set of boy's clothes. 'Boys have nearly every advantage in life,' she told me. So I was to learn to act as one."

"No wonder you fooled me," he said, nodding. "You started so young."

"I'm good, but to be honest, it wasn't that hard." She laughed. "I didn't have any refined manners to begin with. I just had to learn to be brash and bold—and to dig a finger up my nose when anyone looked too close."

He clapped a hand over his eyes and shook his head, while she laughed.

"I spent most of my time as a boy for a while. Hatch took me to London and dumped me in the streets to learn to survive—and it was easier as a male. But she wanted me to be able to pass for a girl at times too. Being able to do both would make me the most valuable runner she ever had. She gave me the name Francis—because it would work for both sexes, but she taught me to spell it with an i. And although I began to act the girl more as I grew older, I kept the masculine spelling. And when Hatch died . . ." she shrugged. "I kept it in her memory." She sighed. "She was not a good person. But she was good to me, in her fashion."

"When did she die?" he asked quietly.

"Years ago, now."

"What happened to you? What did you do?"

She climbed to her feet and shrugged as she looked down at him. "I started my real life."

He would have asked more, but she shook her head and moved

away, back toward the trees. She felt a little raw, after the telling. Thinking of their argument earlier made it worse. Hatch's help might have been crude and largely self-serving, but where would she be now if it had not come?

⊛

R hys knew a retreat when he saw one—and he let her go. He felt a little bruised, himself, after that story. He could imagine how she might feel right now. But he was helpless not to watch her wander along the bank, and not to feel the soft earth shifting beneath his own feet, too.

He kept saying it, but it kept proving true over and over again. Nothing about this felt usual. From the resilient pixie of a girl before him, to his own odd reactions to her.

Something was happening to him—and it was her doing.

She was one of the *sticky* people. Someone who touched and held on to everyone in her path. She would have a knotted tangle of strings leading back and forward and connecting her to everyone she'd ever encountered and befriended.

And he, who had made it his life's goal to live free and easy and without connections at all—should be running at full speed away from her.

Instead he grew more fascinated with every passing moment. He wanted to keep feeding her new things, watch her encounter new tastes, new sounds, new experiences with her senses wide and her mind open. He wanted to wrap her in cotton wool and keep anything from ever harming her again. And he wanted to kiss her senseless, explore her womanly curves and feel the rise and surge of her desire.

He stepped nearer, narrowing his eyes as she bent over a tuft of dried grasses. Even as he watched, she wound a section around her finger and tucked it away. "Francis," he said, touching her shoulder. He rejoiced a little when she turned easily, but he couldn't help but notice the solemn cast to her expression.

"I'd like to go back to the ruins now," she told him without quite looking at him. "That forge area might be worth exploring."

"Of course." He shoved his disappointment away. "But first, I'd like to thank you for sharing that story. You were right—I didn't realize how much I was asking, but I do know how generous it was of you to tell it."

Her head raised and her gaze sought his. "You don't think less of me, then?"

"For what? Your circumstances were not of your making." He took her hand. "We are alike enough, you and I, for me to understand that the telling of it was nearly as hard as the living of it."

She sighed. "Yes, and made worse because I feared you would scorn me for accepting Hatch's help."

"What? No." He frowned. "Do you think me such a monster? You were young. Alone." He shook his head. "I know that must be only one of a hundred stories. I salute you, Francis, for wading through it all and becoming . . . remarkable."

Some of the light returned to her eyes.

Pulling her closer, he let his free hand rise up slowly and slide along her cheek.

She sighed and tipped her head into it.

And there it was, the electric charge back in the air again. It pulled at them and like dancers they came together. Gentle fingers trailed along arms, reached up to clasp shoulders. Lips brushed, soft and in no hurry, sending out the signal to the rest. *Here.* All the pleasure in the world, to be found *here.*

Rhys deepened their kiss. Her mouth parted. Her breath was sweet and hot and he felt privileged to be the one feeling the rise and fall of her breath, the press of her soft curves against his chest.

He tightened his hold. Her hands crept higher, tugged at the ribbon holding his queue—and released it. She pulled away, staring as his hair swung loose, then dug her fingers in, making a sound that was part gasp and utterly carnal.

It slipped into his bloodstream like fine, French brandy, that sound.

And they were kissing again, their tongues teasing, exploring. He bent lower, and she opened further, kissing him back with a hunger that matched his own.

Slowly, he straightened. Moving carefully, he guided her back until she stood against the elm tree. And with the steady strength of it to protect them, they threw caution to the wind. Their ragged breathing grew louder, competing with the gurgle of the stream. Her hands drifted, down to his waist and back again, and around to his back when he buried his face in the curve of her neck.

She made a lovely moaning sound—and then her hands gripped him tight. "Why?" she asked when he drew back. "Caradec—why choose me?"

He drew a deep breath. "I think we've progressed past the point of you calling me by my surname. Call me Rhys." He raised a brow and waited until she nodded in agreement. "And as for why?" He shrugged. "Damned if I know."

Her eyes widened—and then she looked in his face and laughed. "Blackguard," she said, trying to push him away.

"It's no more than you deserve, for asking such a question." He refused to let her move away. "Come here." He gathered her close. "How? That's what you should ask. How *not* you? Francis, you are quick-witted and wry, easy-going and yet sharp as a tack. You are a beautiful woman and a formidably convincing boy. You are completely, utterly unique."

Straightening, he stared down at her. "But what if I put the same question to you? You came here to gather information to Hestia Wright, I presume. To bring me back to her. Well, you may tell her what you like, but you know I will not go with you. So why are you still here? Why stay?"

She closed her eyes.

"Tell me," he urged.

"I came for Hestia, it's true," she whispered. "But it was also for me. I should go, perhaps. It would likely be better. Easier. But I'm staying . . ." She opened her eyes and drew a deep breath. "For the largest part . . . I'm staying for me. But a small part is for you, too."

She made him ache.

But thank the heavens, she was also the cure for his pain—and before he could think further about that answer he was kissing her, touching her, trying to draw her into himself like a drowning man grasps for air.

So good. So sweet. He put his hands in her red-gold curls and tugged her head, just a little, tilting her so that she was positioned exactly right for his ravaging mouth. Feeling primal and possessive he seared her with his kiss, marking her as his.

His hands were moving then, down over her slim shoulders and then back up to the buttons at her back.

"Caradec," she began, muttering against his mouth.

He growled.

"Rhys." She pulled her mouth away. "Here? I'm not sure—"

"I want to see you," he rasped. "Touch you. I don't want to stop until you are throbbing in every secret place, until you are shaking with hunger and as helpless with desire as I am."

Her bodice slipped then, and he pushed it down further, wrestled a bit with her chemise and stays, and at last, with her help, he had her bare before him.

"So lovely." He filled his hands with her and kissed her again.

No one else had touched her like this. He hadn't realized how the thought of it would send his desire spiraling. Pulling back, he gazed at her again. Fair skin, fully rounded breasts and pink-tinged nipples that stood peaked, tempting him. He gave in to the call, reached out and rubbed a thumb across one peak.

She sucked in a breath. This was new to her, he must remember, and rein in his own raging impatience.

Francis Headley deserved patience. She deserved gentle seduction and wild desire.

He meant to give her all of that and more.

"You look like a fairy princess. All pale, silken skin against the rough bark of the tree. You've cast your spell on me. I am helpless to do anything but . . ." He leaned down and ran his tongue over the tantalizing top of her breast. "This."

Pressing kisses around her curves, he paid her homage. And finally, he put his mouth to one pink bud, sucking and teasing while his thumb played idly with the other. Her soft moans and ragged whimpers told him how much she enjoyed it. He'd just returned to her mouth while he rolled each peak between a thumb and forefinger when she turned her head to the side suddenly.

"Rhys."

"Francis."

"Rhys," she said, sounding more urgent.

"Mmmm." He kissed the neck she'd so obligingly offered.

"Caradec! Listen!"

He paused, frowning.

"Yer lordship?" The voice called from not too far away.

Rhys straightened in shock. "Damn that boy!"

"Yer looooordship!"

He threw back his head. "Damn it all to hell and back, Geordie! I thought we had a bargain!"

Francis was frantically wriggling back into her clothes.

"There's someone here, sir." The boy's voice had moved closer.

Rhys reached down to help Francis. He'd just buttoned her back up when the livery boy popped out onto the bank several yards away. Rhys stepped away from the girl and the tree.

"There you are," said Geordie. "There's a girl back there—and she says as how she's looking fer ye."

Chapter Twelve

❧❀❧

Find my own power? I wanted it. I wanted wealth and influence and position because I thought they would bring safety. Security. I arrived in Brittany a determined woman.

--from the journal of the infamous Miss Hestia Wright

A ll of her hackles were raised, and her suspicions too, but Francis took care to smile broadly at Malvi. The maid merely bristled back at her.

Caradec, in his turn, stared at the girl. He looked flabbergasted. "What in seven hells are you doing here?" he demanded.

She faced him and went instantly contrite. "Oh, sir. I'm ever so sorry. It's my half day off." She looked down. "I heard you talking to Mrs. Beattie this morning, telling her about your picnic out here." She lifted her chin and glared at Francis. "I didn't know you wouldn't be alone. I hopped on a farmer's cart and rode along, because I thought you might reconsider using me as your model. I could look good in a rustic setting like this."

Instead of snorting, Francis clapped her hands together. "Such a pretty girl, Caradec! Surely she would make a fine model."

The maid narrowed her eyes at her. "Have we met?"

"Indeed not. I would remember." Francis dropped a cheerful curtsy. "I am Miss Headley."

"Malvi, I've told you I've no need of a model," Caradec interrupted. "I'm to paint the young miss, here." He rolled his eyes. "At the behest of the Duchess of Aldmere."

Malvi pursed her lips and ran an insolent eye over Francis's form. "Well, there ain't much to her. It shouldn't take long to finish her up and then move on—"

"The gig's all loaded, just as you asked." Geordie spoke loudly and stepped forward, interrupting the girl.

Caradec frowned at the boy, but Francis kept her eye trained on Malvi. There was something more here than met the eye. An engagement as a model was a temporary spot of employment. Surely it didn't warrant this sort of zealous pursuit.

Perhaps it was Caradec himself the girl was after. Francis could hardly deny his appeal—not considering what she'd just been up to with him. But she remembered the innkeeper's words from the other night. The maid had asked after Caradec even before she'd met him.

Something was afoot here.

"Everything is ready to leave when you are, yer lordship," Geordie announced. Loudly.

Caradec glanced at Malvi, then at her. Sighing, he nodded. "We'll head back, then."

"Come, Miss." Geordie stepped between her and the maid. "I'll help ye into yer seat."

She smiled her thanks. He was sweet to wish to protect her. She moved off with him, but stopped suddenly and spun back on a heel. "Oh, but what of your young friend?" she asked Caradec, all dismay. "The bench on the gig is so small."

Both males glanced at the maid, neither one appearing to be sympathetic.

"Surely we cannot expect her to walk all the way back to Edinburgh?"

Neither appeared moved, but Malvi suddenly looked alarmed.

"Well," Francis declared. "There's naught else to do. Geordie is small enough. He can squeeze between us on the bench and the young maid can take his spot in the back."

"What? Stand up back there, all the way back?"

"You could walk instead." Caradec shrugged.

"I suppose you could sit backward and dangle your feet," Francis mused.

No one looked happy, but she felt more than satisfied. Until she found out more about that young maid, she wanted Malvi where she could watch her.

⚬⚬⚬

H is axe whistled and wood chips flew through the evening air. At this rate, he'd have Mrs. Beattie enough wood for the winter—before the summer hit its peak.

"Is that frustration or fury?" Malvi crept out of the kitchen door and perched on a nearby ledge.

"Both."

"I came to apologize, if it helps."

"It doesn't." Rhys tackled a particularly knotty log. Sweat dripped down his chest under his shirt. He'd taken off his waistcoat, but he really should have changed out of his good linen. But he'd been so damned frustrated—both at the ill-timed interruption Malvi had managed, and at the fact that Francis had left him tonight at the livery.

Cool as a cucumber, she'd climbed down with Geordie MacNeal and said she'd promised to help the boy with a friend—the sort of help that Rhys had declared himself not interested in. She'd dismissed him without a backward glance and left him with Malvi—after everything they'd said and done to each other that afternoon!

He'd bundled the maid into a hack and stalked off, wandered the city with a black cloud over his head and then he'd come back here to take it out on the innkeeper's woodpile.

"Why do you women have to think with your emotions?" he growled out, pulling hard to remove the axe blade from a knot. "Why must you touch everything, everyone? Put out feelers and roots every-where?" The axe came free and he stood straight and glared at her. "It's much cleaner to slide through life keeping to your own business."

She held out a hand. "Don't paint me with the same brush you are using on everyone else! I'm not the same as every other woman. Do I look like I'd settle for some backwater husband and a parcel of brats?"

He laughed. "You look like the sort of woman who would lead a man on a merry dance all the while making him believe he wants what you want."

She preened. "I knew you were one of the smart ones."

He wiped his brow. "Know many smart ones, do you?"

"Lord, no. But there is one . . ." Her eyes unfocused. "I'm no slouch in that department either—I know who to listen to. And the smartest man I know told me that we are all given gifts. We use them—and whatever else we can—to make our way in the g—" She stopped. "To make our way in life." She hopped down from her perch and posed for him. "I have a body and a face that call to men—and a brain that can outthink them. They'll get me what I want. I'll make sure of it."

"What do you want?" he asked softly.

She grimaced and then shot him a saucy grin. "Right now I very much want you to take me to London."

He let the axe drop. "Is that why you've been chasing me so hard—you think I'm your ticket to London? I hate to disappoint you, lass, but I'm not finished in Edinburgh yet—and London is not on my itin-erary at all. I'll likely head for Italy next."

She sighed. "Damn and blast." But she perked up after a moment. "I heard that you have another artist friend here in Edinburgh. Perhaps he'll be more agreeable."

Rhys shook his head. "Sorry, but you've even less of a chance there." Looking her over, he frowned. "In fact, I'll ask you not to bother the man. He has a new family and doesn't need the sort of trouble that likely follows on your heels."

She pouted. "I won't give up. I will get to London."

"I wouldn't expect it of you, Malvi." He shrugged. "Keep trying, just look in another direction. More, I wish you luck."

Chapter Thirteen

Monsieur—the only name I will give my dear friend here—the artist who took me in—was a lovely man. Older. Kind. He had talent, but had never found a wealthy patron or a large following.

--from the journal of the infamous Miss Hestia Wright

Francis did not go out in search of Caradec the next morning. Her thoughts were too jumbled, her emotions still teetering from longing to anxiety to absolute irritation.

White hot desire sparked and fizzed under her skin anytime she thought about him. Over and again she replayed his kiss, the feel of rough bark on her back even as she reveled in the feel of his hands, his tongue and his hot breath moving over her front. But a bit of panic dwelled in her too. How many times had she seen women blow up their lives for the wrong man?

But was he the wrong man? Her body didn't think so. And the story she'd told—she still couldn't believe she'd shared it. The tale of her mother and her own low beginnings should have sent him running.

Instead, he'd accepted the story with a lift of a shoulder and with sweet, understanding words.

She set her elbows on the dressing table and pressed her fists to her temples. She didn't know what to think. She couldn't be certain of him, of herself, or her ability to keep their relationship even and light.

But one thing she was utterly certain of, however, and that was her distrust of the maid, Malvi. What was the girl up to? Her gut told her it was nothing good—and that she didn't mean to do Caradec any good, either.

So, she put on her boy's clothes and she searched out Angus and his crew—bringing along a sack full of Mab's bridies and a handful of coins. She lolled about in an empty courtyard with them, eating the meat pies and telling them what she knew of the maid—not much— and what she wanted to know—everything else.

"She's not a Scot," she told them with certainty. "But neither can I place 'er accent to a spot in England." She pursed her lips and raised a brow at Angus. "She's a canny one. You won't find 'er an easy mark."

"No worries." Angus spoke through a mouthful of meat and pastry. "We'll crack 'er. We have our ways."

Francis straightened in alarm. "Cor, don't touch 'er! She can't know that we're burrowing out the dirt on 'er."

"Hear that, boys?" Angus raised his voice. "This one's on the sly!"

There followed a chorus of pie-filtered acknowledgements.

"I offer my thanks, as well as good coin." Francis grinned about her and popped the last bite in her mouth. "I knew you all were the best crew in the city."

She returned to Mrs. Spencer's and changed back into a girl, taking time to wash thoroughly and spend time on her hair. When she descended, the lady herself beckoned her from a corner of the shop. "Do join us, my dear Miss Headley. This gentleman is asking after you."

"Mr. Larson!" she said with pleasure and a quick curtsy. "Have you come to select something new for your wife?"

"I have, Miss Headley. And she places me entirely in your hands, as she says you did such a marvelous job choosing for her last time."

"We have cuffs and ribbons that will match that collar," Francis began.

"I had a notion," the gentleman interrupted. "And I hope you will not find me too forward. It is just that, my wife has been a trifle lonely since we came to Edinburgh for my training. It would cheer her immensely to meet another young lady from London, and so I was wondering if you might join us for dinner tonight?"

"Thank you, I would be happy to, if I hadn't already made plans."

He frowned. "I'm sorry to hear it."

"But tell your wife I should love to meet her another time. Perhaps she can visit here at the shop and we can arrange something?"

He nodded, but all of the good cheer seemed to have gone out of him. After a moment he bowed and took his leave.

"Oh, dear," Mrs. Spencer said. "He never did pick another piece for his wife. I hope she won't be disappointed. Ah, well, come in the back with me, my dear. There is tea and I've good news to share! I've had a letter from Emily."

"How nice." Francis followed along, sat at one of the sewing tables and accepted a steaming cup.

"She's coming for a visit and bringing that handsome husband of hers too. In just a few weeks time! I do hope you will still be here to meet them."

She sighed. "It isn't looking likely. The situation with Caradec is . . . difficult."

"Well, he is a man, dear. They are all difficult."

"That's true enough." They laughed a little. "I am sorry to miss your daughter, though. I wasn't at the ball where she made her revelation, but I heard all about it from Hestia."

"Oh, I'm sorry too. I know the two of you would be fast friends," Mrs. Spencer said with a chuckle. "She's full of spit and fire, just like you. And she's always had the soft spot for an underdog."

"Speaking of which—I'm on my way to speak to Janet Grant and her mother. Are you sure you have a place for the woman?"

"You did say as how the girl and her mother were both well spoken and neat—and that their clothes were well-mended?"

"I saw them both several times, and they did seem so."

"Well, then. The mother must be a decent needlewoman, then, aye? I'm in need of one. My embroidered ribbons and sashes have begun to take off here as they did in London. If I'm to hire someone and teach them anyway, it might as well be where it can do the most good. Your Hestia has shown me that, at least."

Francis ducked her head. "Yes, Hestia's an inspiration to us all."

"And you tell the woman that if she'll need shelter as well, then there are rooms upstairs still unused." She sipped her tea. "I enjoy having my own little apartments around the corner, and they would be welcome to use the rooms across from yours."

"You are very generous." Francis leaned over and laid a hand on the other woman's. "Thank you."

Mrs. Spencer merely smiled and patted her. "The thanks go to you and Hestia, my dear, for showing me how to go on. I've been so very happy to come back here and open a shop again, but I admit, my happiness only increases at the thought of sharing it. Now," she said briskly, "why don't you run along and fetch young Janet and her mother and bring them back here? We'll learn all about each other and see if we are a fit. I'll have a fresh pot ready—and I'll send Jasper out for some cakes. Won't that be lovely?"

"It will. Thank you, again." She stood. "I'll return with them shortly."

She left out the front door of the shop. She and Geordie had spoken to Janet last night, so she knew that she'd be in front of St. Giles today with her flowers. Oddly enough, she felt glad that Caradec was not involved today. Scots were a proud people. The situation with the girl and her mother was still precarious. Rhys would undoubtedly end up in a bad temper at her interference and none of them needed him complicating things.

She heaved a sigh. Because if that didn't spotlight their unsuitability, what did? Still, she held out hope. He could learn. And if this worked out well, it might even help her case. Determined, she picked up her step.

She hadn't gone far, though, before she felt it. Her instincts were finely honed. That tingle at her nape . . . the raising of hairs along her arm . . . someone was watching her.

She kept moving steadily. She knew better—far better—than to act like prey. The other side of the street held a larger concentration of pedestrians. She crossed as soon as she was able and lost herself in the crowd. When she reached a corner, she turned along with a group of clerks, pausing only long enough to look back.

Her heart stopped—and then pounded harder than a thoroughbred with the bit in its teeth.

Caradec.

Triumph surged through her first. Clearly, he was as affected by yesterday's events as she was. She hadn't sought him out, so he'd come looking for her. Surely that meant something?

But exasperation followed hard on elation's heels. She had to fetch the Grants and she didn't want him involved until things were more settled.

Suddenly, she bit back a grin. He'd set the challenge for her, earlier. And she'd found him repeatedly. Now, they would see if he could keep up with her.

A narrow close lay ahead. She picked up her skirts and ducked into it, swallowing a laugh as she went.

෨෪෬

W hat in seven hells was he doing? Never in all of his days had Rhys chased after a woman. Now he was literally running Francis down in the street.

Damnation, if Andor or any of his friends could see him now . . .

But everything had ended in such confusion yesterday. He'd been flying so high, with Francis by that stream, lost in heady sensation and throbbing passion. Then Malvi had showed up and he was still reeling from the plummet down from those heights.

Francis had gone so still, and grown so dismissive. A shock—seeing that fey countenance without its usual stream of quicksilver expressions. The lack had settled like a cold weight in his gut—and kept him tossing and turning in his bed last night. He'd had to come by today and try to make things right.

He'd seen her set out from the shop, but he'd been too far away to call. He'd followed instead, but the streets were crowded. It occurred to him that she might be on another errand of interference—the sort inspired by Hestia Wright. Irritation instantly soured his mood. He knew Francis's intentions were good, but like his mother, she likely wouldn't be around long enough to understand all the ramifications her actions might have.

He increased his pace as she crossed the street and strained to see where she went. It was difficult to spot her amidst the hustle . . . and right then something else occurred to him.

She was trying to lose him.

The minx! Was a day going to pass that she didn't throw another challenge at him? She would learn soon enough that he was more than able to handle any of her shenanigans.

Grimly, he set a more aggressive pace. He pushed his way through a passel of dark clothed businessmen and saw her duck into a narrow close. He followed, but she was as fast as she'd claimed and there was no sign of her when he reached the stairs at the end of it.

He climbed and at the top emerged onto a smaller street. It looked more residential, save for a kirk that lay to the left. Just as he looked that way, he saw a flash of green going around the corner of the church.

He raced in pursuit—and skidded to a stop as he encountered a small, walled cemetery. Such a thing would never give her pause or even cause her to change her course. Gripping the gate, he caught sight of another in the corner on the far side.

This one was locked—but it wasn't so high. He scrambled over it and stepped out onto the well-groomed grass, maneuvering his way around the monuments. They were of a large variety and he passed ancient looking stones, a round mausoleum and a tall, thin obelisk.

Not until he approached two curious pedestals did he pause.

Something flashed in his head at the sight. His heart pounded as he examined them closely. Each was a square pedestal as tall as a man, topped with a large, detailed cap. The front of each featured the name of the departed and a profile. Man and wife. But, truly fascinating, the rest of the surfaces were covered with carved images that must be meant to represent their interests and the story of their lives.

His bore a Masonic image, as well as some others that looked vaguely pagan. The sides were carved with a skeleton and a mortar and pestle, as well as a rifle and a quill.

Hers featured a large, complex image of a three-masted sailing ship. A journey? A cross and a dove to represent her faith, yarn and needles, a pianoforte.

Rhys stared. He ran his fingers over the weather worn carvings. Yet it wasn't the unusual monuments that held him fast. Somehow the shape and the very idea of them had broken something loose in his brain. His breath heaved short with excitement. He dropped to his knees, fumbled with his bag and pulled out his sketchbook.

Finally.

There, blazing in his mind, he saw it.

He knew how he was going to paint Francis.

Chapter Fourteen

Monsieur's daughter was a married woman. A childhood accident had rendered her barren, the doctors said. She was to act as caretaker for my child while I was away . . . on business.

--from the journal of the infamous Miss Hestia Wright

Francis arranged the last of Janet Grant's flowers in a vase and set it amidst a display of lacy, fingerless gloves. Behind her, the girl trailed her mother and Mrs. Spencer toward the narrow stairwell.

"Ye've overswept me, ma'am," Mrs. Grant was saying. "An honest job—and rooms as well? It's more than one has a right to expect."

"You are welcome to them," Mrs. Spencer assured her. "Miss Headley will be leaving us, long before we're ready for her to go. Jasper will appreciate having the choice to stay here to watch the shop at night, or to spend his evenings with me."

"Or out and abroad," Francis called.

"Don't give the lad any ideas!" Mrs. Spencer scolded.

"It's not certain we'll even need the rooms," Mrs. Grant said hesitantly.

"Yes, it is," Janet spoke up. 'Ye ken verra well that Uncle will be spittin' mad at the idea of ye takin' on work. No use pretendin' he won't."

"Oh, I've no wish to cause trouble," Mrs. Spencer ventured. She paused with her foot on the first step.

"It's my uncle that's caused the trouble—and we're that grateful to find a way to get away from it," insisted Janet.

Francis saw the girl's mother drop her gaze and then nod in agreement.

"Janet is likely right," she said, her voice lowering.

"Well, then. It sounds as if this will work out for the best—for all of us. Let me show you those rooms."

Francis sighed with satisfaction. The two women had got on well over tea and Mrs. Grant had indeed proven to be a competent needle-woman, and eager as well to learn from her new employer. Janet was happy at the thought that her career as flower seller might not be as necessary, once her mother was earning a good wage.

"Perhaps I'll find a job in a shop as well," she said enthusiastically. "I'd stay warm and dry all day, no matter the weather." Her baby sister crowed suddenly and she brightened. "Or perhaps I'll watch small Helen for mum. Maybe even take in the care of another baby for extra coin." She sighed happily.

But now that the first steps had been taken for the Grants, Francis found her mind turning again to Caradec, where it had been trying to drift all day. Where was he now? Was he furious with her?

"Mrs. Spencer, I need to go out," she called up the stairs.

"Fine. Be careful, dear," her hostess called back.

"I will." She drew on her pelisse and set out.

She didn't find Caradec at the Hound and Hare. He was not to be found along High Street or the major sites, or even the places they'd spent time together. Wandering along, she tried to recall at what point she'd lost him this morning. She'd been full of pride after giving him the slip, but no one appeared to have seen him since. Could some-thing have happened to him? Could he be hurt? Set on by thieves or taken up by constables? Surely not. He was likely just hiding from her, again.

She checked in again at the inn, but they'd had no word. At a loss, she decided to retrace her steps this morning and ask after him.

She bypassed the cemetery the first time, but when she'd paced all along her path, she went back. Using the special twist of the bar that held the lock that Angus had shown her, she disengaged it and went in. She didn't hear anything unusual. Stepping carefully, she wound her way between monuments, and then, as she came around a small mausoleum, she found him.

Stock still, she stared.

Seated on the ground, surrounded by a dozen crumpled sheets of paper, Caradec muttered to himself as he scribbled furiously in his sketchbook. His brows were lowered, his fingers flying. As she watched, he rose up, took a corner of the sheet he'd been using, held it against a tall monument and rubbed a square of charcoal over it.

Even from here she could see the transfer of the texture of the stone.

"No, no," he said aloud. "Not right. Blocks, then. The mausoleum? Or the kirk, perhaps." Turning, he nearly reached the structure she stood beside before he saw her.

"Oh, good!" His eyes widening, he reached out to grab her. "Here, come over here, in the sun. Hurry, before it's gone."

She gaped as he backed up a few paces. Turning over to a new page, he began to draw, glancing between her and the page.

"Let your hair down," he ordered.

She blinked.

"Your hair!" he barked. "Quickly, Flightly! The light is fading. Let it down."

"No."

He looked up at her in surprise.

"Caradec! I cannot!"

"What? Why ever not? I must get it right."

"We are in public," she said through clenched teeth.

"Oh. So we are." He heaved a disappointed sigh and went back to sketching.

"Caradec?"

"Yes? A moment, please."

"What in all the saint's names are you *doing*?"

His expression brightened. "Oh, yes. You don't know, yet! It's wonderful news! I've figured out just how to paint you."

"You . . . what? We are—" Suddenly self-conscious, she didn't know what to do with her arms. "Are we really doing that? I rather thought we were just putting it about as an excuse."

He frowned up at her. "There was never any question of whether I *would* paint you." He gestured with charcoal stained fingers. "That expressive face. That hair." He waved a hand up and down, encompassing her entire figure. "All of your extraordinariness. I just didn't yet know *how* I was to paint you. But now I do."

She supposed she was flattered. She should be, shouldn't she? It was only that . . . she'd been thinking of that kiss by the stream, those embraces . . . and she'd been expecting him to be eager to do perhaps . . . a bit more of that sort of thing. If he wasn't angry with her.

He didn't appear to be angry. He appeared to be . . . distracted. Caught up in his work.

Suddenly, she remembered Mr. North's description of Caradec when he met him in Leeds. How he'd been in the grip of his muse. "Caradec," she began.

"Ah." He held up a hand without looking up. "I thought we were past that sort of formality?"

"Oh, yes." She swallowed. "Rhys. Have you been here all day?"

He looked up at the sun. "No. Only since this morning. And I did have to run back for a few supplies." He sighed and began to sketch even faster. "How did it get to be so late?"

She bit her lip. "The usual way. Come, Rhys. Isn't that enough for one day? Let's get you a drink. Something to eat."

He looked around. "I am thirsty. The vicar gave me a draft of water from the well, but that was . . . long ago." He dropped his charcoal into a pocket and stretched his fingers. "Very well. The light is nearly gone." He flipped his sketchbook closed. "Let's go back to my studio."

She snapped her fingers at him. "Pay attention, Rhys! I cannot go back to your studio like this." She gestured toward her skirts. "Not without a chaperone."

"We'll have Malvi in," he said, stretching.

"We will not," she answered firmly. "Come on, then. There's a coffee shop around the corner and it is supposed to have the city's best Cullen Skink."

"All right. But only if you come to my studio tomorrow." He glanced at her hair. "And bring hair ribbons."

"Yes, fine. Pick up your mess, you great lug, and let's go."

⟨⟩

The next morning, Francis gingerly followed Mrs. Beattie across the threshold into Caradec's studio.

Makeshift studio, she should say. He'd clearly rented two rooms, and had the pocket wall between them folded back to open the space.

"Come on, then, boy. Don't know why ye're so jittery." Mrs. Beattie clearly had other things to do. "He's only goin' to set you mixin' paints, most likely."

"He'll have to learn how to prepare canvas as well," Caradec said. He peered from behind a massive specimen on an easel, situated over in the corner where he could catch the morning light streaming through the shutter-less windows.

"I'm sure he can handle anything ye need," Mrs. Beattie said in a neutral voice, whose tone did not match her encouraging nod. "He seems a quick lad."

"Thank you for showing him up, ma'am. I'll send him down for our dinner, later."

"Have at it, then," she said, closing the door.

Francis had to work not to blush.

She concentrated on the room instead. After all, she'd been alone with Caradec before. This was no different.

It *felt* different, though. Likely because they were closed in, with no passers by or fellow tavern customers—and no easy escape down an alley or through the woods, either. Breathing deeply, she looked around, avoiding the bed, which had been pushed against the right hand wall. She concentrated on his work area instead, running her hands along a desk in the corner. Covered in a tarp-like fabric, it held a collection of palettes, a multitude of paint bladders and a vase filled with brushes. She fussed with the brushes as if they were flowers that needed rearranging, then stepped around a couple of stacks of unused canvas, and over a pile of paint-smeared rags, to move to a smaller table, where she traced her finger along the rims of two porcelain, paint stained bowls.

"Are you nervous?" Caradec asked incredulously.

She shot him a glare. "A little."

He frowned, looked around—and then understanding dawned across his face. "Don't be, Flightly. You're safe here. No escape route needed. If you want to leave . . ." He shrugged. "Just walk out the door."

She flinched, because his insight ticked her panic up another notch. But she refused to give in to it. "How do we begin?" she asked instead.

"Hair," he said, making it an order. "Wig off. I need to see it down."

She had to turn away to do it. It felt too personal, removing her disguise while he watched. She lifted off the wig, then the cap that constrained her own hair, and shook it out, sighing in relief.

The sound he made as her hair fell down her back was altogether more guttural.

She turned.

"Oh, yes." He let loose a long sigh of pleasure and gestured toward a chair set up a few feet before the easel, in the sun. "That's for you."

She took the seat and found it comfortably padded.

"Sit forward, on the edge for a bit, will you?" he requested. He stared avidly and she shivered a little at the intensity. Hidden away inside her boy's clothes, her nipples peaked. But she had to wonder; what did he see? Flightly, the urchin? Francis, the woman? Or had she become just a combination of color and form?

"Pull your hair forward, so that it falls over your breast."

She did and he moved away from the canvas, caught up his sketch-book, stood before her and began filling page after page, flipping them over without letting her see a thing.

"No." He moved at last, trailing around and frowning at her. "Muss your hair a little."

She did.

"No." Stepping forward, he took her hand. "Bend down." When she didn't move fast enough, he helped her along, pushing on her back.

"Caradec! Now that's—"

Her protest was cut off when he dug his fingers into her hair. With strong fingers he rubbed at her scalp, moving them to shake out all of her locks. Saints, but it felt good.

"Now, flip it back up."

She did, meeting his gaze. He stood so close, and there, at last, she saw it. All of the emotion, the smoldering desire, banked like a sleepy, erotic fire.

He leaned in. "First, we paint," he said thickly.

"And then?" She couldn't stop herself from asking.

"And then . . . you decide what's next."

They both returned to their seats—and there followed after that several of the strangest days of Francis's life.

She posed for hours. Sitting. Standing. Hair up. Hair down. Once he asked her to wrap up in a blanket and bare her shoulders, but though she waited in trepidation, he did not ask her to pose nude. At one point he had her stand behind the desk, leaning on it with her hands planted on the edge.

"Push against it," he told her. "As if you were going to launch yourself over it."

"Why?" she demanded. "Come now, Rhys. I'll do it, but surely you'll give me a peek at it, if I do."

He shook his head.

"Just a sketch? Something?"

He merely shook his head and held fast, refusing to let her catch a glimpse of paper or canvas.

One afternoon he perched her next to the window and knelt before her. Taking her hand, he stretched out her arm and bent close, trailing a fingertip along the path laid out by the faint blue of a vein.

Her every nerve ending lit up, pleasure points pulsing across her body like stars in the sky.

"Your skin is softer than silk," he whispered. "And the color of the palest cream."

Leaning forward, he placed a row of kisses where his finger had led. She shivered. Goosebumps erupted all over her.

He looked up. "Your eyes change with the light, but those long lashes—" He sighed and rubbed them with a finger. "They are dusted with gold."

His eyes had gone dark with passion, his expression hungry. And she leaned down and pressed her lips to his.

Such a kiss. Soft and slow. Light as a feather. Deeper than the darkest ocean depths. She wrapped her arms around his neck, slid down to meet him on the floor and pressed her body up against his.

He pulled her in and she gasped as the hard ridge of his manhood met her belly. Sliding her arms through his and clutching his shoulders, she rubbed against him. Sighed his name.

Moaning, he buried his face in the curve of her neck, sending shivers down her with his hot breath. But only for a moment.

He pulled away. "Not yet," he said into her hair. "You have thinking to do, still." He drew back and smiled at her. "And I must paint."

They did leave the studio occasionally. She spent one morning standing against the outside wall of an apothecary's shop, increasingly bored as he scribbled away. Hours, days, he spent staring at her. She wondered if he realized she stared at him quite as long? She didn't think so. And she was grateful that he never seemed to notice that her body hovered continually on the edge of molten desire.

She yawned incessantly one morning, when he picked her up in the pre-dawn black and bundled her into a carriage. Geordie saluted her from the box. She nodded at him and promptly fell asleep in the corner, only to wake as Caradec bustled her outside and onto a thick blanket at the top of Calton Hill.

"I want to see your hair when the morning sun hits it."

It was all the explanation he gave and she huddled in a wrap and fought sleep until the sky lightened in the east and a sudden wailing sounded nearby. She sat straight up, only relaxing when a piper stepped out from behind a tree.

"You did say you always wished to hear a great pipe," Caradec said with a shrug. He took up his brush and set to work.

She nodded, touched, and he painted furiously while she listened and watched the sun wake the city with a soft caress of light.

One evening his hand cramped and they abandoned the canvas, wandering instead all across the city as Caradec examined one sort of greenery after another. He marched them from public gardens to kirk yards, but it wasn't until they passed a private residence in George Street that he found what he wanted—a climbing vine cascading down over an iron fence, covered in small violet flowers. Laughing, he gathered an armful of garlands and carried them back to the studio, where he bade her to put them in water.

She grew comfortable staying alone with him in the enclosed space, although she lamented the fact that she had to spend all of her time in her boy's clothes. It was necessary, though, especially as Malvi lurked constantly about, irritating both Francis and Mrs. Beattie.

"What's he painting in there?" the maid demanded one day, cornering her as she left to fetch water and grabbing tight to the sleeve of her tunic. "Why doesn't he come out?"

"He does. But he's nearly always painting—a portrait of that ginger-haired lady." Francis added a note of disgust, secretly chuckling inside at her success at fooling Malvi. She waved paint-stained fingers at the maid, for she had indeed learned how to mix colors. "And how many shades of red-gold can one girl sprout from her head? It don't make a lick of sense."

"Put in a good word for brunettes in general and me in particular," Malvi said shrewdly. "In return, I'll see you get extra helpings of sticky pudding—any time you wish."

"Won't do a bit of good," she lamented in answer. "The cove is in the grip of . . . something. Paints like a madman. Don't even remember to eat or drink until I remind him—and then I have to poke him several times before it gets through."

The maid sighed in frustration. "Oh, what good are you to me, then?"

"None at all," Francis said, grinning as she moved on. "None at all."

Chapter Fifteen

*But I had time before the child was due. Monsieur and I used the
interval to come up with a mutually beneficial plan.*

--from the journal of the infamous Miss Hestia Wright

Rhys had never enjoyed the creation of a painting more. Francis
had appointed herself his caretaker and proved to be exemplary
at the job. She made sure that he took regular meals and always had a
cool drink to hand. She forced him to leave the studio occasionally to
breathe fresh air and focus on something besides the work for at least
a small portion of each day.

And she turned out to be quite the best model he'd ever had. She
never complained, although she did fidget if he kept her sitting for too
long. She possessed an excellent weather vane for his temper, somehow
knowing when it was acceptable to talk while he worked and holding
silent when he was caught up in a difficult or transcendent bit.

She asked question after question about his habits, about technique
in general and even about all the myriad small tasks that come with the

creation of one presentable portrait. She listened to his answers too, learned and actually became such a help in making things run smoothly that he found himself to be far more productive than ever before.

They discussed all sorts of art, from paintings to architecture, to public monuments and even poetry. She was a reader. He was not—so she shared with him some of her favorites. He loved all of those conversations, because her questions were intelligent and her comments were insightful. And her curiosity was boundless.

"You know, it's no wonder that everyone likes you," he said one evening. They were out getting dinner at a pub. She paused, leaving a forkful of shepherd's pie hanging in mid-air.

"Everyone does not like me," she said carefully.

"They do." He swallowed a gulp of ale. "People are often interested in me. They like to hear about my work, my travels. They ask questions I can't answer about painting, sometimes. But I'm an object of curiosity, something to tell their friends about. Whereas, they genuinely like you. You become their friend."

She shook her head.

"Have you not noticed? Everywhere we go, someone is happy to see you, whether you are in skirts or pants."

"Next time we are both in London, remind me to introduce you to a girl named Jesse. She'll be sure to tell you about my many bad qualities."

"Jealous. Must be," he said with a wave of his hand.

"Talk to Malvi, then."

"Definitely jealous—of both of you, boy and girl." He shook his head. "No use denying it." Cocking his head, he regarded her with thoughtful concentration. "I think it is, in part, because you are like a sponge. You soak up information and are always thirsty for more. You pay attention to all the little pieces that people tell you about them-selves—and you never forget them. You ask questions. You are truly interested in their lives and preoccupations."

She shrugged. "I suppose I am."

"I don't think you realize how appealing it is. Mostly because it is so rare. So many people are interested only in themselves, their own cares, their own world."

She set down her cutlery. "But that is nearly how you describe yourself."

He flushed. "It's different. Entirely."

"How?"

He straightened and flung out a hand. "I'm interested in people. New people, new places and new experiences."

"As I am." Her voice gentled. "You are just not interested in connecting with them."

He fell silent, largely because there was no answer to that. It was true. He'd just never seen the consequences of it so clearly.

They finished their meal without further conversation.

"It's late," he said when they had finished. "Why don't you go home and enjoy your evening. I think I'll take a walk."

"If you're sure?"

Nodding, he waved her off. "I'll see you in the morning."

⁂

Francis walked slowly back to Mrs. Spencer's, her mind awhirl. Perhaps she should not have been so . . . forthright? But she'd stayed because she wanted to show him a different path. She'd begun to make headway. She just wished he hadn't gone so . . . blank.

Still lost in thought, she turned into the alley behind the shop. She always entered at the back when she was dressed in her boy's clothes. But she drew to a halt when she found Jasper and Angus reclining on crates and passing a flask between them.

"Evening, you lugs." She pulled up a crate of her own.

"Angus has come to see you, lad," Jasper said meaningfully.

"Aye." Angus grinned. "But I was countin' on ye takin' a bit more time about it." Ruefully, he passed the drink back to Jasper.

"Keep it. I'm to learn more about the bookkeeping this evening. The two don't mix." Jasper made the announcement with mingled pride and reluctance and climbed to his feet. "Good night to you both."

Angus watched him go and tried to pass the flask to Francis when he'd gone.

She shook her head. "Have you learned something, then?"

He nodded. "Not much, but I've two things to pass on."

She waited.

"First—that girl is nae just a maid."

"What makes you say that?" And did she want to know?

"Twice a week she slips out o' the inn and gets herself to a news-stand a couple of blocks away. Always speaks to the same bloke, who is always there at the same time, reading the papers."

"Well, she is the type to have a beau," Francis mused.

Angus shook his head. "Not her beau. I went myself, with the boys, the second time. Not lovers. Whole thing looked familiar. Just like one of my boys, reportin' back to me after a job."

Not good news. Francis could think of only one person who might want reports on Caradec. "Who's the bloke?"

"No idea. Never seen 'im hereabouts, which means he likely ain't from here. And I can tell you—he didn't look too happy with the chit, either."

"He wouldn't. Malvi hasn't made much headway. What's the second thing?"

"She's got a powerful interest in the new girl working in there with Mrs. Spencer." He jerked his head toward the shop.

Francis straightened. "Angus! You didn't take that maid's money, did you? After I set you to watching her?"

"Aye, I did. But I ain't told her nothin'." He scrunched his nose at her. "You and the girl showed up at about the same time. The pair o' ye related?"

"You could say that."

"Then we won't be telling the maid anythin'. Ye come to us first. And besides which, she treated me like the dirt she couldn't wait to rub off her shoes—and ye're practically one o' us." He offered the flask again and this time, she took it.

"I'm honored you would say so." Raising it in salute, she took a swig.

When she burst out coughing, he deftly took it back. "All right, there?" He stood. "Well, I'm off. Want us to keep watching the chit?"

"Yes, please," she choked out.

"P'rhaps ye should go in," Angus suggested, looking amused.

But she was recovering—and beginning to enjoy the warmth spreading throughout her chest. "No. If the chit is spying on Caradec, he needs to know. I'll go and warn him."

"As it suits ye." Angus nodded. "I'll be in touch."

☙❧

S he found him in back of the inn, chopping firewood. Standing in the shadows, she watched for a moment.

He'd stripped off his coat and waistcoat. Only his linen shirt was left and it was plastered to him, showing off broad shoulders and a strong, muscular chest. His hair hung loose and had gone damp with sweat. *Saints in heaven.* She put a hand on the inn wall, seeking support. Was there a saint that protected young women from sheer, unbridled lust?

There ought to be.

He filled that courtyard. There was nothing to do but look and admire how large, hard and incredibly beautiful he was.

"I see you there, Flightly. Come on out." Pausing, he let the head of the axe rest on the toe of his boot. "I thought I sent you home."

"I came back." She stepped forward. "I have something to tell you."

He nodded, waiting.

She moved closer, trying to shut off all of her senses and remain unaffected by his rugged masculinity. "You aren't going to like it."

He tossed the axe, wiped his brow and made an impatient gesture. "Spit it out, then."

"It concerns Malvi. She's no simple maid."

He scoffed. "Anyone who's met the girl can see that. She's got ambition."

He sighed and she shook her head. She'd thought the Scots were skilled at expressive noises, but Caradec could also say quite a bit without actual words.

"She's likely thinking she'll find a rich man she can seduce into taking her on." Lifting a shoulder, he continued. "She might be right, at that."

"It's worse than that, I'm afraid." She told him what Angus had said about the girl's meetings. "All of her focus has been on you, Rhys. It seems likely that she's watching you for someone."

His eyes closed. "Francis." Another inarticulate sound—this one telling her how weary—and slightly exasperated he was with the topic. "I know what you are going to say. I know you are vested in this private war going on between Hestia and her enemies—"

"Enemy," she interrupted. "One. Marstoke. Malvi must be working for him. Why else would she also be asking questions about *me*? The real me, I mean."

That gave him pause. "That is unfortunate. I hope you are wrong. I know Marstoke is not to be trusted, but—"

"Not to be trusted?" she scoffed. "The man is . . . twisted, Rhys. Broken."

"And you know this because Hestia told you?" Furrows plowed across his brow as pain bloomed behind his eyes. His hands fisted and she saw his knuckles whiten. "I know *you* don't want to hear this, but you cannot believe all that my mother says."

Color crept into his face and she turned away to give him a moment. From the taproom came an incongruous swell of laughter.

"I should think that you would know me better by now," she answered quietly. "Do you think that I would make my life's choices based on second hand information? Gossip?" Fuming, she took a step away before she said anything else. She was both reluctant to reveal any more and resentful that he was making it necessary.

"No." It emerged hoarsely. "You wouldn't. Any more than I would. I only refer to the pain Hestia caused me—and those I love—directly. Through her own words and actions."

Frustration tore at her. She longed to defend her friend and mentor, to demand to know what caused the resentment that simmered inside of him. But she'd promised. Voluntarily agreed not to discuss Hestia.

Seconds passed—and then she blinked.

She'd made no such promise concerning Marstoke.

But did she want to tell Rhys more? Let him in further than she already had? Already the boundaries were blurring—at least for her. *This far and no further.* He appeared to be happily secure on his side of the line.

She whirled around and their gazes locked. The awareness, the hope between them felt so fragile, it seemed less sturdy than a soap bubble.

But it was there—and she was not ready to give up on it.

"I'm speaking from personal experience as well," she said softly. "I met Marstoke first, long before I met Hestia."

Alarm flared suddenly in his face. "How?" It was a demand, born of fear.

She shook her head. "Hatch worked for him, for a time."

His shoulders fell in relief.

"Looking back now, I can see why she was drawn into his games. She was just exactly the type that he likes to recruit for his various strategies. Restless and resentful. Ambitious. Determined to take what fate failed to bestow—so similar to those younger sons he endlessly attempts to convert into lackeys." She raised a brow. "It's a description that fits Malvi as well, isn't it?"

He was honest enough to admit it with a twitch of his lips—and stubborn enough not to say it out loud.

"Damnation," he muttered after a moment. "You may well be right." He threw his hands in the air.

"But why would he send a girl after you? Why not just invite you to meet with him?"

"Invite? The man doesn't know how to do anything so polite. He's more likely to send a summons."

"Then why the subterfuge instead of a summons?"

"Because I wouldn't answer an invitation or a summons," he said with a shrug.

Why not? She wished she knew.

"In any case, I do not care. Let Malvi lurk and ask her questions and make her reports." He stood rigid now. "What will she say? Surely nothing so different from what you will report to Hestia."

He threw it out there—a gauntlet wrapped in simple words.

There was not a chance in a thousand that she wouldn't pick it up.

Stiff-legged, she marched up to him. Stood directly before him—an unyielding monument to male stupidity—and met him gaze for gaze.

"First," she said, low, slow and clear. "Let me say that I am as nervous for Malvi as I am for you. Marstoke is careless with his minions and deliberately cruel when they fail him. Second, I could tell you about the pain I've seen that man deliver, the perversions he has perpetuated out of sheer spite or curiosity or boredom. I could tell you how even innocent facts become weapons in his grip and innocent people become pawns or victims."

She breathed deeply. "Third, I could talk for hours—*days*—about Hestia Wright and how she is his shining opposite. About the good and the relief and the justice she brings to this world. But I'll say only this one thing." Stepping close she met his gaze and tried to ignore the growing buzz of anticipation growing between them. "Hestia has no idea that I am here."

Something in him relaxed, just the most infinitesimal bit. "Is that true?" It came out in a cracked whisper that told her just how much it meant.

And hope surged. Foolish, treacherous, tempting hope. Because she knew suddenly that she had been a fool. *This far and no further.* So foolish to think that she could draw that line and not cross it. A fool to think that perhaps he would.

Except—he might have been tempted, too.

And she knew—she would have to cross it. How could she convince him that life without love was wasted—if she would not risk it herself?

"It's true. But I'll say no more. Because I promised you, on pain of being sent away, not to discuss it." Drawing a deep breath, she let it out on a whisper. "And I am not ready to go."

His gaze softened. The tension between them spiraled—but they could do nothing about it. She was still dressed as a boy and they stood in full view of the inn's back windows.

She jumped a little when he bent at the waist and put his face close to hers. "Get yourself up to my studio," he said in a voice that sounded low and full of promises. He pointed with one long arm. "We'll finish this conversation there, once I'm done here."

She stalled a moment, considering.

He raised a brow.

And with a nod, she scampered off. Before she entered the inn, she paused to look back, saw him stacking logs steadily, as if the world had not just shifted beneath their feet.

She failed to see the figure crouched in the nearby shadows. Caradec missed it as well, when he'd completed his task and followed eagerly after her. Watching him go, it stood silently for a moment, then slipped away.

Chapter Sixteen

He began to paint me. Not full portraits, of course. But the drape of a hand holding a rose, a bared shoulder, the graceful shape of a naked back.

--from the journal of the infamous Miss Hestia Wright

Her heart pounded as loudly as her feet on the stairs, and heat bloomed inside her as Francis made her way into the studio. She'd scarcely been alone in here—no more than a minute or two since Caradec had started painting her.

For an instant she gazed at the covered portrait, tempted to sneak a peek at it. But only for an instant. It was Rhys's work, his creation. She would abide by his wishes.

Crossing over to the bed, she contemplated it—and her own wishes. Was she going to do this? She couldn't pass it off as a selfless act, not even to herself. He'd won her over—made her want him—long ago. And now her heart was thumping and her blood was singing—

She stopped—because she was still dressed like a street urchin.

No. Not like this. Hurrying, she removed the wig and shook out her curls with a sigh of relief. Looking down, she sighed. It wasn't enough. But she didn't have any of her female garments with her. Anything would be better, though. Even . . . nothing? She shook her head. She wasn't that brazen. So she shuffled through his drawers, looking for a shirt.

The short lace at the edge of his sleeves dangled far past her fingers. The hem hung past her knees. But at least she felt like a girl.

A nerve-wracked girl who didn't know what to do with herself.

She paced for a moment, then positioned herself in the middle of the bed. But that felt . . . entirely wrong. She scrambled out, wrung her hands, perched on the edge of the mattress—and froze when the door opened and Caradec paused on the threshold.

"Good Lord, Francis," he said dumbly.

She sprang up and sat back down, fingering the edge of his shirt. "I'm sorry. I'd hoped you wouldn't mind. I just wanted to look . . ." She paused, her words failing and her heart full.

"You look exquisite," he said firmly, before entering and shutting the door. For several long moments they stared at each other across the room.

He'd washed somewhere. His hair and collar were damp and his hands and face were clean. "Aren't you going to come in?" she asked, after some time had passed.

"I can't." The words came out strangled.

"Why not?"

"I want to latch the door, to keep anyone from coming in—but I'm afraid to spook you."

She pursed her lips, touched. "Go ahead. I won't spook. I promise," she added, when he hesitated.

He secured the door and turned back—but kept his position.

"Rhys?" she whispered, her nerves screaming.

"I . . . I could use a bit of guidance here, Francis," he said hoarsely.

She straightened. "Oh, dear. Then we are in trouble."

He winced. "Not that way." He shrugged. "You have the reins. I made that promise and I intend to keep it. I'll stop when you ask, even if it kills me. But I would like some idea of how far you intend this to go—so I can prepare myself."

She blinked. "I'm sure I wish I could help, but . . . I've never ventured down this particular path. I'm not even sure how many steps there are."

"That's no help at all," he groaned.

Her heart sank. "I'm sorry. If you'd rather not—"

She got no further before he'd crossed the room, swung her up and into his arms and around as if she were but a babe. With a gasp of shock she wrapped her arms around his neck and then he was kissing her softly, soundly and with great enthusiasm. "I assure you," he said eventually. "There is *nothing* I'd rather do."

She laughed. "Me either."

Setting her down, he took her former spot on the edge of the bed and pulled her into his lap. "I'm honored to be chosen for your first . . . encounter," he told her. "I vow, it will all go just as you wish."

He meant it. Likely he had the skill to make her want exactly what he wanted—but she trusted him.

"Were you nervous, your first time?" she asked suddenly.

"Hell, yes." He laughed. "But my nerves were as nothing next to my excitement—and my enthusiasm."

An utterly relatable thought. But then a dark idea intruded. "Who was your first? She wasn't a . . . prostitute?"

"No!" She rather thought she'd startled the answer out of him. "She was a dairy maid. Though on second thought, she might have had cause to wish I'd been to see a . . . professional first, to teach me a thing or two." He grinned, then grew more serious as he searched her expression. "Were you wondering if I've ever been on your side of this situation? Well, the answer is yes. Although that first time was just a quick job against the side of the barn, I did eventually spend time with someone who thought she could show me a few lovely things." He raised a brow. "Nor did I have to pay her."

"The first time I saw a pair having at it, they were standing up, too, in an alley in the stews. I thought that's how it was done, for the longest time." She gave a short laugh. "Funny to think I grew up in a bawdy house, and never saw a thing—until I was let loose in the city."

"It's not funny—but it is unique." Bending down, he pressed his mouth to hers and kissed her softly. Gently he brushed her lips. It felt like the slide of silk against bare skin. "Just like you. There is no one like you, Francis. No one as lovely and quick, as endearing and amusing. I am honored to be given a role in your introduction to things . . . physical."

He was so generous, so giving. She knew she'd made the right choice. He would make a fabulous first lover. And she would do her damndest to show him that intimacy—real intimacy—would only make this, and life in general, even better.

She looped her arms around his neck and loosed the damp ribbon holding his hair. They both sighed when she ran her fingers through his thick locks. "I do love your hair," she told him.

"And I'm still surprised by it."

"Don't be." She grinned. "As you are fond of saying, it's unique."

Suddenly they were kissing again. It felt more urgent this time, almost desperate, and he quickly claimed her with his tongue. He tasted of wine and smelled of soap and the faintest lingering of sweat—and that wasn't unpleasant at all. And the ferocity of his kiss, the clear signal that he wanted her as much as she did him—it made her tremble.

"Are you all right?" He pulled back, instantly solicitous, but whatever he saw in her face—gladness, joy, potent desire—sent his warm mouth to savage hers again.

The neck of his shirt hung loose and open at her throat—and he took full advantage of it. Pressing it aside, he easily bared a breast. His broad thumb rubbed the other through the linen. Her eyelids dropped. A rush of excitement flooded her as he closed his lips over the exposed nipple. Saints, but his mouth was hot. He teased her with the tip of his tongue, suckled, and flicked the hard pebble until she was squirming in his lap.

It felt so good, made her so . . . excited . . . that she let it go on for a while. But eventually she grew impatient.

"Rhys," she said. She had to repeat his name. "Rhys! You have far more clothes on than I do."

"We can't have that." He drew back. "Easily fixed, though." He leaned back and wiggled out of his coat, but she reached for the buttons on his waistcoat before he could. Deliberately, she released one after the other, stretching it out and grinning when he impatiently tore it off and tossed it.

She helped him with the shirt beneath, and then she sighed in pleasure and indulged herself, running her hands all over him, exploring his broad, masculine bounty. Such shoulders! And a fascinatingly wide chest, just lightly covered in hair that felt rough against her fingers. And a narrow waist with a darker line of hair leading . . . down.

She grew a little flustered. Unsure. But Rhys sensed it and kissed her again, then lifted her and eased her back onto the bed. With hands and sweet whispers he urged her to scoot back, until they were both stretched out upon the mattress—and she was completely distracted by the taut muscles of his arms and torso as he braced himself beside her.

She ran light fingers down one arm and up again—and delighted in the shiver that ran through him. She was feeling so many new and overwhelming things . . . it felt good and right that she should be able to affect him as well.

He pressed her into the bed when he leaned down to kiss her with slow heat and rich passion. Their tongues danced and their hands slid over each other, touching and teasing blood and heat right to the skin's surface.

So large. He loomed over her. It was daunting—and exciting. She felt small, but not frail. And also utterly safe and protected.

Hot and wet, his lips traced a path down her neck and on to her breasts. Soon enough she was arching, pressing her shoulders back, silently begging for more as he found her taut nipple, flicked it with his tongue and captured it with his teeth.

She never wanted him to stop.

And yet, she wanted more.

Suddenly he stopped, drawing back from her. With a whimper of protest, she reached for him.

"Perhaps we should stop here."

"Why?" she gasped.

He groaned. "Because you are a temptress, Francis. Because you are everything sweetly, wildly desirable. Because if we go further, I'm afraid I won't be able to stop at all."

She sank back. This was it, then. Her moment to decide.

Except that there was no decision. Not truly. What was she to do? Go this far with Caradec and find someone else to finish it, some time off in the future? Mind and body revolted at the thought.

Of their own volition, her arms reached for him, pulled him close again.

"Francis," he said with warning clear in his tone. "Be mindful of what you are doing."

"I am mindful," she said, a little cranky. "I'm absolute aware. Although you'll have to accept it without the wrapping and the bow, I am giving you my virginity."

His breath hitched. "Are you sure?"

"Yes."

He kissed her, pleasure and pride aglow in his expression. "Then no bow is needed." He tugged at the shirt she wore. "And let's get rid of this wrapping."

Her fingers clutched the linen, but she forced them to relax and allow Rhys to maneuver the shirt over her head. When it was off, he sat back, still for a moment, and gazed at her in wonder. "You are so very lovely."

She blushed, more at the compliment than at her nakedness. "There's no need for you to grin like a boy at Christmas."

"On the contrary, there is every need—and I couldn't help it, in any case. Your trust is the greatest gift I've ever received."

Her insides turned to a puddle and she reached for him once more.

He scooped her up and hugged her close and as his mouth claimed her again, his fingers were moving between them, moving down, down, and she gasped as he parted the warm, wet, private folds of her sex.

"Mmmm." Magic. He created it with those fingers as he explored her. All of her focus was narrowed to that feeling of silken paradise. All of it . . . except for one nagging bit.

"Wait," she demanded.

Rhys groaned. "Francis."

But she reached out and tugged at the waistband of his breeches. "Take these off. It's only fair," she insisted. With familiarity and ease she unbuttoned the fall of his garment, eyeing him as he hurriedly moved to shuck everything off.

Her breath fell away. She'd heard plenty of coarse talk. She'd known his member was sizable—she'd felt it pressing her into that tree. But this—she hadn't guessed. He stretched high and hard and long, the head of it pulsing just beneath his navel.

Cautiously, she reached out, questioning him with her eyes, but he groaned in approval. "Yes. Do it. Touch me."

She did and reveled in the soul deep moan he let out when she wrapped her fingers around him. She made a noise of her own—one of appreciation at the velvet weight of him. Shockingly, he grew larger and harder. His hips thrust forward, silently asking for more. So she moved her hand, as he had done for her, exploring the length of him, wondering how he could be both soft and firm.

He laid her back again and edged her legs apart. Their caresses continued, slow now, then quick, faint as a feather and then more aggressive as they learned how to please each other.

"Now," he said, suddenly. Loudly. "Francis."

He braced himself above her. Her mind raced. At last.

But suddenly a look of horror crossed his face.

"Rhys?"

"Damnation. I nearly forgot."

It dawned on her then, too.

"The French Letter!" they said in unison.

He was gone and rummaging through a drawer, but back in moments.

"God in heaven." He fumbled and struggled with it.

"Let me help." She tied the small ribbons and then lay back, meeting his gaze directly.

"Say it," he demanded. "Let us be clear and honest with each other." He sucked in a breath. "I ache for you, Francis, perhaps more than I ever have before. But you must say it. Tell me that you want me."

"I do. I want you. All of you."

He was there, then, over her, breaching her folds, poised at her entrance. She held her breath as he pushed in. He moved slowly, a look of utter concentration on his face.

For a moment, she froze. He was so large and it all felt so . . . tight and full.

"All right?"

She concentrated. Her body was adjusting and it felt . . . "Saints!" she said weakly. "Yes. Yes, all right."

More than all right. She was awash in . . . discovery. And amazement. And the strongest feeling of *want* that she'd ever experienced. And that was saying something.

He looked concerned. "What is it?"

"More," she said. Insisted.

Brightening, he accommodated her, the color rising in his chest and up across his cheekbones. But she had no more than a moment to notice, because she was busy marveling at what was happening. Heat grew within her as he worked himself in deeper—until finally he was fully seated—and she was . . . delighted.

Look at what they'd done.

Feel it.

They were *joined*.

"Rhys," she whispered. His name escaped on a surge of wonder and dizzy excitement. She didn't think anything could be more perfect.

And then he moved, proving her oh-so-wrong.

Her pulse was pounding, her sex fluttering in time with his movements. He gripped her hips in excitement, settling even deeper, and she was lost. Utterly in his thrall.

He leaned down to kiss her once more. "My God. You are perfection."

And the world narrowed to just the two of them. Only this mattered, the curling tension between them. Only this existed.

He reached a hand between them, found the slick, wet nub at the center of her.

It was the last, perfect note. Almost more than she could process. It released . . . something and a storm broke over her, spiraling outward from that spot. She arched into it, every muscle coiled.

Rhys cried out as well, his head thrown back, and they rode the edge, glorying in the tempest.

Together.

Chapter Seventeen

Each portrait contained the elegant shape of a curved half moon. A charm on a bracelet, a pendant hanging from a necklace, a carved hair ornament.

--from the journal of the infamous Miss Hestia Wright

Boneless, Francis lay sprawled, her head tucked onto Rhys's chest, one leg thrown over his. The comforting sound of his heartbeat added to her sense of peace.

She could have stayed in that position for hours, wallowing in the languid aftermath of pleasure—except Rhys was mumbling. It echoed strangely in the ear pressed against him—and most definitely disturbed the calm she was trying to hold on to.

The rumbling grew louder. She tried to ignore it.

"Berry," he suddenly said. "Scary. Hairy."

"Shhhh…" She nudged him. "I'm trying to file away every delicious moment."

"I cannot," he declared. "You have inspired me to new heights.

What I would like to do would be to paint you—frozen forever in the throes of passion. But never could I part with such a piece—or even display it—so I am composing an ode in your honor, instead."

"No need," she said wryly. "Let's immortalize the moment in silence."

"Impossible! I am caught up!" He looked down and grinned at her. "I need something to rhyme with 'velvet-tipped breast, sweet as a cherry.'"

She winced.

"No? Perhaps I'll turn it around and end that couplet with *breast*. Now, what next, then? Fest? Lest? Ah, yes! Crest!"

Groaning, she tried to roll away, but he laughed and gathered her close. "No, you are right. The moment deserves solemnity. Never has there been such a coupling."

She brightened. He had so much more experience. Had this one, with her, ranked so high?

"And never will there be again, no matter with whom you share it," he finished.

And her high spirits dropped, just like that. It felt like a blow, how easily he spoke of her doing this with someone else. She rolled over onto her side, away from him.

He followed, pressing against her back and reaching around to cup her breast. "There is only ever one first time," he said, tucking in close. "I'm proud to have been part of yours—and pleased you won't ever have to associate it with the smell of cows."

She laughed despite herself, and felt a little better, knowing she'd misinterpreted him. But it was perhaps a good reminder after all. She may have crossed that line, but she still needed to protect herself. Especially because a part of her wished for Rhys Caradec to be her last coupling, as well as her first, with a great, goodly number thrown in between.

He bent to kiss her nape and at the same time thrust his hips into her bottom, where she felt the ridge of his manhood rising again. "Shall we take care of your second time, while we are at it?"

"So soon?" She looked over her shoulder and couldn't help but smile at his suggestive grin. "I've always heard that a gentleman needs time to recover."

He pulled her over onto her back and smiled down at her. His hair hung loose, framing that chiseled face and suddenly she marveled at her good fortune. "I'm no gentleman," he murmured. "And it's a good thing, too, eh?"

"Good enough for me," she whispered, reaching up and tracing a finger along his cheekbone. Then she tucked her hand behind his head and pulled him to her.

The kiss was long, languorous and sweet. Another surprise—how easily repletion could turn back to lust.

He touched her again, everywhere, and this time she made sure to do the same and explored him as thoroughly, running curious fingers up and down the fascinating length of him, finding the tender spots, making him gasp and shiver.

What delicious power.

And then he was tossing her back, pulling her legs up and around his waist. She met him eagerly and soon they were both breathless and pulsing with the pleasure of release.

Afterwards, she lay unmoving, tired and happy and in his arms. He fell almost instantly asleep. With a sigh of mingled wistfulness and contentment, she followed him.

❦

Despite their late night, Rhys awoke early the next morning. Because of it, he awoke in a heartily cheerful mood.

Francis slept on. She had every reason to be tired, the poor mite. Feeling utterly self-satisfied, he crept carefully from the bed and covered her well. Dressing quietly, he headed downstairs.

His good mood lasted through breakfast and carried him out the front door of the inn afterward. In the courtyard, he stretched and smiled and walked out to stare at the city beyond the galleried walls. He was nearly finished with Francis's portrait. What would Edinburgh offer to inspire him next?

Not the castle. Andor had taken care of that subject magnificently.

Rhys had the urge to paint something smaller, more intimate. Something that spoke to the proud spirit of the people who lived here. One of the parks, perhaps. Or a pretty little kirk.

"Excuse me, sir?"

He dropped his arms and turned to face a lad who stepped away from a corner of the inn.

"You are Mr. Caradec?"

"I am." He waited—and watched. This was not one of the boys he'd seen with Francis that first day. How long ago it seemed, although it had not even been yet a fortnight.

"My name is Jasper. I work for Mrs. Spencer."

Rhys cast back in his head, trying to remember . . .

"She has a store just off High Street. Ribbons and notions and things."

"Oh, yes." He was here for Francis. Damn.

"She has a young guest. *He* did not return home last night. We know he's been working for you, running errands and such . . ."

"Oh, yes." Rhys nodded, silently acknowledging that slight emphasis. "The poor youngster was so tuckered out last night he fell asleep sitting up, waiting for me to finish work." He lifted a shoulder. "Sometimes I get caught up in a painting and work into the night. I made a makeshift pallet for the boy and he's up there, sleeping still."

"Oh. Fine, then." By the look on his face, it was anything but fine. "Just send him home when he wakes, then?"

"Actually, I'm right in the middle of a portrait. I could use his help today. But I'll make sure he returns home this evening."

After a hesitant nod, the lad turned and left.

Awkward, that. His mood deflated, Rhys turned back into the inn. He'd never before entered into a liaison with someone not as free and unfettered as he was, that was all. Francis was his first innocent. Some things were bound to be different.

He stopped off in the kitchen for a tray, and then climbed the stairs, lost in thought.

Francis was just awake when he entered, still in bed and entirely delectable.

"Is that breakfast?" She asked it with such happy eagerness that he threw aside his intention of crawling in with her and keeping her there a bit longer.

"It is, indeed. Come and eat, lay-a-bed. We have work to do today." He set the tray down and beckoned. "I'm nearly finished with your portrait."

She bounced out of bed and grabbed a roll while he poured coffee. "When can I see it?"

"When it is finished," he answered firmly. "Now eat up and let's get to it."

A short while later, he had her back in one of his shirts, and perched on a stool in the sun. "No, don't straighten your hair. I like it mussed."

She made a face, but dropped her hands. "What will you paint next? A landscape, perhaps? It would be nice to get out of the studio."

He'd just asked himself the same question, but hearing her ask it gave him pause. He'd been in Edinburgh over a month. Long enough, in the normal course of things, for the first restless stirrings to begin. Granted, he'd been uncommonly busy—two paintings nearly completed in such a short time. In another city he might have started another, but he'd also likely have begun thinking about moving on, choosing his next destination, started to make plans.

Yet he hadn't had so much as a thought of leaving. Granted, the city had beauty and interest to keep him occupied for much longer than this. But perhaps it was mostly because his thoughts had been so busy with Francis lately—and that gave him pause too.

"I'd thought one of the smaller kirks. Something with a cemetery. Or perhaps something to do with Calton Hill . . ." His words trailed away and he tried to focus on his work. "Stretch your neck, just a bit?"

But his mood continued to fluctuate. Hoping to focus his thoughts and quiet his anxieties, he began to talk, to tell Francis of his ambition to visit Florence.

"How long have you thought of going there?" she asked. She'd grown quiet and thoughtful.

"Since I first learned to wield a brush at my grandfather's knee. He was an artist, you know. My first teacher. He told me of the bridges, the buildings and their great history of patronage of the arts. As I grew, I learned the work of the masters and I knew I had to walk where they once did, see the sights that inspired Botticelli and Verrocchio, Raphael and Michelangelo and all the rest."

She nodded. "Of course, you must go."

"I will." He painted quietly a while longer, but then tossed down his brush and stretched out his shoulders. Shaking his arms, he flexed his fingers before taking up his brush again. "Come, Francis. I need a distraction this morning. Talk to me while I work. Tell me something . . ." He glanced at the image on the canvas. "Tell me about something that you love, something that makes you happy."

She stiffened. "No."

"No?" His brush paused.

Frowning, she shook her head. "I said it. I meant it. No. Everything between us is upside down. The balance is shifted in your favor—and believe me, I am not used to it."

He thought about that.

"You know a good deal about me—more than most people," she continued. "About my past and my present. And what do I know about you? Your ambition is to live without strings, you like pastries and you want to go to Florence."

"And I'm good in bed," he offered innocently.

She laughed. "Very good, I concede that." She sobered. "As you remarked once before, we are much alike in our desire for privacy—and in preferring to have the upper hand." She shrugged. "I'm not interested in furthering your domination of . . ." She waved a hand. "Whatever this is."

He put down the brush again. "I'm of two minds about an answer to that. First—honestly, I can say that I never thought about it in terms of dominance. I've always been reserved in what I share about myself, but it's always been more in the way of protecting myself."

He chuckled at the doubt she conveyed. "Don't look so skeptical. You, of all people, know that knowledge can be used against you." He set down his palette. "And in any case, it's easier to make a clean break when there are fewer . . . entanglements."

"And thus you prove my point," she muttered.

"But, second—I've never before been in this sort of arena with a woman who so richly deserved an equal footing." He left the canvas and crossed to her, taking in her disheveled beauty. It was true. He'd never met a woman who met him toe for toe before. Who somehow managed to be both caring and independent. And who stood her ground and kept to her word, even when it was difficult.

He touched her chin with a paint-stained finger. "I trust you, Francis Flightly Headley. So, would you feel better if I were to share a secret of my own?"

Her mouth twitched. "If it were good enough."

"Good enough?" He raised a brow in mock indignation.

"Yes. A good secret." She wiggled her fingers at him. "Ripe. Juicy."

He laughed. "You may dress like a boy, but you are so much a woman."

Her chin lifted. "I know."

Unable to resist, he planted a kiss on her sweet lips. "*Such* a woman." He sighed. "Now, wash up my brushes while I mix some new greens and golds? And I'll think of something suitably scandalous for you."

He knew what she was hoping for, but he had no intention of speaking of Hestia, of the little he remembered of her—or the pain she'd left in her wake.

"Hmmm," he began. "Well, you recall how I told you of my first commission—the gypsy wagon."

"Yes." The smell of turpentine wafted over to him, but he kept his face positioned away from her.

"I was thrilled to get the chance to paint anything, really, but I was also happy when they offered to barter my services for a baby goat."

"You were happy about that?" She sounded skeptical.

"Yes. My mother—my foster mother—had long talked of wanting a goat for milk and cheese."

"Oh, how sweet. She must have been touched when you brought it home, your first professional compensation—and all for her."

"You would think so," he sighed. "But suddenly the thing she'd most wanted was transformed into a burden. The little goat was a darling too, but she declared it nothing but another mouth to feed and she declared me nothing but a fool."

"Surely not!"

He gave her a quick glance over his shoulder. "Some people just won't be pleased," he said with a shrug. Especially not if he was the one attempting it. "And she didn't like the way her wish had been fulfilled."

She fell silent a minute and the splash of water ended too. "Ah. She didn't wish for you to paint."

"No. Not at all. Her father was the one who taught me—and she hated growing up a painter's daughter. She told us many a time how horrible it was growing up, never knowing when the next commission would come, when they would eat and when they would starve. She married a solid, respectable farmer and that's what she wished of us— that we would carry on with the farm and perhaps expand it."

"Us?"

"My brother and I."

"You have a brother?" She sounded shocked.

"Well, not by blood, of course. Sebastian was born to my foster parents when I was still in leading strings." And Sebastian had always been regarded as the true son of the house. But Rhys didn't say it out loud. He'd never complained, never protested the unfair treatment he'd received.

"So the goat was sold and I was left back in my usual life, laboring where I was needed and sneaking an occasional few hours to practice with my grandfather. Until a lady came to the village. She took a room at the inn and scandalized all the gossips because she travelled alone with just her dresser."

"Oh, dear. How fast of her," Francis murmured.

"Yes—just think what they would make of you." He half turned and waggled his eyebrows at her. "The lady scandalized them further when she began to ask after the artist who had painted the gypsy wagon. She'd seen it at the next village and inquired about it."

"She must have seen something promising in it, to make her go to so much trouble."

"So she said."

"A lady artist," Francis mused.

"Yes, and she was truly talented. A genuine artist, not the dabbling lady of society to which the world wished to relegate her. She should be showing in London at that Academy event, but they would never allow it. Women are supposed to play at watercolors and take a pat on the head for their accomplishments," he said with disgust.

"So she came seeking you because . . ?"

"She thought she had something to teach me." Both on the canvas and in bed, although he wouldn't share that much. "And she did. Her landscapes were a revelation. She showed me new techniques, discussed new ways of thinking about art, ways that my grandfather, who had been strictly trained in the old school, would have scorned. Without a doubt, I grew more skilled under her tutelage."

"How long did she work with you?"

"Most of a summer. She rented a small cottage and set out to paint all the beauties of the region." It had been a season of revelation. He'd spent the weeks rising early, moving fast to get his work done on the farm, and then he'd rush to Julietta's cottage and they'd spend hours together while she taught him about vision and oils and sex and life.

He glanced over his shoulder again. Francis was no fool. From the look on her face, she'd guessed at least part of that private reflection.

"Did you leave with her? Is that how your wandering started?" She sounded thoughtful.

"No. She would not take me." He said it without emotion. Without the rage and heartache that had torn through him. She'd carried on with her life and abandoned him to plough and harvest. Damn, but he'd been so young and had felt it so keenly. Because it had hurt. Left again, with no thought to what promise might be neglected or his miseries might be. He'd decided then and there that he would go, come what may. And he had. He'd taken extra work at the winery and wherever else he could find it. He'd saved his money and he'd left, eventually, to follow his own path.

He'd not met her gaze or allowed any of what he felt to color his tone, but Francis suspected much of it, all the same. He could see it on her face—and she was right, it was uncomfortable, to be seen so clearly. She was kind enough not to let pity show, at least.

Instead, she smiled at him. "But you did leave. On your own terms." She nodded. "Well done."

Pleasure washed through him. She knew just what to say—and to say it without sentiment, but with simple acknowledgement. And the thought suddenly sprang up, unbidden. Perhaps it was not so terrible to be known. Understood.

He lifted a shoulder. "So, there you have it. Was it ripe enough to meet your standards?"

She didn't smile. "Did you ever see the lady artist again?"

"No." He hadn't even considered the possibility. "I shouldn't wish to."

Silence stretched out for a moment, then suddenly she smiled at him. "Well, then, I would say that was just ripe enough, so I shall answer your question—if you promise that you shall take a turn again, next time."

It was no light question. Next time implied further intimacy, beyond the bed. Would there be a next time? Did he wish for one?

He gave a half nod, half shrug, thoroughly half-committal response, but it seemed to satisfy her. She settled back on her stool and began to tell him about her friends.

About Brynne Wilmott, betrayed by the men in her life, who escaped her abusive fiancé, helped prevent an international incident, married a duke and opened an orphanage for young girls left with no one to look out for them.

And she spoke of Callie Grant, who traveled with the aforementioned duke's brother to save her sister, married the brother and now ran a country inn, and also gave assistance to women who found themselves with child and nowhere to turn.

And he, with his artist's eye, saw the change in Francis as she talked. Her color rose, her eyes grew alight with admiration and excitement.

Rhys was no fool. He knew Brynne Wilmott had been his father's betrothed, but he'd never before heard how he'd treated her. He knew Callie Grant's name too. He'd heard Marstoke cursing it during their own short, tempestuous acquaintance.

Now, watching Francis light up, listening to her tales, he began to wonder if he'd got it all wrong.

He could almost see the hope and purpose these women inspired in her. And from what she said, they didn't poke an oar in and then move on. If she spoke true, then these women showed grit and determination and dedication to their causes. Not a case of interference from on high, instead they dug in and got truly involved.

And these were the women inspired by Hestia Wright? The faintest doubt crept in to erode his righteous and certain anger.

With a start, he pulled back his brush. She had distracted him, and it had been an even greater success than he'd hoped. He'd got her hair right at last, in all of its red-gold glory. And somehow he'd captured the sparkle of her excitement on the canvas. His heart leapt as he stared down at her air of hope and promise and positive conviction.

He sighed. "Well, that did the trick."

She sat up straight. "Is it finished, then?"

"Nearly."

They both started at a sharp knock at the door.

Rhys pierced her with a glare and held a finger to his lips. "I'm working!" he bellowed.

"Yes, yes, I'm sure you are." Malvi's tone came through on the sarcastic side of respectful. "But you've a message."

"Do not move," he mouthed to Francis and went to the door. He cracked it open the smallest bit. Malvi leaned and tried to peer in as she handed over the folded note, but Rhys snatched it up and shut the door. "Thank you," he said belatedly.

He heard her snort right through the door.

"It's from Andor," he said, reading it over quickly. "He insists I come to dinner." He looked over at her disheveled glory and could not resist going over to give her a smacking kiss. "Turn yourself back into a street rat, then and I'll see you're fed properly. I might as well go to him tonight, seeing as I've already promised to see you safely home."

Reaching over, she grabbed his chin and pulled him in to kiss him back, then with a pouty lip and a sigh, she hopped down.

Chapter Eighteen

My mentor-to-be, the courtesan, arranged a showing at one of her
salons. A progressive path, each picture showing a little more
skin than the last.

--from the journal of the infamous Miss Hestia Wright

The next morning, Francis was demonstrating one of Mrs.
Spencer's embroidered sashes to a young matron.

"I've never seen work to exceed Mrs. Spencer's skill and taste," she
said truthfully. "See, wear it just so, at the waist of a plainer gown," she
demonstrated on her own green-sprigged muslin. "And it's instantly
elevated. When you add the matching hair ribbon, you achieve yet
another level of fashion and versatility."

Duly convinced, the customer departed happily, passing a familiar
face on the way.

Francis moved to intercept him as he came in. "Mr. Larson! Have
you brought your wife in to visit us, at last?" She looked over his
shoulder.

"Alas, no. But we were hoping to tempt you to our home for an evening's entertainment, tonight, Miss Headley. Just a small dinner and a bit of reading aloud—poetry and the like."

"Ah, that sounds lovely," she said with regret. "I do wish I could accept—"

Color crept up the gentleman's face. "Come now, don't disappoint us once again," he chided.

She paused and looked him over. "I do hate to do so, sir, but unfortunately I've promised to help out at the store this evening, and then after hours with a project Mrs. Spencer and I have been working on."

"My . . . wife will be sorely upset."

"Well, we cannot have that," she said decisively. "But I know just the thing to sweeten her temper." She crossed to the rack of ribbon and took down a pretty specimen. "This will go beautifully with that collar you chose for her." She wrapped it up in a tiny, charming box. "Please, take it to her with our compliments, and ask her to come in tomorrow morning. We'll have a grand time going over all of the fripperies and I'll arrange a lovely nuncheon. It will give us the chance to get to know each other."

Mr. Larson's lips were compressed as he stared at her a moment. "You are too kind. I shall ask if her schedule will allow it." He bowed and turned to take his leave.

"Oh, but don't forget the ribbon, sir," Francis called.

He waved a hand in the air. "I am off to chambers and cannot take it now. I'll stop back in later, perhaps."

"Very well." Thoughtfully, she followed and watched him leave. He marched up the pavement, his annoyance clear in each pounding step, and climbed into a carriage parked a little way up the street.

Francis turned back, her mind softly awhirl, but she started as she met Rhys on his way in.

Her heart jumped at the sight of him. He'd cracked her open a little more, sharing that story about the lady artist who had tutored him. She was sure enough that there had been more than art lessons going on, but what did that matter? His experiences added together to make his pleasing whole. His pain did, too, and he was harboring anger against two women who had left him. Suddenly his suspicions made sense, because she knew he believed her to be gathering his personal information to share with Hestia.

But that was not the kind of confidence she would ever betray. She already had the news she would tell Hestia. Everything else she could squeeze from this *affaire* now was for her. She was gathering memories like a dragon hoarding jewels—because soon enough, memories would be all that she had of him.

"Good morning, Mr. Caradec!" Mrs. Spenser called out the greeting as she emerged from the back rooms. Jasper gave a nod from behind the ribbon counter.

"Good morning to you, ma'am. Jasper. Miss Headley."

They had all been introduced last evening. Mrs. Spencer had clearly taken it into her mind to protect Francis. The kindly woman's concern touched her, even as she knew it was too late.

"Have you come to fetch Miss Headley to sit for her portrait?"

"I've come to fetch her to *view* her portrait, ma'am." He turned to meet Francis's gaze. "I worked through most of the night. It's finished."

Her breath caught. "Finished?" Was he happy with it? She couldn't tell. His expression was . . . intense.

"How lovely," Mrs. Spencer trilled. "Jasper was telling me how excited he was to see how it turned out. I hope you won't mind if he accompanies you?"

Francis hid a smile at the surprised look on the boy's face.

"Not at all. I've a hack outside if you can spare them both now."

"To be sure!" Mrs. Spencer waved a hand. "I'll see you both back early this afternoon, yes?"

"You will," Francis answered fondly as she took up her shawl. "I haven't forgotten that we've plans for the evening."

"Yes, and there are preparations to be made," she said, raising a brow.

Francis nodded. They all went out to bundle into the hack and set off, Francis and Jasper sitting together and facing Rhys.

"It's truly done?" she asked.

"It is."

"I'm surprised it went so quickly."

"As am I," he admitted. "But some works just grab on and won't let go."

"It's just as well that Miz Spencer sent me along to play dogberry," Jasper broke in. "I heard from Angus this morning and now I can tell you both. He's been followin' that gentleman—the one that your maid meets. Angus didn't like the look of him, nor how he manhandles the girl."

Rhys sighed, but Francis nodded for the boy to continue. "Let's hear it, then," she told him. "Have they discovered his name?"

"Aye. He's Mr. Arthur Welfield."

"The Viscount Cantwick's son," breathed Francis. "He's known to be one of Marstoke's disciples."

"I thought we'd already decided that Malvi was connected with the marquess," Caradec reminded them sourly. "What difference does knowing his name make?"

"Mebbe none," Jasper answered. "Or mebbe you should keep an eye on the maid. Angus and his boys followed the nob to the carriage builder's, where he asked that his rig be fitted out, custom."

"Nothing wrong with that, if a man can afford it." Rhys shrugged.

"Aye—but he asked for fixed windows, a reinforced door and a new latch—one that bolts from the outside."

Francis stilled.

Even Rhys grew sober. "I'll watch out for her," he agreed. "I'd hate for her to be forced into something against her will."

She kept quiet for the few minutes it took to reach the Hound and Hare, her mind spinning with suspicions. She let them fall away, however, when Rhys handed her down from the hack. "You haven't mentioned your dinner last evening. Did you enjoy yourself?"

"I did."

"And your friend's new wife? How did you find her?"

"Very lovely. Intelligent. Sweet."

"A fit mate for your friend, then?"

"Yes." He rolled his eyes. "Do you wish for me to admit I was wrong? Perhaps I was, at that. She was lovely and they seem happy— although she was a bit frazzled. It seems they've had difficulty keeping a nurse maid since they came to Edinburgh."

"Oh?" Francis's mind immediately jumped to Janet Grant and her wish to add on the care of an infant along with her sister's. "But I could help with that, I believe. Do you recall the little flower girl? Wee Janet is looking—"

Rhys stopped in mid-stride, just past the door of the entry into the inn. A gentleman huffed and moved around them, but he didn't appear to notice. "Francis—no. Haven't I asked you not to meddle?"

"But—"

"No. I hope you haven't interfered with that little flower girl, but I definitely do not want you to meddle with this. Andor is perfectly capable of handling his own domestic problems—without any help from you."

His words stung. And it was made worse when Malvi chose that moment to pop from behind the baize door. Her smirk made it clear that she'd heard at least part of that rebuke.

Francis returned her taunting look with a glare, not sure at the moment if she was more irritated with the maid or Rhys.

"Mail has come for you, Mr. Caradec, sir." Malvi dropped into a curtsy. "From *London*," she said pertly. She handed over a small but thick parcel. "Smells like a windfall to me!"

"Impertinence," Rhys growled.

"That's me." She swirled her skirts. "Just don't go forgetting me if you change your mind about going that way."

Francis stared after her as she departed, then turned to follow Rhys up the stairs, determined to continue chipping at his edges. She would get through to him somehow. When they reached the studio door, Rhys paused and Jasper hung behind, on her heels.

Rhys stood a moment, his hand on the latch, and then he slowly swung the door open.

The portrait sat, covered, on an easel in the center of the room. It looked larger, away from the table and the collection of paints and equipment.

Wordless, Rhys gestured for her to continue in.

She stepped forward and contemplated the covering. Ease it off? Or toss it blithely to the floor? In the end, she just gave a tug—and stood, transfixed.

It was unlike any portrait she'd ever seen. She couldn't stop staring at it, wasn't sure how to make sense of it in her mind.

It was a close perspective of a square column, in a garden setting. Ivy draped parts of the stone column. A woman had been carved in high relief into it. Her flowing skirts were visible, caught in stone in the lower part of the scene.

In the upper part—the woman was breaking free. Pushing herself out of the column, emerging from the still, frozen, grey stone into vibrant color and life.

Except . . .

"It's not me," she whispered. Puzzled, disappointed, she turned to find Rhys watching her intently and Jasper staring, unblinking at the image.

"It's you," Jasper corrected her.

Frowning, she turned back. It couldn't be her. Could it? The girl in the painting had fresh, pearly skin, showcased in a beautiful, intricately folded gown of ancient design. Her eyes shone bright and happy, brimming with promise and fire. Her lips were pink, her cheekbones wide and her hair curled in wild, glorious abandon down past her shoulders. She looked full of life and merriment and mischief.

Turning back to Rhys again, she shook her head.

"It's you," he said hoarsely. "How can you doubt it?"

Her gazed drifted back and he came to stand by her as she stared. "The stone . . ." He pointed to the column. "It's the world. Life. Your losses. Your first home, your mother's death, Hatch's plans for you, life in a brothel and in the streets. It is all of the things that have happened to you, all of the events that could have left you hard, frozen, and dead inside. But they didn't. Because . . . this is you. Buoyant. Defiant. Vibrant. Full of beauty and color and hope and care and consideration—"

She swallowed. Gulped. And burst into noisy tears.

"Whoops!" Jasper ran for the door. "I'll be downstairs! Find me when you are ready to go!"

"Coward," Rhys called as he closed the door behind him.

Francis sobbed harder and sank down onto the floor.

"What is it?" Rhys knelt beside her. "Francis? Do you hate it? Shall I cover it again?"

"No!"

"Then what is it? What's wrong, sweet girl?"

Valiantly, she fought to calm herself. He handed her a kerchief and she blew her nose and wiped her eyes. She struggled to catch her breath.

"You . . . you . . ." She breathed deeply and then met his gaze. "You asked me, not long ago, if I looked at everyone and saw a charity case. It hurt. It hurt more when I realized that you look at everyone and see a threat to your precious freedom."

He made a sound, but let her continue.

"Do you know why it hurt more?" she whispered.

He shook his head.

"Because I knew that you felt free to take up with me because I *wasn't* a threat. I didn't tempt you enough to worry."

"No. You are wrong, Francis."

"But . . .but . . ." She looked to the painting again. "If you see me like that—"

"Francis, everyone sees you like that."

She closed her eyes. "I know enough to know that that is not true. But to know that you do? It fills a hole that I never knew existed." Raising her head, she looked at him through her lashes. "If you see me in such a way, then perhaps . . . I am not quite so alone in this. It might even be that you do feel something for me."

"Oh, my sweeting. Don't cry. Of course, I feel so many different things for you. Admiration, not the least." He gathered her close.

And right then, on the floor of his studio, with his arms wrapped around her . . . she let go.

She released her fears and reservations and just let in the profound and humbling feelings she'd been fighting. Just accepted that, for right now, at least, this moment was pure and right—and theirs.

The knowledge of it was in his eyes, too. It couldn't have existed without consent from them both.

But exist it did.

And she reveled in it.

Bowing to the inevitability of it, she reached a finger up and drew it across his beautiful, strong mouth, then pulled him down into a lingering kiss.

"Fascination," he whispered, after a time.

She drew back and looked questioningly up at him.

"The things I feel for you," he reminded her. He curled his fingers around her breast. "Unending desire."

She tucked her hands inside his coat and pushed it back off of his shoulders. He reached for the buttons on her gown, and in moments they were leaving all of their clothes behind as he carried her to his bed.

"Wonder," he said, laying her down and gazing at her for a long moment. But she reached for him and he climbed in beside her and kissed her forehead.

She, however, sat up and curled around and kissed him—right on his straining cock.

"Ahhh," was all he managed to get out then, as she amused herself and pleasured him with gliding fingers and her soft, wet mouth.

"Impatience," he said after a time and pulled her back up before looming over her. And soon enough she was arching against him and pulsing with the extreme pleasure of her release—even as he silently shouted his.

She clung to him afterward and they lay quietly in each other's arms.

Their breathing, slowed, steadied, took on a joined, languorous rhythm. Her eyes drifted closed. Just as she drifted off to sleep, she heard him speak. "Infatuation," he whispered in her ear.

Chapter Nineteen

✤

It was a huge success. Who was the model? What was the significance of the moon? Men were wild to know.

--from the journal of the infamous Miss Hestia Wright

Rhys allowed Francis a short sleep, then he woke her. "I promised to bring you home," he reminded her.

Sweetly disoriented, she dressed. She'd become alert and focused, though, by the time he dropped her and Jasper back at the shop. "We are busy tonight," she said without really looking at him. "Perhaps I'll see you tomorrow?"

He nodded. "I'll likely be wandering, trying to find a new scene to paint." Though it was raining heavily as he left them, he sent the hack off, wrapped himself in one of Mrs. Beattie's plaids and set out to roam the city. The painting was done. The firewood was caught up and stocked in advance—but still, he needed an outlet for the restlessness in his soul.

Francis's reaction to the portrait had been gratifying—and nerve-wracking. But her response had not been nearly as worrisome as *his* reaction to *her* reaction.

She'd touched him. More deeply than he had intended to allow. But this was her first encounter with passion, and she was feeling it all so intensely. He must not get caught up in it. He must slow things down.

He scoffed at his own thought. There had been no resisting that vulnerable tear in her formidable armor. But there had to be a way to resist her—and he must find it. Or else he'd have to leave Edinburgh —and her.

He wandered for most of the afternoon. The city's inhabitants, inured to the weather, went about their business, while he attempted to convince himself it was time to get to Italy. But with all her temptations, that country did not have a particular maiden with saucy smiles, soft, hazel eyes and tangles of golden hair streaked with red.

The rain stopped and the shadows stretched out long—and at last Caradec found his way back to the inn. He found Malvi waiting on him. She made a sympathetic face and held out a hand for the plaid.

"Glory, but I'll be glad enough to get somewhere where it doesn't rain every second hour." She held the soaked plaid away from her and hung it on a hook to dry.

Rhys raised a brow. "I don't know who you've been talking to, but you're sadly mistaken if you think to find London dry."

She startled and a look of alarm passed over her face. "Oh," she said with a smile, clearly trying to rally. "I meant later on, of course. Once I find a cove to spoil me, we'll travel to all the warm places." She sighed and he tried to move past her, but she trailed along behind him as he climbed the stairs.

"You know, I was that glad to hear you giving that ginger-haired chit what-for over her meddling. I know she had something to do with that little flower girl leaving the streets and her flowers behind. I'm all for moving on and bettering yourself, but I saw the consequences of the girl's attempts myself."

"Consequences?" Rhys stopped on the landing. "What do you mean?"

"That girl's got an eye darker than the thunder clouds that blow in here from the sea." She shook her head. "My own dad was known to darken my daylights if I got out of hand, but she's got a specimen on her."

Rhys whirled on her. "Where is the girl now, if she's no longer selling flowers?"

Malvi shrank back, her eyes growing large. "I saw her at the ribbon shop, where your red-haired girl stays. She's working there, or something like."

Without another word he rushed past her, back downstairs and outside. The rain had returned with a vengeance. A torrent hit him at his first step, but he stalked on. His anger and disappointment would keep him warm.

Arriving at Mrs. Spencer's shop, he found it dark and locked. He would not be thwarted. Searching out the nearest alley, he wound his way to the back entrance and marched right in.

Francis sat there, at a small table, sewing pleats into a length of fabric. Next to her, a colorful rug spread out on the floor. A girl sat there, with her back to him, entertaining a laughing baby with a toy.

"Rhys!" Francis looked up, startled—and grew more concerned when she saw his expression. "What is it?"

He didn't answer her. Instead he knelt down next to the rug and studied the girl seated there. "Who did this to you, little one?" he asked gently, indicating her swollen face and bruised eye.

She looked to Francis for guidance. Seeing her nod, she whispered, "My uncle."

"Whatever possessed him to do such a thing?"

Glancing over at Francis again, she answered. "He did not wish my mother to take a job here. Or for us to leave his lodgings."

Rhys stood. He couldn't prevent the accusing glare that landed on Francis. "I warned you not to meddle. I told you that you would get her in deeper trouble. Now, look at the result of your interference."

The girl straightened, alarmed. "No, sir! Miss Francis is not to fault!"

Rhys gentled his tone as he asked, "Where does your uncle live, child?"

"Do not answer that, Janet," Francis ordered.

He stared over his shoulder at her, exasperated. "I told you that it was easy to make a mistake. Men like that won't stop at a black eye, Francis. He must be dealt with. I will handle him."

"You will not."

"I will," he insisted. "This must be brought to a finish. You think you are helping, I know. But you are meddling with this girl's life. It's not a lark. It's not a means to make yourself feel good. Or to garner Hestia's favor."

"Stop." She shook her head and her tone tightened with irritation. "This situation, this sort of thing—this is my life's work. I've told you that I know what I'm about. You know enough about me. I should think you would believe it."

"You've pulled this girl out of her element—and that is no small thing! It takes more than a new position to truly change someone's life. It takes time and attention and true caring. If you interfere without offering all the rest, you can bring ruin and heartache—and worse." He thrust both hands in his hair, frustrated and incredibly annoyed at his own pain resurfacing and her refusal to hear him. "I know of what I speak, Francis! I know you want to help, but—"

"There's no *but* to be had, Caradec. I want to help. I *do* help. Yes, I'm still learning some things, but I'm learning from the best." She crossed her arms. "But you don't want to hear that, do you? For some ungodly reason you believe that Hestia is shallow and thoughtless—and so must I be, too."

"It's not—"

"Enough." She cut him off again, her face white and her lips pressed together. "It's clear. You will insist on thinking the worst of me, of the work I do, unless you are finally forced not to. Nothing will convince you, I can tell, except what you see with your own eyes. Very well, then." She stood. Taking up her wrap, she went to the back door, opened it, then stood on the threshold and let out a long, piercing whistle.

After a long moment, someone came to the door. A large young man with brilliant red hair and the beginnings of a bristly beard.

"Er . . ." She hesitated and a furious blush of color rose in her cheeks. Rhys had never seen her stumble so, but she clutched her skirts and he wondered if she'd forgotten she was wearing them. "I . . . My, uh . . . that is, Flightly asked . . ."

The burly young man laughed. "We know it's ye," he said shaking his head. "Ye and the boy, one and the same. We've all knowed ye was a girl since the time you brought food with ye, when ye wanted us fer a job. T'was a sure sign, ye wantin' to feed us up."

Her mouth twitched and her color began to subside. "A novice mistake. I should have known better."

"Ye should," he agreed. "Otherwise, ye might have took us in completely." The young man jerked his head in Rhys's direction. "Should we not 'a let him through? I figgered—"

"It's fine," she cut him off. "He's fine. But we have to go out. I need you to stay here with wee Janet." Francis turned to the girl, who had gathered the sleeping baby up on her hip. "Janet," she began. "This is Angus. He—"

"I know who he is," the girl avowed, her eyes wide.

"Oh, yes. Being on the streets as you were, I suppose you would know." She pulled Angus in and then crossed to the girl and knelt before her. "You know he has a gang of boys?"

Janet nodded.

"They are ranged all around our building tonight, watching and keeping us safe. Angus is a friend. I trust him to keep you and little Lizzie safe, while I go to the Gulls with Mr. Caradec. Will you trust me —and him too?"

Janet looked between them. Angus gave her a wink. Solemnly, she nodded.

"Fine, then. We'll return soon, with your mother and Mrs. Spencer."

Angus stepped toward the back door. "You'll need a hack to make it in time. And I was thinkin', out there, that it would be just as well to send a coach fer the women. I already rustled Geordie to fetch a rig, so he could wait fer the ladies at the Gulls."

"Wait." She frowned at him. "Geordie? From the livery?"

"Aye." He smirked. "He's my cousin, did he not tell ye?" At her look, he shrugged. "I 'spose everyone has secrets, don't we? He can take you along as easy as ridin' empty, and bring you all back." He went to the threshold and spoke to a figure that instantly melted out of the evening gloom.

Francis glanced sharply over at Rhys. "Come along, then."

He scarcely recognized her flat tone and still expression, but he followed as she pulled a wrap about her and left through the storefront and the front door. She headed east and after a block, a hack pulled over next to them.

Geordie grinned down at her from the box. "In you go," he said brightly. "I'll have you at the Three Gulls in two shakes."

The boy laughed at his own wit, but Francis sat stone-faced while they headed toward the docks and made their way into the maze of buildings behind them—and Rhys began to wonder just what they were journeying into. Only when the hack began to slow did she shake out her wrap and drape it over her head, hiding her face in shadows.

"In here," she said, after he silently handed her down. Without hesitation, she stepped into a low tavern. He glanced up to see a disreputable sign that might once have represented three white birds flying against a cracked blue background.

The taproom was fully occupied by dockworkers come to enjoy a pint, and perhaps a pinch of a barmaid's back end. The noise was loud, but the mood appeared genial.

A harried serving girl hustled up to them. "No tables left, but the pair of ye can take stools against the wall, should ye wish to stay." She sounded as if she'd be surprised if they did.

"The stools are fine." Francis slid onto one and ordered two pints of ale. The maid shrugged and left to fetch their drinks.

"Sit." Francis motioned for Rhys to take the next stool.

"What are we doing here, Francis?"

"We are watching. *Only* watching, Caradec. You are to follow your own advice and not to interfere. Do you understand?"

He merely raised a brow and took his seat.

The stevedores were singing now, and laughing at their own wit. Another serving girl joined the first and kept the ale flowing and cups filled.

The song wandered toward its end and Rhys noticed another female figure emerge from the back and stand at the edge of the bar.

The last verse trailed off and she stepped forward into the center of the room.

Others noticed her. They elbowed their companions. She said nothing, merely stood proud and silent and slowly the room grew still as all attention focused on her.

"Wee Janet's mother," whispered Francis, leaning in.

Reaching up, the woman pulled back her hood. A soft sound of disapproval went around as her sleeve fell back and revealed a wrapped wrist, and as the low light hit her cheek, which sported a violently purple bruise and a laceration where the skin had split over the bone.

Rhys's gut turned over in anger.

"My name is Jean Grant. Many of ye ken me—and a number of ye were fine, fair mates to my own Ewen before he passed."

"Aye!" someone shouted. "A toast to Ewen Grant!"

Cups were raised around the room.

"Ye'll most all know that I was left poorly off when he died—and with two bairns, one a new babe in arms. I'd nowhere to go until Ewen's brother Roddie stepped up, kind enough to take us in."

A smaller murmur went around—and Rhys saw one man shrink a little as his booth mates raised their glasses to him. He straightened. That was the worm who had used his fists on this woman and her child?

Suddenly a hand gripped tight around his arm. "Sit back," Francis hissed. "Allow her to do what she came here to do."

"We've done what we can to help earn our keep. I was that grateful —and still am," Jean Grant continued. "Nor do I begrudge a hard-working man his drink of an evening. And I know there's scarce a family out there that doesna' raise a ruckus now and then." She drew herself erect. "But when too much drink leads to regular beatings?" She shook her head. "Some of ye will ken why I took a good job with good lodgings elsewhere for me and my girls."

She threw off her cloak suddenly and quiet reigned again as the crowd of rough men took in the layers of bruises, old and new, covering her arms and creeping up from beneath her bodice, crossing her thin collarbones.

"Now, I'm strong and can stand much." She took a step forward and her voice changed, ringing out harder. "But I willna see a hand laid on my blameless bairns—or stand by while anyone vents a drunken spleen on my little ones."

She raised a hand and pointed around the room. "And so I am here tonight to put each of ye on notice. Wee Janet carries an eye dark and swollen nearly shut—and it willna happen again." Her chin lifted. "I will *kill* Roddie Grant myself before he touches either of my babes again."

Low muttering went around the room. Roddie Grant stood at his seat.

"The crown will see me swing for it, most likely—and I'll go gladly to the rope, to protect my girls—but if I do, then I charge all of ye who loved my Ewen to see that his girls are taken in and cared for."

Across the room Roddie stepped away from his table, a little shame-faced, but looking thunderous with anger. Before he could move or utter a sound, another man, large, muscled and weather-beaten, stepped into his path, several feet away.

"There willna be need of ye to be takin' matters into yer own hands, Jean Grant," the man rumbled.

Around the room, other men stood as well.

"Ewen was a good, braw lad, and one of our own. It fair shocks me, to hear of his brother takin' on so."

"Aye, it came as an unpleasant surprise to me, as well, Broderic Carr." returned Jean Grant.

"It should worry ye nae longer, lass, for I say here and now that ye and yer bairns are hereby placed under our protection."

He gestured and around the taproom, a step was taken here, a shift in position there, until it was clear that a loose circle had formed around Roddie Grant.

"*Anyone* who raises a hand against any of ye will answer to us." He raised a brow at the glowering man.

Rhys tensed. The bastard looked defiant. He could react a number of ways, none of them good.

He snarled something low and mean, but the circle tightened. Roddie Grant, it seemed, knew when the odds were against him. His shoulders slumped, his head lowered. The circle opened and he stalked out of the taproom.

Jean Grant's head went up, proud and glad. The men then gathered around her. She exchanged quiet words with them, then embraced them, one by one. Wiping a tear from her eye, she headed for the back room and Rhys saw Mrs. Spencer step out to meet her and gather her in her arms.

Rhys watched, his thoughts wheeling.

The taproom slowly returned to its noisy rhythm.

Francis hopped off of her stool. "Let's go."

Chapter Twenty

And then my pains began. I was so frightened, after the early difficulty, but my fears were unfounded. The birth was as any other first time—that is, difficult, long and painful. But so worth every moment of it.

--from the journal of the infamous Miss Hestia Wright

Outside the tavern Francis put up her hood and set out, walking. Jean Grant and her girls would be safe now. Relief enveloped her as thoroughly as the mist in the air. She let it sink in. Maybe it would wash away the pain of what was coming.

"Francis. Wait." Caradec was striding along purposefully behind her. "We have to talk about what just happened."

"No, we do not."

Roddie Grant was angry, it was clear to Francis and anyone else, too. But he couldn't show it, could never act on it, not without appearing weak before all of his friends and fellow dockhands. He would likely posture a bit, proclaim how happy he was to be on his own again—and there would likely be some truth to it.

A clatter of hooves sounded behind her and the hack drew up next to her in the street. "Coming aboard?" Young Geordie grinned down at her from the driver's seat.

"Is everything all right at the shop?" Mrs. Spencer peered out. Jean Grant spotted her and panic raced across her face. "Wee Janet? The babe—?"

"Everything is fine," she reassured them. "Angus and his crew are guarding the girls. Mr. Caradec just needed the proof of his own eyes to believe our plan was sound."

"*Your* plan, you mean." Jean Grant put a hand out the window, reaching for hers. "Thank you. You were right. It was just what was needed. He'll never look twice at us now."

Mrs. Spencer was looking from her to Caradec. "Come along, the two of you, and ride along to the shop with us?"

Francis shook her head. "Thank you, but Mr. Caradec and I are overdue for a discussion. One that will require a bit of privacy."

The older woman frowned. "I don't like the idea of you out alone this late, and it's a long way back to High Street." She craned her neck out and looked around. "There's a kirkyard ahead. Have your discussion there, dear, and I'll send the nice boy back to pick you up after he's deposited us. That should give you plenty of time."

Sighing, Francis agreed. The ladies closed the coach windows and the carriage moved off. She started off after it at once.

Rhys hurried to catch her up. "It was your doing—that scene tonight. How? How did you know?"

"I did what was needed. I asked. I found the right questions and answers."

"Francis, slow down a bit, will you? Clearly I owe you an apology. At least let me offer it up."

"I'm going into the churchyard. I am not going to argue with you in the streets."

"Must we argue?" he asked plaintively.

"I'm afraid we must."

She reached the low, stone wall surrounding the kirk and followed it to a simple wooden gate that opened easily. It was dark and quiet inside. There were trees and green grass, a wide stretch of tombstones on one side and a tall set of steps leading up to the closed doors of the church. She took a seat on the stairs. Caradec leaned against a nearby tree and watched her.

"I do apologize," he said softly. "But won't you help me to understand? How did you know how to handle Roddie Grant—which tactics to use against him? I know you didn't know him before this."

"No. But I learned what I needed to know," she said impatiently. "I investigated the man, the entire situation, as best as I could. I watched him a bit, took his measure, talked to the people in their lives. I found a way. It seems that there's only one thing that Roddie values, and that's the company of his mates. His standing amongst his fellow dockworkers is everything to him. They've a hierarchy, a ranking, as well as a bond between them. The last thing he would wish to compromise is his place in the brotherhood."

"And you turned that reluctance into the perfect weapon. And you let his victim wield it." He was not much more than a broad shadow next to the tree, but she could see his head shaking. "It was masterfully done. I was wrong. I should not have doubted you."

"Accused me, I think you mean?" she asked shortly. "I did tell you that I knew what I was about. You just chose not to believe me."

"You're right," he said dully.

She sighed, and all the stiff indignation slid out of her. It left only sadness—and dread for what still must be said.

He stepped closer and peered at her in the dim light of the moon. "Francis, are you crying?"

"Only a little." She wiped at her face. "Damn you."

He knelt and tried to take her hands, but she pulled away. "I can't touch you and say what I have to say."

Silent then, he moved away and sat a few steps below her.

"That damned painting," she groaned. "It fooled me utterly, gave me false hope."

"What does the painting have to do with any of this?" he rasped.

"Everything!" she said wildly. "It made me feel as if I was not in this alone. But I should have known," she said on a bitter sigh.

"Known what?" he asked, a bit defensively.

"Caradec," she said, softening her tone. "I know I've told you that I like the way you see the world. I've said it more than once. But it's only now that I understand—it's not the same when you are looking at *people.* You don't engage all of your senses then, you don't open yourself the way you do when you are taking in a mountain range or a scenic view. You shut out everything you don't want to see."

"Don't be absurd."

"I'm not. It's true. I've watched you do it with your painter friend. And with Malvi. But you saw so much of me that others miss—I just didn't realize how purposefully you were doing the same with me."

"That painting *is* you."

"No. Not really. It's the bits of me that you wish to see. And it's so humbling and sweet of you to notice parts that others do not. You see the fighter in me, the survivor, but you also see the girl who hides behind breeches and work—and you portray them all so beautifully."

"You are beautiful."

"I thank you for thinking so," she whispered. "I do. But I'm so *angry* at you for refusing to look past those parts you are comfortable with—for refusing to acknowledge the rest of me."

He made a sound of protest.

"It's true. Yes, I've been through hard times. I fought. I survived. But the work I do with Hestia, doing my best to give back—it is *who I am.* What would you have me do instead? Sit back and lap up my improved situation? I'm trying to be better than that. Learning to be more than that. My life needs aim, purpose, fulfillment."

"Are you saying I lack purpose?" he asked incredulously.

"No. I'm saying that I need it as much as anyone else."

"Yes. But your work . . . the places you go and people you want to look out for. A mistake could be . . . so dangerous."

"I make mistakes! But I promise, so far as I can know, I've never harmed someone more than helped them, nor left them in worse circumstances."

"It's not only them I worry for!" he said, exasperated. "It is you, as well. You throw yourself into the fray. All of yourself—heart, mind and soul."

As she'd done with him. She had to admit it, if only to herself. And it was tearing her heart out. But she could not regret it.

"I must," she said gently. "Just as you must throw yourself into your work. Art is your purpose. There can be no doubt of that. Your art breathes. It comes alive and makes things come alive in those who view it as well. Wonder and awe and so many feelings—but you run from those reactions, or avoid them entirely."

"I don't—"

"You do. Danby told me how you refused to listen to his family's admiration of those portraits you did for him. How you put down your brush, took your commission and ran. Mr. North told us how you waved off his admiration. And I saw how you reacted when you realized how much of your art I had seen."

"I don't paint for others." His words came out flat and he wasn't looking at her anymore.

"Of course you do. Somewhere. Some part of you wants that connection. But you cannot make it." She sighed. "It's why you cannot face the rest of me, too, isn't it? If you truly understood me, you would have painted that column in a sea of similar structures. There are so many people trapped, held down by birth, circumstance, poverty, lack of choices. I might have wiggled my way free, but to be happy I have to help free as many others as I can."

She stopped, gazing down at him, wondering if he could see her longing and heartbreak. His head dropped. Silence pulsed between them, nearly a living thing. "You cannot approve—because you cannot ever be truly intimate, if you do not. "How can you develop deep and real feelings for someone if you don't acknowledge all the parts of them?" She paused to breathe against the ache that came with understanding. "You don't want to see all of me."

"That's not true."

"You know it is. And there's more to it, isn't there? You won't see that part of me, cannot approve of it—because of some misconstrued notion you carry about, regarding Hestia."

He shook his head.

"I know it. I feel it. The anger and disapproval you feel for her bleeds onto me. But I don't understand. Won't you explain it?"

He turned to glare up at her, then stood and walked away. "Don't ask me to speak of Hestia Wright!"

"I must! I'm sorry. I've held to our bargain. But it's reached its end now." She choked back a sob and hunched a bit over the pain of saying it out loud. "So I must ask. I must know, Rhys. Surely your resentment cannot be because—"

"Because she abandoned me?" he interrupted. "Left me without looking back? Never once inquired about my well-being, my achievements, dreams or miseries? I assure you, I can resent that quite easily."

"Oh, no!" She could feel his anger welling up and out of his deepest fathoms. "It was not like that!"

"I lived it, Francis," he answered bitterly. "I assure you, it was just like that."

"But she had to leave you, to break contact! She had to hide your very existence. Marstoke never let up. He had people following her—he still has spies set on her, all these years later! They came, snooping, insinuating, and asking questions." She paused. "You have spent at least a little time with Marstoke, I know."

"Very little," he acknowledged. "As little as I could manage."

How she longed to hear that story. But there were more important issues to be hashed out first. "Then you know what he is. Twisted. Wrong. No mother could let him have the raising of her child. You see why she could not risk him getting his hands on you." She sat quietly a moment, remembering the very few unguarded moments of pain she'd seen from Hestia. "You cannot know what it did to her."

"Perhaps not," he said, lifting his head. "But I know what it did *for* her."

Francis frowned. "What do you mean?"

He shook his head. "Do you think I conjured up a sense of injury from nothing? Pulled it from my imagination the way Andor did his idea of a fairy bower? No, Francis. I've felt the jagged edge of Hestia's neglect for myself."

"She has missed you, as well," she insisted.

"Do you think that I don't remember her? Did she not tell you that she used to visit me, when I was small? I have hazy recollections of it. Hestia would come to pose for my grandfather, a smiling, blonde angel, who would pick me up to hold me close, smelling of flowers and bearing gifts."

He swallowed. "So very different indeed from my foster mother, the long-barren daughter of Hestia's dear artist friend. *Maman* agreed to raise me, and yet she could not hide the distaste she felt—for Hestia, and for me."

"Oh, no," she whispered.

"Yes. She held me at arm's length, watching, waiting for signs of my bad blood to show. Every day she expected to see the signs of my breeding. She held her breath, searching for the wanton, lazy, wicked ways that were sure to breed true." He shrugged. "She tried to hide it, especially at first, but when her prayers were answered and she at last bore a child of her own . . . it became less important."

Her heart broke at the image he conjured.

"Even so small, I treasured Hestia's visits. So beautiful, she was, and always bearing gifts—sweets, toys, soft embraces and kind words. But she stopped calling on us. She stopped sitting for my *grand-père*. I didn't understand. I waited for her. I asked after her. I cried for her. But she never came."

Francis swallowed against a rush of tears.

"Hestia had forgotten me, my foster mother insisted. Abandoned my grandfather. After they had been good enough to take me in when she chose not to keep herself."

"She never forgot you. Never," Francis insisted.

"Certainly, no one forgot her," he spat. "If Hestia missed me, she found ways to console herself. Even in our small village her exploits were talked of. Her extravagant, debauched lifestyle. The pranks, the jewels, the rich and powerful men. No one knew of the connection but my family—and their eyes narrowed at me as they whispered to each other, each time another story came along from the village gossips. But the worst—"

He bit off the words and she waited, breath held, while he reached for calm.

"The worst was what her desertion did to my grandfather. He'd made a name for himself, immortalizing the famous Hestia Wright. His portraits and sculptures of her were highly sought after. But when she stopped coming, refused to sit for him any longer—then fashionable French society followed her lead. The commissions dried up. The money stopped coming in. His reputation disappeared, along with any chance of finding a more permanent patron. But Hestia's repute shot as high as the stars." His brow furrowed. "It hurt him. Deeply. I think it injured something bright inside of him."

"I am so sorry."

"Oh, he still sold pieces here and there, but he never reached the level of appreciation and recognition that every artist dreams of. It affected everything. His work turned darker, he suffered moods. He felt like a burden, dependent on his daughter and her husband—and she felt much the same. Resentment fostered on both sides and it all turned on an ugly, vicious wheel."

She could imagine how he'd been caught up in the middle of so much ill feeling, how it must have hurt him, too. She didn't dare say it out loud, though. "It was not easy for Hestia, either. You must understand that much, at least. We never knew, those of us who live and work with her, just what her private hurt was. We knew something profound pained her. There were signs, although she fought not to let it show. But we never understood—not until Marstoke unveiled that sculpture. Your sculpture—the depiction of the child and the woman reaching for him from the painting. The marquess made sure to announce your name loudly to the room—and Hestia nearly fainted away."

"There! You see why I don't wish to see or hear of either of them? I won't be a pawn in their game or a weapon they use against each other."

"She feels your loss deeply."

In the dark, she just caught the motion of his shrug. "I've never seen any sign of it."

"I have. Not until after Marstoke's stunt, but then I understood why she would get wistful and sad when she met with young, blonde gentlemen. Why she was so very tender with mothers who left or lost their infants. And now I know why she looks so very lost when she stands over that sculpture, when she thinks no one is watching."

"She has it, still?" he asked. A quiet question. An infinitesimal and fragile break in his wall.

"She took it from the hostess of that ball, who knew better than to raise a peep over it. It is her only link to you." Francis would be careful not to push too hard at that crack.

She gathered herself a moment, then moved closer to him. "Rhys, Hestia is strong. She gives so much, to anyone who asks, anyone in need. And to no one more than myself. In the work we've done, I've seen things—things that shredded me. Things that struck like a blow until I had to cry. We all cry sometimes. Except Hestia. She never cries. She takes the blow and soldiers on, always adapting, always making things happen. Except for one time—once I've seen her shed tears, when she thought herself alone. It was over your sculpture."

He stood and walked away to stand by the tree again. "I'm glad that she's done so much good with all that she's gained," he said, speaking outward into the kirkyard. "It helps a bit."

She hopped up onto her feet. "Rhys, come with me. Come back to London and meet Hestia."

He took a step back and fetched up against the tree again. "No."

Francis would not give up. "She's away on business now, but will return soon and I know she longs for you. It would make her so happy to see you, to get to know you."

"No." He said it flatly, definitively. "I'm not going with you. I'm not going to see her."

"She's given so much, Rhys. And your presence alone would mean so much to her—the best present you could ever give her."

"Or the best present *you* could give her?"

She flinched at the cynical bent of his tone.

"Are you going to wrap me up in a metaphorical bow, like you did your virginity?"

Her shoulders drooped. She'd pushed him too far. She was frightening him away. "No, Rhys. It's more than that." She lifted her chin. "And do you know? I think it would be good for you, too."

His lip lifted in a sneer. He breathed deep—and she braced herself.

But then he deflated. Heaved a sigh. Shook his head. "I think you are tender-hearted, Francis. And you mean well. But I think you've overestimated how much I could ever mean to Hestia, after all that has happened."

"Absolutely not." She said it with utter conviction.

"You are too close to the situation to be able to see the truth. I don't think Hestia has a need to become acquainted with me at all, anymore. I think perhaps she's found another way to console herself."

"What do you mean?" She narrowed her eyes to peer at him. He sounded so serious, so *pained*, and she could not puzzle it out.

"Perhaps, having left her own child behind . . . perhaps she needed only to find another to care for."

She frowned. "Whose child would it be? I don't know of—"

And then his meaning grew clear and she flushed—first hot and then cold. "Oh. No. It's not like that."

He said nothing and she stood abruptly and strode over to peer into his cold, still face—and suddenly she knew the futility of it all. She done it—crossed the line even as she knew how dangerous it was. She'd opened her heart and shared her all with him—but he would never do the same. He would never let her in.

Was it too much anger built up in there? Too much hurt? It didn't matter, in the end. He'd do anything, twist anything, to keep from adding to it.

"Oh that is rich," she said softly. "Damned rich." She would have laughed if it hadn't hurt so much. Her heart wrenched. She'd so wanted to be the one to meet him, to bring him home to Hestia, and it turned out that she was exactly the wrong person for the job.

"That you could say such a thing," she marveled. "Feel that way . . ." She bit out a sharp, bitter laugh. "Oh, but that makes things so much easier for you, does it not? Accuse her of neglect and me of stealing your place and you are free to resent the hell out of both of us, are you not? And it leaves you in no danger of stepping beyond your rules, opening your walls." She let it all out then, allowed hurt and anger and scorn to round out every syllable. "No need to risk real intimacy or allow someone a glimpse of your heart."

Spinning about, she marched back to the stairs. She snatched up her reticule, hesitated, and shot a disdainful glance over her shoulder.

"I should thank you, I suppose. You've made it easier for me to say goodbye, as well."

Perhaps later, someone else could approach him. Callie, maybe, with her no-nonsense ways.

She paused, her head bowed. "Thank you, Rhys, for all the ways that you were kind to me."

"Francis," he said softly. "I . . ." His words trailed away.

Her chin lifted, then, and she walked away, opening the gate and stepping back out into the street without hesitation. It was late, and she was in her skirts, but she would welcome the chance to let loose her anger on anyone who tried to approach her tonight.

But there was the hack, after all, tooling toward her out of the night, Geordie's welcoming grin shining right along with the carriage lamps. He pulled up and she climbed in. Settling into the sparse cushions, she let him take her back.

No, that was not right. The coach moved ahead, taking her forward. Into her future. Alone.

Chapter Twenty-One

My child was beautiful. More wonderful than any other in the history of children. The midwife said every mother felt so, but I knew better. He was big and healthy and looked like an angel. Only five weeks old when he first smiled and I lost my heart utterly.

--from the journal of the infamous Miss Hestia Wright

"Of course, I will do just as you ask." Andor put a hand to the top of the painting. He'd placed it on an easel and now lifted a brow, silently awaiting permission to unwrap it. "But first, may I?"

Rhys scrubbed a hand over his face and waved his consent. He sank down onto a low seat and deliberately looked away. He didn't want to see it anymore.

He heard his friend's intake of breath, but he didn't turn. The silence stretched out. And out. At last, he broke and turned to gauge Andor's reaction.

His friend stood still and silent, studying the painting. Francis smiled out at him, vibrant and alive. Not cold and distant, as she'd been when Rhys last saw her, walking away. He glanced away. He couldn't look at it. It filled him with anger. He was furious—and yet also . . .

Damnation. Parts of him wanted to feel all of the emotions her image dredged up and out of him. Practically ached for it.

He didn't know if he could forgive her for that.

"It is quite brilliant, my friend," Andor said quietly. "Utterly unique. As is the subject, I'll wager?"

Rhys gave a short nod of agreement.

"Who is she?"

"She's . . ." His lover. His friend. He thought of her last words to him. His nemesis. "She's no one."

Andor frowned and leaned closer to the painting. "She has the same pointed chin as your young apprentice. Are they related?"

"Something like that."

"I shall, of course, mail it to this duchess you mention. But what of you? Are you on the search for your next subject? Perhaps you should go tramp about Calton Hill. Plenty of inspiration to be found there."

"No. I'm leaving the city."

Andor stilled. "Oh?"

"Florence calls."

"Ah, she does, does she not?" Andor sighed. "I do regret that we cannot sample her joys together, as we so often discussed. Alas, my Lorette and I are bound here for a while yet."

"And you are all the happier for it, I know." Rhys said, squeezing his friend's shoulder. "And I am happy for you, my friend."

And it was true, finally. Francis had given him that much, at least.

Andor glanced at the painting again. "I hope you find happiness in Florence, Rhys."

Rhys sighed. "I hope so, too."

⚜

R hys sorted through his brushes, discarding the worn ones, choosing which to pack for the long trip. He went over his paints next, picking an assortment of colors to take along. He had to be prepared for inspiration to hit, even though it felt now as if he'd never have the desire to wield a brush again.

His palettes were a mess. Choosing one, he grabbed a knife to scrape it clean, but found himself faltering. A dozen shades of red gold graced the thing. He dropped the blade and ran a finger over the dried residue.

How long did he sit there? It didn't matter. In his mind his finger followed her trailing curls once more. He breathed in the sweet fragrance of her and buried his hands in the bright beacon of her hair—

Thump. Thump. Thump.

Startled, he jumped and dropped the palette as if it were on fire, flushing like a guilty lad with his first racy book. "What the devil is it?" he snarled.

"A gentleman to see you," Malvi called.

Not Andor. There was no one else he wanted to see. "Send him on his way."

"He's looking for your red-haired chit."

She said it quietly, as if she knew that's all it would take for him to open the door—and she was right, damn her.

He yanked it open. "What are you talking about?"

Malvi smirked at him, her arms crossed. Behind her stood a man who looked vaguely familiar. His beaver hat was in his hands and he worried it as he gave a nod of greeting, turning it around and around in his hands.

"Mr. Caradec? We met once in High Street. Miss Headley introduced us . . ."

Rhys scowled. "I remember." The man who had halfheartedly suggested Caradec might paint his wife. "What's this about Miss Headley?"

"It seems she's gone missing. I've volunteered to help Mrs. Spencer look for her."

"Missing? That's absurd." He rolled his eyes. "That girl can take care of herself."

Malvi rolled her eyes and turned away. Her footsteps sounded loud as she ran down the stairs.

"That does seem to be the prevailing view," the man said. Larson? Was that his name? "But Mrs. Spencer is worried."

"She likely left and headed back to London," he said gruffly. But he knew she wouldn't leave without a proper goodbye to Mrs. Spencer and Jasper—and to her tamed pack of street rats.

"Without her bags?" Larson asked doubtfully. "In any case, I've just come to ask if you've seen her in the last two days? Perhaps she came to make arrangements for delivery of her portrait?"

"Two days? Mrs. Spencer hasn't seen her in two days?"

"As I said." The man was beginning to sound impatient. "Have you seen her?"

"No." Not since she'd raked him over the coals and left him smoldering. "Has Jasper had the boys out looking? Has Mrs. Spencer notified anyone?" His heart was pounding. Hadn't Francis said Malvi and her contact had been asking questions about her? He stepped into the passage and let the door close behind him. "Malvi!" he roared.

No answer came. He pushed past the other man and started down the stairs. "Where have you looked?" He shot the question over his shoulder.

"All over the city," Larson answered, following.

"Not all over, I'd wager. I know a few places to try." They'd reached the empty entry hall. "Malvi! Come out!"

"I just saw her head out into the courtyard." Mrs. Beattie poked her head out from behind the green baize door. "What's amiss? What's the girl done now?"

"I don't know yet, but I'm bound to find out," Rhys growled.

"If you think you have somewhere new to look, you should travel with me." Larson followed him out into the courtyard. "It'll go quicker in my coach, and delay does not seem advisable."

"Thank you," Rhys nodded, looking around the quiet courtyard. "Where did that girl get to?"

"Isn't that her?" Larson frowned. "What in bloody hell is she doing in my carriage?"

The big vehicle was parked near the entrance to the courtyard.

Malvi's face looked small in the open window. Rhys stalked over and threw open the door. "Malvi, if you know anything about this—"

Stars exploded in a bright shower in front of him. A shrill ringing started in his ears as he fell forward, his upper half landing on the floor of the coach. He struggled, trying to prop himself up. Malvi was above him. He could see her lips moving from the corner of his eye as she bent over him, but he could not hear her.

He pushed sluggishly, trying to stand, and another blow hit him from behind. His skull might split in half, the pain was so bad. He slumped forward again, landing near Malvi's shoes. They looked fuzzy. As his vision blurred, but his hearing returned.

"Get him in," Larson said behind him. "Before someone notices."

His cheek scraped along the floor as he was pushed from behind. He noted it as if from a distance.

"Damn, but he's a big one. Why did you not tell me we'd need an extra pair of hands?" Larson griped.

"Stop complaining," she snapped back. "If it were not for me you'd still be trying to actually kidnap that chit. I told you all you had to do was *tell* him she was gone. And I was right."

A soft, caressing touch moved over him, turning his head. He looked up to see Malvi with a vial in her hands. A soft, sweetly cloying scent filled his nostrils. The world fuzzed even further, then faded to black.

Chapter Twenty-Two

*My figure slowly came back. Monsieur began to paint me once
more. A little more tempting, now. The swell of a breast, the curve
of a hip, a long leg lifted from the bath.*

--from the journal of the infamous Miss Hestia Wright

The miserable, pounding thrum in his head woke him. Moving,
even just a little, brought on waves of sweat-soaked nausea, so
Rhys didn't. Dazed, he lay still and wondered where he was and why
was he semi-prone upon the floor and why the regular thumping also
seemed to come from outside of his brain box.

Eventually—it could have been minutes or hours later—he felt well
enough to open his eyes. The light brought a fresh stab of agony, so he
went back to dozing for a while. He might have stayed like that for a
very long time indeed, had it not been for a loud crash, distinctly out
of rhythm with the tempo in his head.

"Hellfire and damnation! Where is that miller's boy?" It was

Larson. No, Welfield. He'd made the sound, entering with a slam of a door.

Suddenly, Rhys recalled his predicament. Miller's boy? His hands were bound, but he stealthily felt about, discovering what he could. And it made sense at last. A stack of flour sacks propped him halfway into a sitting position. The creaking, rhythmic thump was the turning of the mill wheel.

"He's likely gone back into the city. Laudanum is not so easily come by in many small villages."

Malvi. She'd been so quiet and still, Rhys hadn't even realized she was in the room with him. A storage room, he guessed from what little he could see. He didn't look around. No reason to rush to let them know he was awake.

"Why not just dose him again with whatever you gave him earlier? We need to get moving."

"The effects only last a short time. We need something that will knock him out and keep him out."

"God's blood, but I can't wait to leave this blighted place behind and get back to civilization."

"I can't wait to get truly warm," Malvi agreed.

"I want to get a hold of one of Marstoke's special cigarillos," Welfield said on a sigh. "I'll sit in the library and wallow in good tobacco and brandy." He shook his head. "Lord, does that man know how to live. My exalted brother can keep the moldy family pile, damn him. I'll stick with Marstoke, who serves the finest wines, keeps the best cooks, owns horseflesh to tempt a pasha, entertains distinguished visitors, has powerful men dancing upon his strings—and the women!" He laughed. "And he's doing it all now, living on that fine estate, under the very nose of the government scrambling to find him."

"He is like no one else," Malvi said quietly.

"And I'll earn a permanent place at his side when I deliver his reluctant son, as ordered." He rose to look out of the window. "But we'll need that damned laudanum. The devil's too big to bother fighting all the way to London. Where is that boy?"

Silence reigned for a few moments, then Welfield said sharply, "What? Do not glare at me!"

"I don't think—"

"Don't think," the man interrupted. "No, don't say a word about your wonderful insight. We would have been on the road days ago, had you done your job and seduced the man."

"How should I know he's partial to redheads? Had I known, I would have found a bottle of dye before I met him. And in any case, you were not so successful in luring the girl into your clutches either, were you? We both made mistakes."

"And now we run the risk of arriving late and bollixing up the whole plan." Another slam. "Where is that damned laudanum?" he shouted out the window.

The floor shook a little as the man began to pace. "Damn Hestia Wright for changing her plans, but we will arrive on time. Even if we have to travel day and night." The footsteps stopped. "We will make it in time, and when we do, you will say *nothing* to Marstoke."

Malvi laughed. "So I should keep quiet while you pump yourself up in his eyes? If you wanted the credit, you should have done something to earn it. I more than made up for my part—changing sheets and scrubbing dishes and chamber pots, peering through keyholes and listening at doors, watching this oversized idiot fall for a grubby girl child dressed as a boy." Her chair scraped. Rhys could imagine her dark eyes flashing as she stood to face her foe. "So no, I don't think I will keep quiet."

"You will," he insisted.

"It seems to me," she said softly, "that Marstoke is a man who is willing to get his hands dirty. In fact, I rather think he enjoys it." A little silence. "Who do you think he will respect?" she asked softly. "The one also willing to get messy? Or the man who sat back and watched?"

The stomp of Welfield's boots echoed loud and sudden in the small space, but the smack of flesh meeting flesh sounded louder still.

Another crack and Malvi stumbled and fell, landing half across Rhys. He could not suppress a groan at the jostling of his head. He shifted a little and looked up at Welfield as he came to stand over them. The man ignored him, focusing his hate-filled gaze upon the girl.

"Look!" He flung a hand toward Rhys. "You woke the lout!"

She wiped a hand across her mouth. "The lout has been awake for some time, you fool."

Welfield gawked at her. "You think you know everything." He sneered. You are nothing but trouble," Welfield said with a growl. "And you are bound to be even more of a problem later." He pursed his lips, thinking. "So. You can stay here." Utterly unexpected and swift, he kicked the girl in the side. "Make your own way to Marstoke, if you can." He pulled back a foot to strike again.

But Rhys lifted his bound hands and caught his boot before he made contact. Sitting up, he ignored the screaming pain in his head and pushed hard, unbalancing the bastard and sending him sprawling.

Fighting dizziness, he made it into a crouch, and then fell on Welfield. The air whooshed out of the other man. Rhys took the advantage and moved to straddle him. Fisting his bound hands, he swung them hard, striking a blow to Welfield's jaw from one direction and then from the other.

The man scrambled beneath him, but could not heave Rhys' bulk off. He managed to get a hand to his boot, though, and pulled out a knife.

Rhys knew he was in trouble. Welfield started to raise the blade. Malvi, still coiled around the pain in her gut, kicked out and knocked it from his hand. The knife skittered across the floor toward the doorway.

Rhys followed its progress—and then frowned. The door stood open and a lad was silhouetted in the frame. At first he thought . . . but no, it wasn't Flightly.

"Geordie?" He frowned. Had his pounding head played him false?

"Aye, yer lordship." The lad picked up the knife and strolled inside. Casually, he stepped on Welfield's wrist, pinning it to the floor. "Hold the rest of 'im," he ordered. "And keep yer hands still."

The boy sliced Rhys' bindings while Welfield wriggled and spit and cursed and threatened beneath him. Rhys shook his hands free and held one out. The boy slapped the knife into it.

Rhys pressed the point to the man's throat. "Be quiet!" he ordered. "I didn't think my head could hurt any worse, but you are managing it."

"Good!" Welfield shouted. "I hope it hurts like hell. I hope it falls from your—"

With a sigh, Rhys flipped the knife and struck the man in his temple.

Welfield slumped and the flow of vitriol stopped.

"I hope his head aches like the very devil when he wakes up," Rhys muttered. He rolled off the man and touched the back of his head. His fingers came away covered in blood. "Grab that sack," he ordered Geordie, pointing. "Rip some long strips from it."

He struggled to his feet, reached over and almost casually grabbed Malvi, who had begun to inch toward the door. "Don't be in such a hurry," he told her.

She just sighed.

"Francis," he said to her, pulling her close. "She's not truly missing, is she?"

Malvi rolled her eyes. "No. She's sitting in that ribbon shop, just as you were sitting and twiddling your thumbs in your studio. Both of you waiting for the other to leave the city before you moved on. So, I sped things up a bit."

Rhys breathed a sigh of relief.

"How did you get here, lad?" he asked Geordie when the boy brought him a handful of ripped lengths of flour sack. He tied Malvi's hands together and pushed her over to her abandoned chair.

"I was at the livery when they called for the coach. I delivered it, then followed. I seen what they did to ye and knew they'd be lighting out o' the city. So I sent word to Angus by one o' the inn's stable lads, then jumped on the back." He grinned. "They never knew I was there."

Rhys nodded—then grimaced and made a mental note to never do that again—or at least until the drums in his head quieted down. He bound Malvi, hand and foot, to the chair. His head hurt so that he could scarcely think, but he knew that eventually Francis and Angus and his crew would track them down.

For a long moment, he considered just leaving them all where they were. He could just take off, leave for Italy, leave it—all this mess and complication and the many emotional quagmires associated with it —behind.

But looking around, he touched his head again and contemplated the lengths to which Marstoke and his followers were willing to go—and he knew he had to find out more.

"When Francis and Angus and all of them get here, tell them what happened. Make sure Francis knows what they said about intercepting Hestia," he told Geordie.

"Why don't ye tell them?"

"Because I'm taking these two and heading out. This one," he nudged Welfield with a foot. "This one I'll leave with a constable at the next town big enough to boast one."

Geordie nodded. "Did ye want the laudanum he sent for? It's here. I took it off the miller's boy." He shrugged. "T'weren't a bad idea—and a sight easier than listening to him gripe."

Rhys considered. "Fetch it. I'll take it, just in case."

The boy nodded and went out. Rhys bent carefully and began to tie Welfield's feet.

"Leave me here," Malvi said quietly. "Don't take me with you."

Rhys snorted. "What, after all that wheedling to get me to take you to London?"

"It's too late to go to London. It's all happening now—and you'll travel faster without me."

"Travel faster into what?" he asked. "You dragged me into this, damn you. Now you can help me get through it." He cocked a brow at her. "You can be my ticket into Marstoke's little club. You might even get credit for it."

"You're the prodigal son—you won't need a ticket. And if the truth comes out . . ." She shrugged.

"I need to know what's going on. You can share your insights."

She laughed. "How much do you think I know? You were my first real test. Luring you there, all unsuspecting, that might have won me a place in the game." She looked away. "But helping you to thwart him? It won't go well with me."

He knew enough to know she was right. "I could arrange protection."

"For the rest of my life?" she scoffed. "That's what it would take. He never forgets an enemy."

Rhys knew that was right too. It was only one of the many reasons he'd tried to avoid both of his parents. "Tell me what you know, then, and I'll consider leaving you here."

"You mean letting me go, do you not?" she asked silkily.

"I do not. Francis will be along soon enough. I'll let her decide what to do with you."

She didn't like the sound of that. "Hestia's girl," she said with scorn. And perhaps a bit of . . . wistfulness?

"Yes."

"She'll just let me go. She's too soft-hearted to do anything else."

"It's likely." Eventually. But she'd probably hold the girl until this mess was settled.

"You might as well save her the trouble."

He didn't respond, just tied off his knot with a flourish.

Malvi tilted her head. "You know, I've met your mother."

Rhys stilled. Then he grunted and stood, reaching for more fabric so he could bind Welfield's hands.

"I was a naive fool, just like any other," she said dispassionately. "Pretty enough to know I was meant for bigger things than small village life. But stupid, like so many others. I answered an advertisement for an opportunity in London, wiping the country dust from my feet and leaving with a small case and two shillings to rub together." She sighed. "They were long gone by the time I discovered the agency wasn't truly looking for girls to train up to serve in great houses. They took one look at me and hauled me off to Mother Gretel's."

He could well imagine the sort of place that was.

"They locked me in the basement along with the other new, recalcitrant girls. Softening us up, so we wouldn't balk at the sort of clientele Mother Gretel catered to." She shuddered. "We'd only been down there a couple of days, hardly long enough to get really hungry, when Hestia and her people raided the place and set us free."

Pausing, she looked him over. "People talk, but she truly is a beauty. Breathtaking." She nodded. "I can see her in you."

He folded his arms. "Have you changed your mind? Shall I haul you out to that carriage? Or are you going to tell me what I need to know about Marstoke?"

"I'm getting there." She looked away. "Hestia gave me a bit of money and offered me a place at Half Moon House. I told her I'd consider it."

His lip curled. "And yet you ended up with her enemy."

"Yes. He does that sometimes, did you know? Approaches those that Hestia has helped, tempts them away or subverts them to his cause. He gets a perverse pleasure out of it."

"I hear that's the least of his perversions."

"True enough," she said simply, and with the tone of one who knows.

"So why choose him?"

"Why not? You heard that one enthusing." She tossed her chin toward Welfield. "Intrigue. Adventure. The trappings of old money. Entry into a new world and a game played by the highest and wealthiest. How can hard work and learning and the service of others compare to that?"

"You chose poorly," he said with a significant glance at their surroundings.

"At least I picked a side," she shot back. "You think you can skate through life tasting only the beauty—the art, the food, the wine and women. You think you are safe that way?" She laughed. "There's always a price to pay. That red-haired chit got her claws in deep enough to hurt, didn't she?"

The truth of it slammed into his chest, but he batted it away. "None of that is your business. Just tell me what I need to know."

"No. You two were clearly made for each other, but you were too stubborn and afraid. We might both be defeated and miserable now, but at least I had the stones to reach for the brass ring."

"Malvi." Her name emerged a harsh warning.

"Oh, no. You won't quiet me any more than that idiot did," she pointed her chin at Welfield. "I know you are suffering from some fool notion that walking the middle between your parents will keep you from harm." A corner of her pretty mouth lifted in a sneer. "You could not be more wrong. Do you want to know what Marstoke is up to?" She gave a bitter laugh. "If you will not join him, then you are of no use to him—and there exists the chance that you'll join the other side. So he's devised a way to *make* use of you."

"He cannot make me do anything," he began.

"You are a bigger fool that I thought, if you think that is true," she interrupted. "You are going to end this long war for him, once and for all. And you are going to give him the ultimate triumph, too."

"I highly doubt that."

"He's not going to ask you, dolt! Your fate was sealed the moment the idea occurred to him."

Rhys waited. And tried to imagine what the idea of ultimate triumph might mean to the man who was his father.

Malvi stretched the silence out for a few minutes. Rhys finished tying Welfield, who had begun to moan a little. He propped open the door so he could carry him through unimpeded.

"Oh, very well!" Malvi capitulated. "It's not as if I can ever return, in any case." She gazed pityingly on him. "I don't even know very much. He knew where we were going," she nodded at Welfield. "I only know that the timing is deliberate. Why do you think that Welfield is in such a hurry? Hestia Wright has been out of London, but she will return shortly. We have her travel plans. We were to arrive at the destination, sit tight and wait. Help the others set the trap. I know she will find she has to stop —and she will encounter *you*." She looked away. "I don't know the particulars, but the end result is to be her death. And *you* are to take the blame for it." She tossed her head. "And doesn't that sound like Marstoke's idea of a great victory? The sensational murder of his oldest enemy—and at the hand of the son she spent her life protecting and pining for."

His breath caught. His heart clenched. It took a moment before he could swallow against bile and denial and horror.

His father would frame him for foul murder? Only because he might, perhaps, someday turn against him? Francis had been right all along. The man was a monster.

He refused to consider what this made him.

Too, the thought of anyone harming Hestia—he shied away from it with a shake of his head that set the drums to throbbing again. Rhys might harbor a noxious mix of hurt, anger, longing—and yes, a bit of ridiculous jealousy towards his mother—but he'd be damned if he let anyone hurt her. Especially Marstoke, who appeared to have made a lifelong habit of it.

And Francis—she would be gone as soon as she got wind of this. Where Hestia was, she would be. And Rhys would be thrice damned before he let his father's taint harm that girl. *His* bright, hopeful, generous, maddening girl.

Damn it all to hell. Francis had been right about this too. Sometimes one must step into the fray. And this was more his fight than hers.

Malvi watched him closely. "You should run. Leave quickly. Go to Italy. It's what you had planned already, is it not? It's your best hope of escaping his clutches, at least for a time."

Rhys sank down onto a stack of flour sacks and rested his aching head against the wall, considering her words.

"He'll still kill her, won't he?"

"Yes. But that's always been her fate. You cannot change it. You can only save yourself." She grinned suddenly. "I could go with you. It's warm in Italy, is it not? And there is a good deal less rain."

A month ago, he might have taken her up on that offer.

Now. He stared at her for a long moment, the wheels in his brain creaking slowly. Now, he wasn't the same man. Flightly had got under his skin. Her voice whispered in his aching head.

He closed his eyes. There were times, when he painted, when he would come to a moment that he knew was vital. Chose one angle of light or depth of color and get one image. Choose another and he would find himself with a completely different result, in the end.

He was there. He'd reached just such a defining moment in his life. He could continue on as he'd come, treading the same path. Safe. Uninvolved. Unfettered.

Or he could shift his thinking. Embrace the difficult and the unknown and allow himself to truly feel.

He frowned at Malvi. She was nothing like Francis. She was cynical, like him. He'd always thought love was a dark emotion. Something that would restrict him, tie him down, keep him from tasting the joy in life. But it hadn't been like that with Francis. She exuded joy and light.

Francis wouldn't be a burden, would she? She'd be someone who would share it all—the fun and experience and adventure—and the hard times too. Yes, she'd left emptiness and aching when she'd gone, but this time it had been his choice.

Why hadn't he seen that?

He stood. Bending, he hoisted Welfield, tossing him over one shoulder. He stalked out, threw the bastard into the same carriage he'd meant to confine him in, and threw the bolt.

Geordie approached, watching in awe. "Here's the laudanum."

Rhys paused, and then unlocked the bolt again. "Get a dose down him, lad, and then hitch up the horses. I'm going to travel fast and I've no wish to delay to deal with that buffoon." He walked back toward the millhouse. "Don't choke him, now," he called back. "I want him to live to face justice—and his father's wrath."

He stood on the threshold of the storage room. "Goodbye, Malvi. Hestia gave you a second chance and you wasted it. Now, it seems you're getting a third. I hope you will use it wisely." He turned to go.

"Wait! Untie me before you go, Caradec!" She made a sound of frustration. "At least tell me what you are doing! Where are you going?"

"I'm following your very good advice, of course, and I'm heading south." He walked away, gave Geordie a few more instructions, and then climbed up on the box of the carriage. *Picking a side*, he thought as he shook out the reins and urged the horses on.

Chapter Twenty-Three

WILTSHIRE

*We never showed my face or full form. The moon was a beauty
mark, a reflection in the mirror. Always there. The unveiling of
each painting brought men flocking to the courtesan's salon. My
fame—if not my name—spread beyond Vienna.*

--from the journal of the infamous Miss Hestia Wright

A graveled path led from the Duke of Aldmere's stables. Francis's
footsteps crunched loudly as she ran, taking the offshoot that
wound through the kitchen gardens.

She still felt as frantic as she had when Geordie's message had
arrived at the shop, as she had when they'd found the old mill and she'd
forced Malvi to tell her everything.

Where was Rhys? Malvi had laughed in her face when she'd asked.
The maid might not have been able to tempt Caradec, she'd gloated,
but Francis hadn't been able to keep him.

Was it true? Francis had been so angry after their last argument.
The man was good for a laugh, she'd told Mrs. Spencer. No one better

for a witty conversation and a thorough knowledge of the best food in the city.

She hadn't told the older woman that Rhys made for a stupendous lover in bed—but was too emotionally stagnant to allow himself to be more.

Lesson learned.

Her first heartbreak earned.

But her anger had faded when she realized what had happened to him. Had he run away to Italy as Malvi insisted? Had he chosen to stay distant and unattached behind his cursed line and abandoned Hestia to her fate?

Francis pushed away the sudden rise of unshed tears—again. She could not believe it of him. But where was he? And where was Hestia?

Without pausing, she burst through the servant's entrance, taking the stairs two at a time and startling Billings, the Duke of Aldmere's staid butler.

"What's this, then?" he exclaimed, curving a protective arm around a bottle of wine. "Oh, Flightly." He frowned. "Wait. I thought it was Miss Headley now? Are you not supposed to be in skirts?"

"Not tonight, Billings. I've no time, although you know I dearly love to shock your sensibilities. Where is the duchess? I need to see her right away."

He shook his head. "Already gone to see to Half Moon House, and the duke with her. Your note arrived today—as did a visitor—who is likely awaiting you, upstairs."

Her eyes widened. Hestia? Could it be? She flew past the butler and up the servant's stairs, emerging into the main corridor, where she paused. The formal parlor lay dark. The door to the library stood closed, with no light showing beneath it.

"In here, Miss." Further down the passage, a footman bowed. He stood outside the morning room and opened the door. She hurried through to find—

"Isaac?" She stopped, her mind whirring faster than broken clockwork. "What are you—? How did you—?"

"I already knew something was amiss." The butler from Half Moon House, who also acted as protector and sometime bodyguard to Hestia

Wright, held out an arm. She rushed over to give him a long, tight squeeze.

He set her back after a moment and looked her over, as if checking for damage. "You're all right, then?"

Sudden tears welled, but she refused to let them fall. She nodded. "But I don't understand how you are here?"

"That letter Hestia sent," he said, shaking his head. "I could tell by the wording that things were not right. And the work she's doing shouldn't be so challenging." He paused and glanced over at the closed door. "You know I arrange all of her travel."

"I do know."

When Hestia traveled she rarely took the common roads and never the same route twice. Isaac made her arrangements himself, and they were ever varied and kept quiet. If Marstoke and his minions knew where to find her, then Half Moon House likely had a traitor in the ranks.

"She wouldn't make changes, not without letting me arrange it. Not unless there was good reason. So I set up a patrol of guards at the house and through the neighborhood and I came to intercept her." He lifted a hand, indicating the house. "I stopped here this afternoon, to see if the duchess had had any word. Your note arrived right after. I sent Brynne and Aldmere on to Town, but waited, hoping you'd come in tonight." He shot her an approving glance. "You must have traveled like the wind."

"I wish I had. I wouldn't ache so." She frowned. "But Isaac, where do we go now? I was hoping to discover her here. If she's taking a new route, how can we possibly find her before Marstoke does?"

"We discussed alternatives before she left. She'll take one of those routes—and I believe I know which one." He nodded. "We'll find her. But we'll have to move quickly."

Francis slumped a bit in relief. She grabbed up a biscuit from a nearby tray. "Are you sure you set enough watches on Half Moon House? It would be just like Marstoke to entice us away and strike there as well."

"They are safe. Callie and her Lord Truitt had not left London yet. They are moved in and I left him in charge of a small army," he said blandly, pouring her a cup of tea. "I know you are tired and hungry, but if I feed you up and spoil you with blankets, pillows and warm bricks, can you leave with me tonight and sleep on the way?"

She yawned and snatched up another sweet. "Fill my belly and I'll likely sleep on the roof of the coach, I'm that tired."

"No need for such heroics," Isaac said blandly. "The duke has left us his posh traveling carriage and arranged for fast horses after that."

"All right, then," Francis said, stifling another yawn. "Let's go."

⚶

I t hadn't been a gentlemanly thing to do.

But Rhys had left neutrality behind and jumped with both feet into a war. In war, one used guile and lies when one must. One took advantage of foolish men, circumstance—and laudanum.

Easy enough, then, to slap the drugged Welfield into a state of semi-consciousness and sit back in the shadows of the darkened coach. Imitating his father's sharp, clipped tones, he harangued the man with his failures until, protesting, Welfield let slip where the confrontation with Hestia was to occur.

Rhys turned the man over to the first village constable he found, leaving him to sleep off the rest of the drug and to await charges on kidnapping. He'd left the coach behind and hired a big, fast horse and he'd ridden hell for leather, switching horses several times, barely stopping to rest until he reached Kendal, a market town situated in the southern end of the Lake District.

The Smithland Arms was a smallish inn at the western end of the town. The ostler who came to take his latest hack told him they only had two guests at the moment.

Two guests? If this was a trap, wouldn't there be more? Tired and travel worn, he'd stood in the courtyard and fumed, furiously convinced that Welfield had sent him to the wrong spot.

But then a man had moved to stand at the window of the taproom. Awash in relief, Rhys had spun away to face the ostler. He knew the man inside. Cade. One of his father's lieutenants, as he liked to call them. A misnomer. They were mere chessmen, pieces in Marstoke's

Great Game. Less than that. They were checker pieces, interchangeable and disposable.

No way to stay inconspicuous as one of only three guests at the inn. Rhys watched the boy lead his horse away. The stable sat a little way beyond the inn, the doors facing the courtyard. Doubtless a design that lent itself to speed and efficiency, if not beauty. And it might also lend itself to Rhys' needs.

Following his horse, he went in search of the stable master. He offered to work a few days in return for a bed in the barn and board for his hack. The man eyed him up, doubtless weighing the complicated equation of his size, how much work he might wring out of him and how much he'd have to feed him. After a moment, he shrugged and agreed.

Rhys set to work. It was a good arrangement. He kept busy, but was also able to keep an eye on the comings and goings at the inn. More of Marstoke's men arrived as that day and the next wore on. They were smart enough to come in from different directions. Disappointing, as he couldn't make a guess as to where his father's latest hideaway might be. All of the men booked rooms, and the inn began to fill. They settled in, playing cards, flirting with the taproom maids and keeping them busy fetching drinks.

Rhys was called to carry more than one keg from the storeroom. Judging by the relaxed attitude of the group of men, he figured that nothing was expected to happen today. He was relieved, too, to see no sign of Francis. He'd left her with no way to discover this rendezvous point—which was exactly how he wanted it. She could stay safe for once. He would handle this confrontation between his warring parents.

Somehow. Sometime. His nerves were wearing thin and he wanted this over with so he could find Francis and tell her—everything.

The next morning, it looked as if he would get his wish. He brought out a horse for an early-departing guest and found a well turned out traveling coach recently arrived in the courtyard. Several of yesterday's arrivals spilled out of the inn to greet a new gentleman standing next to it.

"Did Welfield arrive? With the son?" the new arrival demanded.

Rhys stepped around to the other side of the horse.

"No. There's been no word," one of the men answered.

"They've all just disappeared," the other said. "Welfield, the girl, the son. There's no trace of any of them."

"Damnation." The newcomer reached into the carriage and pulled out a rich looking, lined cloak. "Well, then, our orders have changed."

"What? After we've set everything up?"

"Marstoke's changed the game. A new plan, in case Welfield didn't show. That's why I haven't traveled alone." He sighed. "Where's Cade?"

"Inside, seeing the old man set up—and seething. You know what he's like. His interest is the revolution. He's impatient to get to the politics and violence. He gets riled when Marstoke goes off on these personal tangents."

"Who could blame him?" the newcomer said bitterly. "The last time he ended up in Newgate and *we* had to get him out." He shook his head. "What did they do with the old man?"

"They've put him in the private parlor. He's already ordered breakfast."

Rhys' grip tightened on the horse's lead. The old man? Surely Marstoke's minions wouldn't speak of him in that way? Who had arrived with the newcomer?

The horse's owner emerged and Rhys helped him mount, plans whirling in his head. The inn was only large enough to boast one private parlor. Last night, Rhys had carried firewood there and laid the fire. As the room had been empty at the time, he'd taken the opportunity to unlatch the window, just as he'd done in the storeroom in the basement, when he was fetching kegs.

"I'll take my meal in the taproom," the new arrival was saying as the guest moved off and Rhys stopped at the edge of the building to pretend to pick something from the sole of his boot. "And I'll have a damned large glass of ale to wash it down with."

"I'll join you," one of the others told him with a shake of his head. "This whole thing is a bloody nasty business."

"Yes? Well, you may ride inside and listen to the litany of complaints on the way back," the newcomer snapped. "I'll ride outside and be glad of the quiet." He looked over at the groom unhitching his team. "Feed them lightly," the gentleman called. "We'll be needing them again, later today." He moved toward the inn, but stopped and turned back. "And leave the doors open to let the inside air out!" he shouted to the boy.

Today. Rhys' heart tripped into a gallop. He got to his feet and strode off before the three men headed inside. Once they were gone, he slipped around the side of the inn, moving quickly to the back. Bending low, he approached the window, crouched beneath, and waited.

No sound from within. No one spotted him out here. Slowly, slowly, with two fingers at the corner of the window, he swung it outward, opening it just the smallest bit.

No alarm rose. He could hear the faint click of silverware on china. With luck, no one would notice the slight opening.

Tension swirling like a live thing in his gut, he went back to work.

For hours, nothing happened. He mucked stalls and got harangued for stopping to go to the stable door at every stray noise. He could scarcely keep his eyes from the inn. Was it Marstoke, in there? Briefly, he considered dunking his head in the trough, putting on the clothes in his saddlebag and going in there to find out. But truly, he had no desire to confront his father. Anger and disgust lay too close to the surface of his skin. He didn't think he could go in and act as if he didn't know that the man who had sired him planned to murder Hestia and let him hang for it.

He saddled up mounts for a couple of Marstoke's men. Were they being sent on errands? Or on watch? He pitched fresh hay and fetched a bucket for water. Standing at the pump, he looked up when one of the lackeys returned, riding in fast. Breathing heavily, the man threw Rhys his reins and ran into the inn.

Automatically, Rhys began to walk the horse, cooling it down. He had to get to the back, to see if he could hear anything at that window. He motioned for one of the young ostlers to take the horse—and then froze.

Two more arrivals cantered into the courtyard. A great bear of a man, dressed impeccably, who dismounted and called for the innkeeper in a haughty tone. And behind him, his servant, a young man who glanced casually about as he dismounted.

Flightly.

A series of complicated sentiments whipped through Rhys. Relief, fury, resignation, affection and a deep, abiding joy. He felt them moving fast, like he was riding full tilt again, through a whirlwind of Francis-inspired emotion.

He wasn't ready for her to see him. And what if the sight of him jarred her out of character?

Stepping behind the horse, he watched, waiting to see what she would do.

Chapter Twenty-Four

I had to go to Vienna. Almost, I could not leave my son. Only the thought of keeping us safe and fed allowed me to go. I learned from my mentor, all of the ways to keep a man happy and wanting more, in secret. When I was ready, she announced an auction. Men from across Europe bid to be first to see my face, to meet me in person, to become my protector.

--from the journal of the infamous Miss Hestia Wright

Francis had worked with Isaac countless times. He was the silent, hulking threat behind Hestia's right shoulder. Usually, his bulk did the persuading for them all. Occasionally, he allowed his fists—and his pugilistic skills—to chime in.

Today, though, she had to fight to keep her mouth from hanging open as Isaac climbed down from his horse and turned into an urbane, cultured, utterly annoying nobleman.

He gave the ostler detailed instructions on how to store his tack and how to rub down his horse. He requested a precise mix of grain for his mount's feedbag, right down to the percentage of barley and oats. He lectured at length against the evils of too-cold water for heated horses.

And it worked. Because they were still there, lingering outside the inn's doors when Hestia Wright walked around the curve in the road and into the courtyard.

It was all right to stare, because that's what any young groom would have done—but no stranger's heart would have been filled with the relief, longing and trepidation that Francis felt, seeing her mentor once again. Nor would a random boy have felt the same pride.

Slowly, Hestia drew close, moving at the head of an odd procession. She looked a little flushed, but otherwise just as beautiful, calm and regal as she always did—despite the horse she led, the man slumped over its neck and the tired, bedraggled looking woman at her side.

Isaac didn't even glance in their direction. He moved into the inn, calling for the proprietor. Francis looked after him, then back to the dust-covered group, as if torn. Finally, she ran to help ease the injured man down from his horse.

"Thank you, young sir." Hestia betrayed not an ounce of recognition. Neither did Francis. "As you can see, we've had a bit of trouble on the road."

A maid came running from the inn, wringing her hands over the injured man. One of the stable boys took the horse.

"Our driver has been injured. His leg is broken. He'll need a doctor." Hestia kept her arm around the man on one side and Francis helped support the other side. He moaned with each step, one leg dragging uselessly. The woman trailed behind as they followed the maid into the building, untying her bonnet and holding it by the enormous brim.

"We'll send someone to fetch the doctor," the maid said. "The innkeeper is with another patron, but I'll send for a lad to help us carry him up to a room."

"Take them into the private parlor," a haughty voice ordered.

Bloody, sodding hell. The old street expression crept up on her, along with a shocking jolt of surprise and fear. The man who emerged from a shadowed passage was Cade, one of Marstoke's most trusted men—

and also one of the most intelligent and ruthless. He might easily recognize her. She ducked her head, pretending to grip the poor man more securely.

"We left our carriage a couple of miles back," Hestia told the maid. She ignored Cade. "The driver's assistant is waiting there with it and with our luggage. I told him we would send help."

"As he is the man who arranged your accident, I assure you that he has been taken care of and is not lingering there." Cade looked them all over with a detached gaze. "Into the parlor with them. All of them."

Two men stepped up close behind them. Marstoke's flunkies, no doubt, although she didn't recognize them. They crowded close, but didn't offer to help with the burden of the wounded man.

Hestia stood a moment, still and straight, her chin lifted high. Francis glanced between her and the door. Was Marstoke in there? She knew Hestia and the marquess had glared daggers at each other across theatres, ballrooms and receptions, but this might be the first time they'd come face to face in years.

"Let's go," ordered Cade.

Hestia set her shoulders. Then she bent down to support the injured man once more. They all moved awkwardly into the room.

A man sat in a chair facing the door, straight-backed, proud, dressed in fine clothes and wearing a fur draped around his shoulders.

He was not Marstoke.

"You!" Hestia dropped, all color leeching from her face.

The driver groaned and leaned more heavily on Francis as Hestia's support faltered. There were two other chairs near the unlit hearth. She maneuvered the poor man into the closest one. His head fell back and she turned to leave.

One of the two men following them stepped in her way.

"'Scuse me, guv," she said, low. "Gotta get back."

"My God! It's true!" The older gentleman in the chair had locked his gaze on Hestia. He half arose, then sank back. "You've scarcely changed at all. In all of these years!" Everyone turned toward him, he sounded so frightened, and perhaps a little in awe.

"Well, I cannot say the same for you," Hestia said bluntly. "Captain —No, it is *Mister* Wilson now, is it not?"

Francis fought not to react. Captain Wilson? Her fists clenched. The man had betrayed Hestia, lied to her. He'd seduced a young Hestia into eloping, a girl not yet old enough for her come-out into Society. He'd pretended to marry her and turned her over to Marstoke instead, allowing the marquess to take his place in her bridal bed and leaving her trapped in the wicked man's clutches.

Hestia's brow elevated. "So changed you are—and without even suffering the prison time you deserved. Something has sucked the health and vitality out of you, sir. What could it be?"

"Hard living, my dear." He coughed. "Hard living. And the pain and regret that come with it."

Hestia's expression did not change, her calm remained unruffled. "Pain? I dearly hope so. But regret? You've never showed an ounce of it." She folded her arms before her. "How did you avoid a court martial and hanging, by the way? Did Marstoke intervene? Or was it that you included an admiral's son in on your scheming when you cheated the navy and endangered our brave lads at sea?"

"A bit of both, my dear. A bit of both." The words were followed by a long, eerie wheeze.

"I'm not so sure it was a blessing," Hestia said directly. "You look like death warmed over."

The old man laughed, but it turned into a nasty cough that got the better of him and went on and on.

Cade sighed. One of the other men went to pound on the old man's back—and Francis tried again to slip out of the room. She had to get out of here and bring Isaac back to help—preferably before Cade looked too close and recognized her.

"Here, now." The man who had stopped her before grabbed her by the wrist. "Cade, do we need to keep these others?"

"Yes! That's it exactly," the old man rasped, his cough finally under control. "I am that precisely—death warmed over. I daresay I would be entombed already, had Marstoke not forbade me to die before I met you here."

Cade stepped forward, motioning the other man away. "Sir, do you know any of these other people?"

Wilson didn't look their way. He scarcely shifted his gaze from Hestia. "What? No." He flicked his fingers dismissively.

Cade turned. Francis stayed put, her face turned toward the door. Slowly, the tall man crossed the room. He paused next to her, and then moved on to the drab, tired woman who had accompanied Hestia.

"How do you know Hestia Wright?" Cade asked her.

She looked up at him, her shaking fingers setting her hat atremble. "Who?"

Francis gave her credit for trying.

Cade gripped her chin. She gasped and tried to jerk away. Shock showed on her pale face and Francis knew that, whoever she was, she'd never been handled roughly before.

Lucky woman.

"Her." Cade pointed her toward Hestia. "What are you to her?"

"We just met this morning," she answered shakily. "At the inn, where we stayed last night. I am journeying to London. During the night, the wicked man I hired left me. Took the coach and my money and left me behind."

Real tears showed in her eyes. Francis would have been impressed, had she not worried that they were a sign of weakness.

"That lady was traveling to London as well. She offered to share her carriage."

Francis knew she was lying. She wondered if Cade had picked up on her little slips, as well.

"That's no lady," said Cade. "What is your name?"

"Excuse me?"

"Your. Name."

"Oh." The woman started to tremble. "I am Miss Smy—." She twitched. "Miss Smith, that is."

Cade raised a brow at her, then glanced in Francis's direction. She deliberately suppressed any reaction except impatience. "My master will tan me if I don't find him soon," she said, pulling away from the man who held her.

"Take the driver upstairs and let the doctor see to him," Cade told the henchmen. "Keep the other two here."

"Here, now!" she protested. "I only helped carry the bloke in—and got claret spilled on me fer my troubles." She swiped at her blood stained trousers. "And now yer goin' to get me whipped!"

"Take them all away," Wilson fretted. "It's her I want to see." He still gazed at Hestia.

"Why are you here, still dancing to that old reprobate's tune?" Hestia asked him. "All of this effort to acquire me—I should think Marstoke would be here himself."

"You know the man," Wilson complained. "He is attached to his little dramas."

"Drama? That's what this little reunion is meant to be?"

"It's meant to be a *reenactment*," he told her. "I'm to bring you to him, just as I did, so long ago." He raised a hand and beckoned. "Come here to me." Wilson reached for her. "I've longed to touch you again, after all of these years."

Swift as a flash, Hestia grabbed his hand and twisted it back as she spun around and stepped behind him. Her other hand reached into her bodice, pulled out a small, shining blade and pressed the point to the older man's neck.

"Keep back," she warned.

One of the lackeys took a step toward them.

"Do you think I won't bleed him?" She raised a brow at Cade. "Do you *know* what he did to me, so long ago?" She gave a short, bitter laugh. "And the most important question—do you want to return to Marstoke with only one of your trophies?"

Cade shrugged. The others held still and watchful. Wilson struggled to free his arm, gasping like a fish out of water.

"You never married, did you, *Mister* Wilson?" Moving quickly, Hestia folded his fingers down, leaving his ring finger pointing back and down towards the floor. Sun streamed in the window behind her and flashed on the metal of the knife as she quickly ran it in a line all the way around the base of the finger.

The other woman gasped. No one else moved. Wilson's rasping breath and stream of feeble curses were the only sound in the room.

"Did you know that he marked us?" Hestia asked in a conversational tone. "All of us, those that he falsely wed? At times he was a pretend bridegroom. Occasionally, he masqueraded as the clergyman.

But the brides were all marked in the flesh, to show his triumph, his ownership, his claim. Mine is a burn."

Francis's stomach turned when all the men's eyes turned toward Hestia's blood spattered glove. Their curiosity was casual and sickening.

"Others have brands, tattoos. Or scars, as you will have," Hestia continued. She tossed his hand back in his lap and put the bloodied blade back to his neck. "But the scars on our hearts and minds were where the true damage lies."

"Enough." Cade had a pistol pointed at her now. "Throw down the knife and step away from him."

"No need for firearms," Hestia said clearly, and a little louder than necessary. Nodding, she did as she was bid. Leaning down as she went past him, she told Wilson, "That's what I've been longing to do to you, for all of these years. You are far more his creature than I ever was. You should be marked as well."

Wilson, clutching his hand, struggled to breathe. His skin tone had gone grey and he looked to be in real distress now.

Cade sighed in disgust and shot Hestia an accusing look. "Have that doctor fetched in here when he arrives," he told the men. "Before he sees to the driver." He waved the pistol. "Lock the three of them in a room upstairs."

Francis tried to protest again, but Cade cut her off. "Save it, street rat. I know who you are." He walked over to Miss Smith and held her chin once more, turning her head to examine her profile. "Miss Smythe is it?" He gave Hestia a look. "We'll see what Marstoke has to say about it."

Hestia ignored him, but she shot Wilson a look over her shoulder as they were all ushered out of the door. "Feel free to pass on now, Mister Wilson, despite what Marstoke has to say about it. Certainly, you have my blessing."

⚙

Slowly, moving on silent feet, Rhys backed away from the window.

A tangle of emotion lodged in the back of his throat. Oh, damn, but he was in it now.

His lifelong mantra of caution, pride and distance peeled away. He was leaving it behind him bit by bit, like a knight divesting himself of armor as he strode from the field of battle.

Except, this time, for the *first* time, Rhys was running straight into the fray.

Because he had to. He must. What good was a defining maxim if it meant that he could not have Francis?

No good at all. Rubbish.

He would not let her fall prey to the tangled, wicked mess his father had created. Lord, but she was brave. He swallowed down pride mixed with fear as he sprinted toward the stables. Hestia, too. He knew who Captain Wilson was. Marstoke had told him the story himself, watching avidly for his reaction to the story of his conception.

He ran faster, a plan forming in his head.

Francis was his—and he'd be damned before he allowed Marstoke harm her. All of those rules he'd lived by, they'd been his shield as a child, kept him safe as he'd grown, but he would gladly toss them aside now—as long as he could live with her.

Chapter Twenty-Five

The final amount was staggering. I was a success. My fame skyrocketed. I could choose between the men who wanted me. Ask anything of them. I chose kind men and treated them well. And I traveled to Brittany as often as I could. Visiting Monsieur, allowing him to paint me, and spending time with my son. Those days were the best in my life. My reason for living.

--from the journal of the infamous Miss Hestia Wright

"Quit dragging your feet, girl." The lackey prodded her from behind, urging her to climb the stairs at a quicker pace.

But Francis craned her neck as they passed each landing and deliberately moved slower. Where was Isaac? She listened intently for the rumble of his voice.

Nothing.

When they reached the top floor, they were shuffled to the end of the passage and shoved into a tiny room, made smaller by a deep-edged dormer window. The door slammed behind them and they all heard the key turn in the lock.

Hestia pushed away from the bedpost where she'd landed, straightened and turned—and gave a *whoof* when Francis launched herself into her arms, hugging her tight.

"I was so afraid we wouldn't make it in time," she whispered.

Hestia smoothed her hair and cupped her face for a moment. "It's good to see you, too. Who is with you? Was that Isaac I caught a glimpse of, entering the inn?"

"Yes. He's in the building somewhere, I think." Francis marveled. Hestia appeared her usual composed self, unruffled by her confrontation with one of the men whose vile betrayal had altered the course of her life.

"Who was outside the window, then? I could have sworn I caught a reflection of someone skulking out there."

"I don't know. One of Marstoke's flunkies?" Her heart sank. If she hadn't been so rash, so over-confident, she might have been able to tell Hestia that her son could be counted on to help them. But she'd driven Rhys away instead of bringing him home, and now she was going to have to confess her failure.

She had to lower her head and blink away a swell of tears.

"Anyone else we might expect?" This was Hestia, adding up resources, making plans. "Aldmere? Truitt?"

Francis shook her head. "Callie and Lord Truitt were already in London. Isaac sent Aldmere and Brynne to help them at Half Moon House."

"Very wise. It would be just like Marstoke to strike on two fronts." She smoothed the tousled locks of Francis's wig. "Any sign of Stoneacre?"

"No." Francis stepped back. "Not that I know of."

Hestia heaved a sigh. "I suppose I should not be surprised." She was still calm, still in control, but there was something pensive behind her eyes, and Francis felt her own well with tears once more.

"Here, now. What's this?" Hestia grinned at her. "We've been in worse scrapes, my dear."

"Yes, I know."

Hestia's expression turned suddenly knowing. "Have you been up to something, Francis? Is that why your name has been conspicuously absent from the reports I've been getting from Isaac?"

She could not suppress the rise of a sudden sob.

"Oh, dear." Real concern showed in her mentor's face. "That bad, is it? I can see we are overdue for a talk." She glanced about the room. "Let's get out of here first, though, shall we? I suspect we'll need time and tea for this discussion." She turned and went to the window. It lifted easily. "I suppose they thought it too high to worry over," she said, looking down.

Francis wiped her face and went to open the wardrobe in the corner. "It's big enough," she said peering inside. She withdrew and gave Hestia a look, raising doubtful eyebrows toward the third member of their group.

"Oh, yes." Hestia left the window open and crossed over to the bed, where Miss Smythe sat, slumped in misery. "Miss Smythe, I would like you to meet my associate and dearest friend, Miss Francis Headley. I know you'll overlook her scandalous attire, since she assumed her role in order to come to our aid."

The woman didn't even glance at Francis. Instead, she raised a teary gaze to Hestia. "I'm sorry!" Anguish rang true in her words. "I've ruined it, haven't I? I'm no good at any of this. Worse than useless! And now, I'll never be left alone!" She buried her face in her hands.

"Now, do not worry." Hestia patted her arm. "We'll get out of this quandary and we'll see you settled quietly. Somewhere small and out of the way, where no one will bother you."

Hestia addressed Francis, then, with a serious expression. "My dear, I need you to hear me. I trust that nothing will go wrong and we will worm free of this, as we have before. However, if something does go awry, then I am telling you that Miss Smythe's safety is your mission. See her away safely and into Stoneacre's hands. That is your priority."

"But—"

"No," Hestia interrupted. The look she wore meant she would brook no opposition. "I'll have your word."

Francis nodded.

Hestia stood and drew her away, back to the window. "And if something does go amiss, and I cannot do it myself, then you tell Stoneacre that I have noticed the pattern." She frowned. "He will likely pretend not to know what you mean, but you just tell him to ask the Prince Regent, if he needs further enlightenment."

"I understand." She didn't ask questions. Hestia had her methods and Francis had learned long ago that there was no need to question them.

"Now, then. Let's get to work," Hestia said briskly. "Can you braid, Miss Smythe?"

The woman stood and looked around. "Yes, of course." She looked puzzled. "But braid . . . what?"

Hestia pulled the blanket from the bed and stripping a sheet from it, ripped a large strip. "This, to begin with," she said with a grin.

It took both sheets, a couple of pillow shams, the lone blanket and the effort of all three women, but in an hour they had a braided rope. They tied one end to the bedpost and took the rest to the window.

Francis looked down and pursed her lips. "Even if we pull the bed to the window, it won't be long enough."

"Close enough," Hestia said with shrug.

"Close enough?" Miss Smythe repeated, horrified. She peered downward again. "We'll break our legs."

"You must trust us, my dear. And do everything we say." Hestia straightened suddenly. "Listen!"

Francis leaned out. Their window faced the back of the inn. Off to the right, she could hear a commotion. Pounding. Shouting.

"The horses!" someone cried.

She looked back at Hestia. "Something is happening. We have to get ready now."

Hestia nodded, then threw the rope out of the window.

"We need something else," Francis said, frowning. "Something convincing." Inspiration hit. She stood, yanked the wig from her head, held it out and let it drop to the ground beneath them.

"Good. But there must be something more, I think," Hestia mused. "Oh, yes." She retrieved Miss Smythe's hat where it had been placed on the side table. Bringing it back to the window, she drew back and sent it sailing out. It drifted a long way, the brim having caught the wind, and landed near the edge of the inn, towards the stables, from where shouting still echoed.

"Very nice," Francis said, approvingly.

"I don't understand," Miss Smythe said, bewildered.

But Francis drew back from the window, pulling the others as well. The yelling was drawing nearer.

"Hurry, now." Hestia took Miss Smythe's hand and led her to the wardrobe. "In you go, my dear. It will be close, but we will all fit. With luck, we won't be in there long—but we must stay utterly still and silent."

Miss Smythe blinked. "Are we not climbing down the rope?"

"No," Francis told her. "But they will *think* we did."

Understanding dawned, and the lady climbed in willingly. Hestia followed. Francis pulled her cap from her head, stuffed it in a pocket and ran her fingers through her hair, listening. Another shout rang outside, rather nearer their window. A moment later, footsteps sounded on the stairs.

She stepped in, pulling the door closed after her. It was a tight fit.

"Be still, now," Hestia whispered. "Someone comes."

The pounding grew louder. Nearer. The key rasped in the lock again and someone rushed in. They all crouched, frozen, hardly daring to breathe.

The footsteps crossed to the window. "They are out," a man's voice said, sounding muted from their hiding spot. He yelled it louder. "They are out! They've flown the coop! Damn the sneaky wenches!" He left the room at a run and they could hear his shouts echoing up the stair-well as he hurried downward.

"Did he lock the door?" Miss Smythe whispered.

"I don't think he even closed it," Francis answered quietly.

'Shhh . . . someone might come checking after him," Hestia warned. "We should stay put for a few moments."

But no one came. They exited the wardrobe quietly and found the door left open a crack.

Francis heaved a sigh of relief. "Let's go. Isaac and I were watching the inn from a spot a little up the road, waiting for a sign of your arrival. We left two horses tethered there. If we go out the back of the inn, we can go through the woods and get there unseen."

Hestia nodded. "We'll move quickly, but quietly," she told Miss

Smythe. "Keep to the wall and walk on the side of the stairs, rather than down the middle. There will be less chance of creaking, there. Stay close and do whatever we ask, right away."

Miss Smythe nodded, looking determined.

Francis put her hand on the latch of the door. Nodding over her shoulder at Hestia, she drew it open, stepped out—and straight into a solid wall.

She reeled back in a panic, but found herself swept up, arms pinned, before she could pull back for a blow. Struggling furiously, she jerked back, looking up . . . into a familiar set of blue eyes.

Chapter Twenty-Six

Until the day that Lord M—s men came, following me to Brittany, asking questions about the child in Monsieur's house. My fame had spread too far. Caught Lord M—s attention. We were successful in deceiving them, but they would be back. I knew what I had to do—but I fought the certainty of it for several months.

--from the journal of the infamous Miss Hestia Wright

Francis's legs nearly crumpled beneath her.

Ironic, as her heart lifted like a balloon she'd once seen aloft in Hyde Park.

"Rhys!" she gasped. She let him hustle her back into the room and stared as he closed the door again behind them. "What are you doing here? I thought you'd gone to—"

"Don't say Italy," he interrupted crossly.

Joy erupted inside of her. Heat rushed over her. She lifted her chin. "Or what?"

He glared down at her.

"What will you do?" She couldn't help herself. She had to poke him a bit. "If I say . . . Italy?"

His confusion cleared. His brow lifted and the scorching look he gave her curled her toes. "I'll kiss you senseless," he threatened.

"Italy," she breathed.

His arms went around her and he pulled her in tightly against him. His kiss was hungry and rough, and then tender and loving. His tongue caught and tangled with hers and she kissed him back, fierce happiness fizzing through her veins like champagne bubbles.

He was here! And she knew what that meant. How difficult it had been for him to make the choice. But he had—and her heart sang with it.

"Are we going?" Miss Smythe asked, sounding puzzled.

Francis pulled away. "Thank you," she breathed.

"For that kiss?" he grinned.

But he knew. Just as she did.

"For crossing the line."

His head shook. "I crossed it long ago, truthfully, and I was too daft to realize it. But I'm over now," he said frowning down at her. "And it's unfamiliar territory. I'll need your guidance. So don't you dare leave me alone out here."

"I never will. I promise."

"Fine. And I know now that you will not jump lightly or without thought into difficulties—but you should know—you won't do it alone. I'll always be with you. And I promise to only haul you out of trouble if you need it."

"Why don't we concentrate on getting all of us out of this predicament, right now," said Hestia.

Francis felt Rhys tense as his mother eased past Miss Smythe and laid a hand on his arm. She saw the tiny tremble move through her mentor and saw her much-vaunted serenity waver as a raft of emotion moved behind her eyes. "And then, I think, we should *all* talk."

Rhys nodded. Francis stepped back and they all grew serious.

"I let loose the horses," he said.

"Yes, I thought you smelled of stables." Francis leaned toward him and sniffed. "Not even a hint of linseed oil."

"I've been here, waiting, working in the stables. I heard what happened in the parlor this morning."

"Outside the window. I knew someone was there," Hestia murmured.

"I wanted to create a distraction and reduce the number of Marstoke's men around here. But I didn't count on your brilliant maneuver. It worked a treat. They are out there chasing horses and looking for you, but it got them *all* riled—and even the horses I had kept back for us were found and confiscated."

Francis took his hand. "We have two mounts hidden down the road. We were going to go out the back and strike out through the woods to get to them." She glanced at Hestia. "But where is Isaac?"

"And the innkeeper—has anyone seen him, either? Have Marstoke's men locked them in somewhere, too?"

Rhys was thinking, she could see. "Yes. Our first thought must be to get all three of you out of here. We'll get you to those mounts and then you can all head out. Don't go east or south, instead head west for Underbarrow. It's a scant three miles."

"But there's nothing there," objected Miss Smythe. "Just a bridge and some farmhouses."

"But they won't be expecting us to head there. They'll think we'll ride hard south." Hestia nodded her head.

"Yes. And I'll come back here, as if I've been out searching for the lost mounts, and I'll see what I can discover about Isaac and the innkeeper, and then I'll steal away a carriage. I'll meet you at the bridge, as soon as I can."

"It will work," Hestia said with a nod of approval. "If we can get safely out of the inn."

"We will." Francis stood. They were not going to be defeated now. "Let's go."

◈

R hys' every nerve stood on edge. He'd been in a thousand scrapes before—but he'd never had so much to lose. Francis, and his admiration, affection and this aching need of her, had awakened something primitive in him. He pulled her close as they cracked the door and listened.

And Hestia. His mother. He kept looking at her and sliding his gaze away. There was too much there, most of it uncomfortably intense and not all of it pleasant. No time to think about it now, in any case. Francis had to be his focus.

Silence reigned outside the door. Many of the men had been lured away by the combination of their two subterfuges. Hestia and the woman who had accompanied her here slipped out into the passage, but Rhys grabbed Francis's hand and held her back a moment.

Cupping her face, he kissed her, quick and hard. "I love you," he whispered. "I love your biting wit and your changeable hazel eyes. I love your smart mouth and your fiery strength and your honesty and even your ridiculously long eyelashes. It's a damned idiotic time to tell you, I know, but it also the perfect time. Because we are going to get through this today—we'll get everyone out safely." He shot her a wry grin. "It doesn't even feel hard to do, after the difficulty I had getting here."

"Rhys—"

"No. The hard part is over. Behind me. We'll get out today—and then we'll have the future—and each other. You will marry me, Francis Flightly Headley, and I am going to take you to Florence. To Paris. To my home in France. I am going to paint you in every one of those places and a thousand more. You can wear breeches, if you like and you can rescue troubled women in every country, and I'll help. I like the way you see, Francis—as if everyone could be a friend and deserves your best. And I am going to go to sleep every night with your laugh to soothe me and wake every morning to your smile."

Francis, his direct, forthright girl, grasped his wrists and said, "Yes, to all of it. And more." She stood on tiptoe and kissed him. "I'll give you all of the details on *more* when we are safely away."

He nodded and opened the door for her. "It's a bargain."

He held her hand as they eased out and toward the stairway. They all moved silently downward and he kept her hand in his when he called a halt on the last landing. The entry hall and main corridor below lay empty.

"The doctor is at work in the private parlor," he whispered. "The door is closed, so we should be able to move toward the back of the house unseen. Follow the passage that leads back the way we came." He gestured above. "In the middle, you'll find a door that leads to the outside—to a covered utility porch where they store firewood and empty kegs."

They all stepped quickly and quietly down the stairs—and they all froze as one when voices sounded in the courtyard outside. Several male voices, all coming closer.

Francis's grip tightened suddenly. "There, too," she whispered. She nodded toward the parlor door at the back of the house. The click of the latch sounded loud in his ears.

Rhys made a split decision. No time for anything else. "In here." He pulled Francis into the taproom, and then hustled them all into the small pantry behind the bar. Along with the shelves and pints there was a door to a narrow, turning stairway leading to the storage room.

A pounding echoed in, coming from the entry hall. "I locked the door to slow them down," said Francis.

It didn't last. Shouts followed.

"Search the place!" It was Cade's voice. "Every room. Every nook."

Rhys pulled open the door. "Let's go."

The storage room was crowded and dim. He led them toward the high window he'd unlatched the other day. "Let's move quickly," he urged. "We can get away outside while they are searching inside."

"Boost me up," Francis ordered. "I'll help pull Miss Smythe through."

Rhys lifted her and she propped the window open. Scrambling up, she turned around and peered back in. "It's good—the utility porch shields us from anyone in the direction of the stables." She held out her hands. "Send Miss Smythe up."

The other woman went up and Francis poked her head back in. "Your turn, Hestia!"

Rhys gazed up at her, his heart full. "I'm going to paint you like that," he told her. "Peering in, with your eyes full of excitement and that mischievous smile on your face."

She grinned and started to answer, but then her gaze went wide. "Shadow on the wall behind you," she whispered. "Someone's coming. Hide!" She pulled away and lowered the window back into place.

Hestia was already moving toward the darkest corner. Rhys followed and they crouched in behind a stack of brandy barrels.

"There's no one down here." The complaint came in before the man who made it.

"It's a waste of time," his companion agreed. "You saw where I found that bonnet, nearly to the stables. They stole the bloody, damned horses. I'll put paid that they crossed the River Kent and are headed south on Aynam Road."

A few footsteps sounded, but none drew near. "Let's get this farce of a search finished, then go after them," the first one said.

Their voices faded as they climbed the stairs.

He and Hestia stayed put, waiting. After a moment, Hestia reached over and placed a hand on his arm. "Thank you for coming," she said softly.

He didn't quite meet her gaze. "I wouldn't have, had it not been for Francis." His shoulder lifted. "I would not have been able."

Slowly, she nodded. "I understand."

He ducked his head. "She did it for you, you must know. Came looking for me. She told me all that you have done for her."

"Then we have that in common, at least. For I can see how much you have also done for her."

Francis stuck her head back in before he could answer. "Come along," she called. "I'll take Miss Smythe to the woods now, before any of those lackeys decide to come back out. Be careful when you cross the open space between the end of the inn and the trees." She twinkled at him. "And don't forget to duck when you go past the windows."

It nearly went just as she said. Rhys and Hestia climbed easily out of the window. Crouching, Rhys ran along behind her, away from the stables toward the other end of the inn. He saw Francis and the other woman dart into the copse ahead and breathed easier when they disappeared into the wood.

He slowed as they approached the corner—but then plowed into Hestia as she skidded to a sudden stop.

And then he saw the reason for it.

Cade had stepped around the corner. He had a pistol aimed straight at her heart.

"Enough," the dour man said on a sigh. "Enough. I am beyond weary of these theatrics. I—we—so many of us—were lured to Marstoke's service by talk of change. Of *revolution*. There is serious work to be done." He sneered. "A broken and antiquated regime to pull down. A new one to build from the ashes. And yet, we are continually derailed by these personal vendettas."

Hestia, straight as a poker at Rhys' side, shook her head. "I am sorry you have not yet discovered it, Mr. Cade, but Marstoke is naught but a personal vendetta on two feet."

"Which is why you will come smartly along with me. We can finish this and move on to important business."

"You might be surprised to find that I am eager to put an end to this, as well, sir."

"Good." Cade nodded. "Then come along." He waved the pistol at Rhys. "You too, prodigal son. I have conflicting orders concerning all of you, so I'll just cart the lot of you to Marstoke and let him sort it out." He aimed his scarecrow's grin at them both. "It appears he'll have his family reunion, after all."

"If you didn't have that pistol, I'd snap you in half," Rhys growled.

"Fortunately, I do have it. And I will shoot your whore of a mother myself, and be rid of Marstoke's biggest distraction, if you do not do just as I say."

Rhys' fists clenched, but Hestia held out a hand, preventing him from moving forward. "No. Let's see to this the end, at last." She turned and raised the brow that Cade could not see.

He tensed.

Turning back, Hestia stepped forward, moving past the man—but she stopped suddenly and reached up to grab his pistol hand and push it high. With her hip, she rammed him into the corner of the building.

Rhys jumped forward, but not before Cade raised his other fist and slammed Hestia a hard blow to the head. She crumpled, and Rhys stepped in, smashing the pistol out of his grip.

Cade tried to go after it, but Rhys drew back and delivered a massive blow to the man's jaw. He held nothing back. Cade's head bounced off of the corner behind him. Rhys struck again and the man's eyes rolled back in his head. With a moan, Cade slumped down to land at his feet.

Rhys took a moment to toss the pistol farther away, then rushed to help Hestia sit up.

"Thank you." She smiled. "I knew you'd know what to do."

"Are you all right?"

"Of course." She allowed him to help her to her feet—and then she kept a hold of his hand. "I've suffered worse."

"I know." He looked down and placed his other hand on hers. "I'm sorry."

"You have nothing to be sorry about, Rhys Caradec," she said, abruptly fierce. "It's true that I endured much at your father's hand, but I would have withstood far more in order to bring you into the world."

He frowned and searched her face. He thought of Francis and her bravery, the way she faced the most difficult problems head on, flinging her all into the resolution.

Breathing deeply, he allowed his love to inspire him. He asked the hardest question. The one that had formed the foundation of every wall he'd ever erected around his heart. "Then . . . you don't hate the sight of me? Seeing me doesn't . . . bring it all back?"

"Oh, Gods above. No, Rhys!" She touched his face. "You've always been the only one that could chase all of that darkness away."

Emotion washed over him. Something hard and ugly and tight inside of him just . . . loosened and slipped away. He straightened—and caught sight of Francis—flying toward him out of the wood. "Rhys!" she shouted. "Hestia! Behind you!"

He turned to see Cade pulling himself up, his nose bleeding freely and another, smaller pistol in his hand. Again, he had it pointed straight toward Hestia.

It was not a conscious choice. It came as naturally as drawing his next breath. He heard the report as Cade fired at the same time that he stepped in front of his mother, pushing her away.

The impact hit, hard and low. His left side jerked backward. Off balance and dazed, he fell.

"Rhys!"

He found himself staring up at Francis and Hestia. Both looked a little fuzzy around the edges.

"Rhys?" Tears flowed down Francis's face. "Are you all right?"

"Of course." He tried to reach up to wipe the tears from her face, but his arm fell back. "It doesn't even hurt." Gathering his willpower, he tried to sit up. *Damnation.* Pain erupted in his hip, shooting down his leg and across his back. "Oh, hell. There it is."

"Just lay back," Francis insisted. "We'll get help."

"The gun," he gasped through the rising red haze. "The other gun." He looked beseechingly at Hestia.

She understood. With a nod, she rose and ran to fetch it. Through the fog he saw her point it at Cade.

"Don't let her." He grasped Francis's hand. "Not worth . . ."

"Hestia!" Was that panic in his love's tone? His calm, capable Francis? He must be worse off than he thought.

"There's too much blood, Hestia!"

Someone fumbled with his breeches. He winced as someone sawed at the fabric.

"Pull the edges together. Press down tight and don't let up."

Hestia sounded tense, too.

He reached for Francis. "Love," he whispered.

Then the pain flared again and his head spun and darkness rose to pull him in.

Chapter Twenty-Seven

In the end, I did what I had to do, to keep my child from ever falling into a monster's hands. Monsieur and his daughter and her husband moved back to France, to a farm bought with money I gave them. And then I had to say goodbye. For good. I could not leave breadcrumbs leading back to him. I have never felt such pain. Torment that never ends, never fades. But there were no tears, this time. I was beyond them.

--from the journal of the infamous Miss Hestia Wright

He woke to silence and a soft bed beneath him. Fatigue felt like a hook, dragging at the center of his chest.

His left hip throbbed, but the pain was manageable. His other side, however—his other side was warm and comfortable and damned lucky to have Francis Headley curled up against it.

Stirring a little, she glanced up at him—then sat bolt upright. "You're awake!"

Rhys nodded. "Thirsty, too."

"Yes." She rolled out of bed and bustled about, pulling a kettle from the fire and propping him up on pillows. "Drink this tea. Yes, I know it is very sweet, but the local doctor has a very good nurse and she insists you must have it." She heaved a sigh once he'd finished, a satisfied look on her face. "You are going to be fine, you know."

"Good to hear," he said, tired from only taking a drink of tea. "How bad is it?"

"The bullet entered in the front, ricocheted off of your hip bone and went out the side, opening up a large wound and nicking an artery. You lost a lot of blood, more than the doctor likes, but we were very lucky he was so close. He closed it off quickly enough."

Rhys looked about the empty room. "Hestia?"

"It is late. Isaac finally convinced her to go and rest."

"You found them, then. Good." He settled back, already feeling drowsy.

"He rode in just after you passed out. He'd informed the innkeeper of the situation and they rode out to fetch some local rein-forcement."

His eyes snapped back open. "Did Marstoke's men fight back? Was anyone hurt?"

"No. Just you," she said with irony. "Without Cade's leadership, the men were reluctant, and then Isaac made it clear that Cade had shot Marstoke's son, and that spooked the lot of them. Most rode out right then. Trying to beat each other to Marstoke with protestations of innocence, Isaac says. A few stayed on, tired of Marstoke's great game, and have asked for help escaping his wrath."

He nodded, satisfied.

"Now, don't you go falling asleep," she admonished, slipping into bed beside him again.

He chuckled and rubbed his face in her hair. "You're not helping."

"I want to ask a favor, now that you are all right and we have a moment alone."

"Anything," he replied contentedly.

"I want you to paint me a miniature. Your own image."

He peered down at her. "I've never painted myself," he said, interested.

"Could you try?" Her eyes filled. "You frightened me, you know. For a moment, I thought . . ." Tears spilled over and her lip trembled.

"Shhh . . . I am going to be fine, remember? And I will paint you anything you like."

"Thank you," she sniffed.

"I wouldn't have died, in any case. I could not have."

"Oh? I'm glad to hear it."

"I could not possibly leave this mortal plane without knowing."

"Knowing what?" she asked, mystified.

He took her hand. "Your true name," he whispered. "It's been niggling at me since that day in the forest. I can't bear it any longer, Francis. Won't you tell me?"

She flushed. "I'd forgotten! Well, I suppose I'll tell you . . ."

She didn't sound enthusiastic.

"You must!" he insisted.

Her color rose. "I will, but you must promise to keep it to yourself." One of her shoulders lifted and she wiggled a little in discomfort. "It's not really me anymore."

"It's part of your past though," he said. "A lovely memory of your mother." He gave her a wry grin. "I'm learning how precious such things are, thanks to you."

Her expression softened. "Very well." She hesitated. "It's Aubrey."

He touched her hair. "Perhaps you were born with this glorious mix of color in your hair, and your mother named you after the auburn," he ventured.

"Perhaps. But, please, do not call me by it? Francis is who I am, who I have worked hard to become."

"I understand. And I promise."

"Good." She sounded satisfied. "And I warn you, you'll have to get used to such demands."

He laughed. "Planning on becoming a nag, are you?"

"Yes. A nag of a wife," she corrected. "For I'll be holding you to your declaration."

Her words startled him. "I did declare, didn't I?" His fingers rested on her arm and he moved them in a soft circle. "Would you like me to ask you, instead?"

"No need. I've already agreed. And I'm afraid I'll be insisting on other things, instead."

"Now you've sparked my curiosity. What is it you insist on?"

"Oh, more kisses behind doors and in alleys and up against trees. Maybe a few in a bed, as well?"

"We can start now," he assured her.

"I'm not done. I can't wait to make love with you in Paris and Florence. You'll have to get used to me tidying your studio and forcing you to eat during marathon painting sessions." She took his hand and slid it to her belly. "I fully expect you to give me several children and I'll probably teach them to pick pockets and wheedle you to paint them, too."

He smiled. "I confess, I look forward to being a hen-pecked husband, if that's how it is to be." He moved his hand up to cover her breast. "Shall we begin on a few of those demands?"

Laughing, she pulled his hand up to kiss it. "I'm afraid the doctor says you must keep quite still for a while, until that wound begins to knit." She placed a kiss into his open palm and then licked his wrist where his pulse had quickened. "We will have to wait."

"Give me some more of that tea," he rasped. "I swear, I shall be the quickest healing patient the good doctor has ever encountered."

Her eyes shone. "Do you promise?"

"I do." He ran a finger along her jaw. "You broke me out of my self-imposed prison and taught me to love. Now I can't wait to get started."

Sighing in happiness, she snuggled down at his side. "Me either, Caradec, me either."

Epilogue

✦❦✦

I threw myself into the loud and gaudy life of a celebrated courtesan. I laughed when I didn't feel like it, learned to mimic every emotion, but my heart was dead. No man could touch me inside—so of course, they all wished to try. I let them fling themselves against the rocks of my sorrow. I played their games and I took their money. But it was a long time before I felt anything again, before I discovered what I truly wanted to do with my power.

--from the journal of the infamous Miss Hestia Wright

They were married two months later. Rhys still had a limp, but he would not be put off another month, another week, or even so much as another day. They were going to Florence on their bridal trip, he insisted, and they had to leave before the stormy season began.

Francis agreed with him. She was happy to give him the timing of the ceremony and the plans for the trip, because, as she'd warned, she had all the rest of the wedding just as she wished.

It had to be at Half Moon House. They were married in the parlor, after Hestia escorted her down the stairs and to her groom. Brynne and Callie and their husbands sat in the front row next to Isaac, who cried.

Francis had personally invited all of the Half Moon House girls, even Jesse, who had discovered that it was the butcher's boy who had sold information on Hestia's travel plans, after using her infatuation with him to gain access to the house.

She invited all of the messenger kids and even a street rat or two from her old gang.

Mrs. Spencer and Jasper came from Scotland and brought Angus. The Earl and Countess of Hartford attended, and the Duke of Danby sent a fine set of luggage as a wedding present.

Mrs. Spencer insisted on fashioning the wedding gown. *Not* white, Francis insisted right back, and so she was married in a lovingly embroidered confection of soft green.

"You're sure you don't mind?" she whispered to Hestia for the hundredth time, taking her mentor's hands after the vows—and the kisses—were exchanged.

"I could not have hoped for better," Hestia told her again. She kissed Francis's cheek. "You are my daughter in truth now, my dear. I could not be more proud."

Francis sniffed, but Rhys whisked her away to greet Andor and his family and Hestia smiled after them.

"Is that the truth?"

Lord Stoneacre sidled up beside her and she raked him with a jaundiced eye. "Do you think I would lie about such a thing?"

The earl pursed his lips. "Yes."

She laughed. "Well, I did not. I did not have to. Apart, the two of them were my best legacy. Together?" She looked after them, both happy and smiling and nearly glowing with love. "They are the greatest gift I could have been given."

"My sincere congratulations, then." The earl lifted her hand and placed a kiss upon it.

"I sense you are here to offer something besides congratulations. News, perhaps? Is the girl safe?"

"Yes, and bound for America, where no one will ever know her true lineage." He shook his head in admiration. "All of the rumors, for all of these years—but leave it to you to ferret out the true daughter of the Prince Regent and Maria Fitzherbert."

"I didn't. It was Marstoke who sent his people sniffing around her skirts. She knew enough to be frightened and she sent to me for help."

"Yes, she told us everything." He sighed. "But it's not just news that brings me."

"An offer?"

"A command. He wants to see you."

"I don't think that the Prince Regent will enjoy hearing what I have to say."

"Please, be careful, Hestia. Our regent has many faults—and one of them is a vindictive bent. You have enough powerful enemies."

"I have more powerful friends," she said, her chin in the air. "But I am not stupid." She took a flute of champagne from a passing footman. "When?"

"Next week. I'll escort you."

"Fine." She drained her glass. "Next week we begin. But not today." Her gaze softened as she looked at her family.

She had a family.

"Today is about love." With a nod, she moved away.

She didn't see the yearning look he sent after her, or the salute Stoneacre raised after her departing back.

Also by Deb Marlowe

Don't miss the other books in the Half Moon House Series!

About the Author

USA Today Bestselling author Deb Marlowe adores History, England and Men in Boots. Clearly she was destined to write Regency Historical Romance.

A Golden Heart Award winner and Rita nominee, Deb grew up in Pennsylvania with her nose in a book. Luckily, she'd read enough romances to recognize the true modern hero she met at a college Halloween party--even though he wore a tuxedo t-shirt instead of breeches and boots. They married, settled in North Carolina and produced two handsome, intelligent and genuinely amusing boys.

A proud geek, history buff and story addict, she loves to talk with readers! Find her discussing books, movies, TV, recipes and her infamous Men in Boots on Facebook, Twitter, Instagram, and Pinterest. Find out Behind the Book details and interesting historical tidbits at deb@debmarlowe.com

Sign up for her newsletter for first peeks at new books and fun contest information!

Connect with Deb!

www.DebMarlowe.com

Deb@DebMarlowe.com

90866292R00159

Made in the USA
Columbia, SC
12 March 2018